The Package

by

Tanya M. Cooper

Soft Cover
Boomerang Publishing, Toronto, Canada
ISBN: 9781712911068

Dedication: To the people on the island of Roatan who helped inspire this novel and who shared of themselves while I was writing it.

Tanya M. Cooper's Books

The Revolutionary's Daughter

Beneath the Stone-Cold Floor

The Wayward Daughters

Waiting on Postcards

The Package

Doll in the Woodpile

Teenage Trouble & Toil

L.O.V.E: Live a Life Of Vibrant Energy

Chapter Outline

Forward: Waterfalls
Chapter 1: Delia
Chapter 2: David
Chapter 3: Prison
Chapter 4: Dry Butts
Chapter 5: Pre-Prison Delia
Chapter 6: Chihuahua
Chapter 7: Bridgette
Chapter 8: Muttonhead
Chapter 9: Velvet
Chapter 10: A New York Minute
Chapter 11: Ghost
Chapter 12: Machete
Chapter 13: Petero
Chapter 14: The Queen
Chapter 15: Chacarron
Chapter 16: Osito
Chapter 17: Pablo
Chapter 18: Bam Bam
Chapter 19: Guatusso
Chapter 20: Eye
Chapter 21: Nickname

Prologue: Waterfalls

Don't go chasing waterfalls
Please stick to the rivers and the lakes that you're used to
I know that you're gonna have it your way or nothing at all
But I think you're moving too fast.
Lisa Lopez (Left Eye Lisa - TLC)

The story we tell ourselves - and others - if we tell it enough times, becomes our truth.
{Scott Harder - Journalist - New York Times}

March 29, 2007

I was desperate.

Not for money. Not for success, a relationship or even happiness.

I was desperate for peace - within and without. So, I left New York and escaped to the Bay Islands of Honduras.

One would think peace on a Caribbean island would be a ubiquitous commodity, but not where there are few rules and fewer people to enforce them. In the end, this may have worked in my favour - at least for a while.

After ten days at a frenetic pace on the smaller of the islands, I had to find a quieter place to hide away, so I jumped islands. I thought I finally found it, spending my days hanging out, meeting new friends, partying like there's no tomorrow and passing almost every day lying on a beach listening to the sound of the surf hit the volcanic reef and enjoying its salty spray misting my face.

Four months into my peaceful getaway, I was passing one more blissful, smoldering afternoon, my eyes closed and drifting off to sleep. Inevitably, however, something - not a noise, but a *knowing* awoke me. A knowing that something was about to float into my life and change it forever.

I lifted myself on my elbows and rested my Versace sunglasses on my forehead and looked out over the white rolling caps produced less by wind and more by the wake of boats.

There it was.

The *something* that had no business being in paradise, but was one of many residual effects of Hurricane Wilma. The surf was bringing it closer and while an excitement erupted within me; so too did trepidation.

It was as if I'd lived in Latin America all of my life and I had some knowledge of how things worked there. I knew what it was - or rather what it could be, that was floating towards me.

I looked around to see if anyone else had witnessed it being tossed to and fro in the surf.

There were a few people wandering the beach near where I was laying and a few metres away, there were some others hustling a bartender for drinks, but no one else was near the surf. I raised my arms to stretch as if it was just another day in paradise and I was getting up to cool myself in the ocean surf. I slowly walked the concrete path over the encrusted reef and stood by the iron ladder and surveyed the object.

My heart was pounding. I knew if I took those few steps into the ocean - if I reached out - if I touched it, there'd be no going back. Who was I kidding? There was no going back.

Chapter 1: Delia
{Present Day}

I first met Delia at the Penitenciaria Nacional Femenina de Adaptacion Social - the only women's prison in Honduras. It was well known - at least on the mainland for being a holding tank for not only women, but mothers and their children - most of whom were conceived during conjugal visits by the very men who had used these women as their drug mules.

Delia was not a mother; nor was she Honduran. She was an American who found herself *in* way over her head in every sense of the word. I, Scott Harder, was a keen journalist working for the *New York Times* in my early thirties, hot on the trail of stories that were inconsequential to most Americans, but nonetheless, worth telling.

I first heard about Delia from an unsuspecting older gentleman - we'll call him *Blue* as that's where I met him - at the Blue Note Jazz Club down on 3rd street. We were sharing a drink they call loneliness - yeah, I'm quoting from none other than the Piano man - when he struck up a conversation with me about politics or some such shit, which quickly turned to something he was a lot more passionate about.

He told me he'd met a girl down in Honduras on one of his many visits to scout out property and that despite no one listening to him, he was convinced she'd been kidnapped by some Central Americans and hadn't been seen again - at least by him on all his subsequent visits to the island. For some reason, she had made quite the impression on this guy.

When I went back to my tiny cubicle to finish writing a final draft for the paper, I found myself instead, doing some further digging about this girl - his description of her had made quite an impression on me. Apparently, she'd been a stunning blue-eyed blonde, the long-legged type who tanned that creamy, bronze colour and when she sat at a bar - or anywhere for that matter - she became every man's secret fantasy. As it turns out, this guy's fantasy wasn't so secret. He seemed desperate to tell me all about her. I sensed for some reason that he genuinely cared about her and wanted to know what had happened to her. Maybe they'd become friends, who knows?

In any case, in my digging, I discovered that she hadn't been kidnapped, but had somehow wound up in a Honduran prison for not only possession, but dealing narcotics in the Bay Islands. She'd been sentenced to 15 years and according to records, she'd served almost three years of her time before escaping, while being transported from the prison to a half-way house for women. Apparently, she had been assigned to a less secure prison for good behaviour. I would hazard to guess it was more likely due to the fact that she was a foreigner and someone had probably pulled a few strings for her.

As it turns out, she was caught a few days later and was sentenced to ten more years for her escape and subsequently, recommitted to the women's prison. Even more interesting was that she too had been an aspiring journalist for the *New York Times* and about three years before I got hired, she'd left for parts unknown, not being able to handle the chaos of New York City. Imagine that!

Hell bent on breaking through the journalistic glass ceiling, for some reason I thought telling this woman's story and heck, maybe finding her a decent lawyer to get her sentence lessened, would put me at the top of my game as a journalist and a humanitarian. If I'd been honest with myself at the time, there was something else fueling my desire to follow this story.

Of course, life has a funny way of turning out in ways you don't expect. I'm only telling her story now because she's long gone and besides maybe a few drug smugglers still looking for that elusive package they lost, there isn't anyone looking for her anymore.

***

I have to admit my research skills needed some work - and it's incredibly time consuming, so I supplemented by normal channels of information with a friend - I use that term loosely - named Woody. He was a private eye who had a knack for finding people - nefarious and law abiding alike. I asked him to do some digging for me on Delia's history while I managed to get permission to investigate the lead and embark on a trip to Honduras to meet her in person.

As it turns out, it isn't like a hot knife in butter trying to visit someone in a Central American jail. It takes some time, a little help from some friends and some good old hard cash to break down those red taped walls. Good thing I had a little of all three.

When I arrived in Honduras, I had to show my passport first to the U.S. Embassy who had been contacted when Delia was first arrested. They had an initial report on her case - which I was not authorized to see. They did offer to have one of their officers accompany me, but I declined. When I finally gained permission to visit Delia in prison, she initially refused to see me - or anyone for that matter. She was a palisade all on her own.

When I arrived at the prison, I had to identify myself to the guard officials. The first time I was honest and said I was a journalist from New York wanting to tell her story. I couldn't lie to them about who I was, but I could, for a small fee, arrange for the prison guard to lie to the inmate I was intending to visit. Her response was an adamant no.

The second time, I made up some shit that I was an author and was willing to write her story and share half the royalties with her. This had no apparent impact on her either, which was surprising when surviving in a Honduran prison depends upon how much an inmate can afford for her daily needs. Basic food like eggs, bread and beans are provided, but from what the locals told me in a few conversations I had with them, the inmates had to pay for everything else, even meat if they wanted it. I figured out pretty quickly that the one thing this girl did have a lot of, was pride.

In the end, I pretended to be a family member. Thanks to Woody, I discovered she had an older brother, James, who was a prominent lawyer from New Jersey. That seemed to be the key to opening the door. Little did I know that her only itch to see him was to spit in his face and tell him where he could shove his legal services. Her need to have revenge on him did manage to get me further than telling the truth or my offer of money.

Of course, as soon as she saw me and realized I wasn't her brother, she got up to leave. Panicked, I spewed out the only thing I could think to say: "Delia, I have a message from David!"

The woman with patchy - it appeared to be falling out - dirty blonde hair pulled back in a ponytail, wearing tattered jeans and a yellowed, sweat soaked t-shirt stopped and turned back to face me. While some residual youth still clung to her, the wrinkled forehead, dark, puffy eyes and pursed lips betrayed her once apparent beauty. I didn't need to hear her story - I could see it all over her face.

Whatever dynamic, blue-eyed blonde might have begun her adventure in Honduras a few years earlier, had faded just as a vibrant piece of furniture does when exposed to relentless light. I suspected however, that it was darkness that had diminished her spirit.

As she walked towards me, she never took her eyes from me. She was skeptical, but curious. This curiosity, I would soon learn, is exactly what got her in over her head.

Chapter 2: David

Back in New York, before I left for Honduras, I asked around the office at *The Times* if anyone had remembered a Delia Russell working there. No one could remember her which was strange as she'd worked there for ten years. However, I suppose her stint at the newspaper was short enough that like so many who had come before and after her, she was soon forgotten.

It was the fate of many writers who dreamed of wanting to work for the prominent newspaper, but discovered the reality of what journalistic reporting took from one's soul. It's not that it lacked excitement. Hell, there was plenty of that; competing with others for breaking stories, constantly worrying about becoming obsolete and simply going after that next high. There are certain people who thrive on it and others who just can't hack it.

At the time, when I first heard about Delia Russell, I wondered if perhaps we were kindred spirits as there'd been many a day, I had thought about quitting and becoming an English teacher or a full-time writer. So, I couldn't blame her – in fact, I made the mistake of thinking perhaps I could understand her. She was one of many who voluntarily removed themselves from the frenetic rat race of journalism and New York city.

Apparently, there was a time when she had been very ambitious and was being mentored by none other than David Fisher himself – a well-respected and much emulated thirty-year columnist at the paper. Interestingly, even though word got out that I was trying to find out more about Delia, he never approached me regarding her. It was one of his support staff - Angelica - who came to my cubicle one afternoon.

Angelica had never met Delia as she'd only been at the paper as David's assistant for the last six months, but shared with me that David had been quite close to Delia and he might be the one to speak with if I was interested in finding out more about her story. According to her, David had kept apprised of Delia and had asked her to call the U.S. Embassy in Honduras at least once a month to check on her. I thought this was an interesting request to make of one's assistant but when you're a top journalist, who's going to question you about your demands?

I approached David later that afternoon in his office, which was about six times the size of my tiny cubicle. He had surpassed all of our journalistic dreams and had his own column for years detailing and commenting upon the cultural and political infrastructure of our city. He was known to be quite well-travelled and a very wealthy man. I admired him and his column greatly.

He was on the phone when I rapped on his half-open door. Instead of shooing me away, he waved me in to sit down. His conversation was quick and when he put down the receiver, he looked at me with inquisitive, blue eyes from a weathered, but whimsical face, his silver hair pulled back in a ponytail.

"Yes, young man. How can I help you?"

"Sorry, David - to bother you. My name is Scott Harder and I heard you might have some information on Delia - Delia Russell?"

"Ah Delia!" He sat back in his broad, leather chair and tapped his fingertips together. "Yes, she was quite the aspiring journalist. It's such a shame how it all ended up."

"That's why I'm here. I've recently heard a bit about her story and that she had worked here once, but is now in a Honduran prison."

"Yes, that's right. She left New York city to find her bliss, as they call it. I'm not sure that's what she found."

"Can you enlighten me at all about her? What would have made her get involved in the drug trade?"

"Well, that my boy, you would have to ask her. Circumstances sometimes bring us to a fork in the road where we must decide which way to go. The truth is, Delia's either exceptionally brave or extremely stupid, but from what I know of her, she always struck me as an exceptionally bright person, so whatever she decided, she must have had a good reason for it."

"I heard that you tried to help her, when she was first incarcerated. Is that right?"

"Well, as much as one can help when you're dealing with a justice system in a developing nation. I happened to have some friends at the American Embassy in Central America so I certainly did what I could to get her the help she needed. As you know, things don't happen very quickly

there.   I thought I might expedite things if I could.
Unfortunately, even the Embassy's hands are often tied.

"She'd been arrested for not just possession, but
trafficking and it's a highly serious offence in Honduras.
There was really nothing I could do, except see that at least
her needs were being met and she was being treated properly.
I tried to find her a proper lawyer - but she chose one of her
own."

"Was that her brother? I read that he is a lawyer here
in New Jersey."

"No! In fact, her brother wasn't much help during her
trial - the dumb schmuck!   Anyway, money seems to be the
language in prison of course and really, that's the only way I
could help her in the end." He began tapping the tip of the
pen he was now holding against his temple. "May I ask what
your motive - or should I say, interest is in her?"

"I haven't really figured that out yet to be honest. I
heard about her from a guy in a bar of all places. It's not like
it was some breaking lead. I just felt the compulsion to look
into her story."

"Well, as journalists I can certainly relate to that –
compulsions and hunches are sometimes the only thing
we've got. However, in my experience, I have found that
it's important to understand our own motives as journalists
before we go digging into a story. How far do you intend
to take this interest, in her?"

I got the distinct impression that David was asking
me something else in that moment, something of a more
personal nature and I became suddenly very uncomfortable.
I thought it better to just be honest and see what would be

his reaction. "Well, I'm doing some investigating at present, but I'm contemplating traveling to Honduras as I'd really like to hear her story in person."

"Well, let me make a suggestion to you, young man. I went to visit her in prison and it's not for the faint of heart. It's not easy to see her there or the conditions in which women live in that place. I also wouldn't hold out too much hope of talking with her. She doesn't trust anyone and certainly doesn't take kindly to strangers showing up and asking questions."

"I understand. May I ask you something else?" I hesitated broaching this subject, but reporters cannot stand down from confrontation.

"Fire away!" He folded his arms and sat up in his chair.

"When Delia escaped from prison when she was being transferred, do you know how she managed it?"

"My dear boy, how could I possibly know that?"

"Well, just hear me out. We both know that the only way to get anything in prison - particularly a Honduran prison - is by bribing or paying off the guards. I'm just wondering if you have any insight as to how she could have pulled that off?"

"Well, all I know is what I heard. There was an accident - mudslide or some such thing - and the bus she was on ran off the road and the driver and guards were killed. I suspect she or the other inmates she was travelling with, saw an opportunity. Really, if you want to know what happened, I suggest you visit her yourself. Who knows, maybe you'll get lucky and she'll talk to you, but I wouldn't bank on it."

"Well, that was the other thing I wondered if you could help me with. I know you were one of the few people she made a connection with here at the paper - and I thought maybe you could talk to someone - pull a few strings - and get me into see her a little easier. I hear only family or close friends are allowed to visit and there's a whole rigamarole getting in."

David breathed in deeply, unfolded his arms, leaned over his desk and clasped his fingers in front of me. "I'll make a few phone calls to the U.S. Embassy, but even if you get into the prison, I can't guarantee Delia will see you. If you happen to manage that, will you do me a favour?"

"Sure. What is it?"

"Give her a message for me."

"I can do that. What is it that you want me to tell her?"

David's next words had very little meaning to me at the time, but I had to trust that if I were to get close enough to say it to Delia, it would most certainly mean something to her.

Chapter 3: Delia in Prison

The promise of a message from David seemed to be enough to make Delia agree to see me. She gave a simple head nod to the guard that was accompanying me and I was ushered to a small table on an outside patio - not the type of patio you find at a resort, mind you. It was a concrete slab with a few metal benches and tables, which also served as a mess hall for the women's meals. There was litter and trash strewn about in every corner and the tables didn't look like they'd been wiped in days.

I waited for Delia to initiate sitting down. From what I gleaned from David, I shouldn't take anything for granted and probably just as quickly as she'd agreed to talk to me, she could change her mind. She pulled over one of the metal chairs and I cringed at not only the scraping of its legs against the concrete, but the disdain in which she purposely did it. She turned it backwards, straddled it and hugged it's back with her arms. I didn't take it as an affront, but could tell she felt more comfortable with some kind of protective barrier between us.

She waited for me to speak. I was hoping that she might ask how I knew David or what message he had for her, but she said nothing. She simply sat there, staring at me, daring me to come up with something that wouldn't make her get up and walk away. I knew I had to choose my words carefully. All I could think to do was hold out my hand and introduce myself. She didn't reciprocate.

"I'm Scott. Scott Harder. I work for *The New York Times*." She remained silent. It was most definitely on me to explain why I was there wasting her time. I continued. "I heard about your story from a man who said he'd met you in Honduras about ten years ago. He thought maybe you'd been kidnapped, which of course, made me curious about you and what happened to you. That's how I came to know you were here." I waited for some visceral or facial reaction, but she didn't even blink. "Anyway, I talked to David Fisher at NYT and he made some calls to the Embassy to get me into see you. I thought maybe there's something I can do to help you."

She sat up, straightened her back and pushed herself away from the back of the chair to create more space between us. I thought perhaps she would swing her leg from over the chair and get up and walk away. She didn't.

"You think you can help me?" Her voice was raspy and I could hear the contention with it. I suspected she hadn't always sounded so gruff or surly because despite her trying to hide it, there was an element of gracefulness in her movements and the way she held her head.

"Well, I don't know. You're in here and I'm not - so yeah, it's possible I might be able to help you." I intuitively sensed I needed to match her surliness for some reason.

"What kind of help do you think I need?"

"I know how things work in here. Money is the language of choice. And it speaks loudly. If there's someone - a family member or -"

She held up her hand. "There's no one." She looked at me with a blank expression, but I caught sight of something in her eyes. Sadness perhaps.

"Well, what about your brother? He's a lawyer, right? Surely, he can help you."

"My brother is dead to me. I've been in this hellhole for almost six years. Do you see him helping me?"

"I'm sure he would if he could."

"How the hell could you know what my brother would do?"

"Yeah, I'm sorry. I don't. I just think if I was a lawyer and my sister was sitting in a Central American prison, I'd do anything I could to help her - to get her out."

"My brother wants nothing to do with me. He wants nothing to do with my case. It might jeopardize his reputation trying to help a convicted drug dealer out of prison. Like I said, there's no one."

"There's David. He seems to care a great deal. He mentioned he came here a couple of times. Perhaps I can talk to him and let him know what you'd like him to do."

"I don't need anything from David. I'm not his problem. You said you had a message from him?"

"Yes. I mean, it didn't mean anything to me, but perhaps it does to you."

"So, what did he say?"

I hesitated offering this piece of information up so soon into our conversation, as I figured she'd be gone in an instant.

"Well? Are you going to tell me or are you going to waste more of my time?"

"He told me to tell you to 'look into the hourglass.'"

She leaned further back holding on to the chair's back with her hands, her arms outstretched. She smirked.

"Does that mean something to you?"

"No. Should it?" Of course, she was lying. It would be the first of many lies that Delia would tell me. I guess that's the only thing one can do, considering where she was.

"I don't know. I guess it was important enough for him to want me to relay it to you."

"So, tell me Scott, why are you really here? What's in this for you?"

"I'm really not sure. I just got the sense that I needed to meet you. Find out what really happened. You don't strike me as a girl who ends up in a place like this."

"No? And what *kind of girl* ends up in a place like this?"

"Well, not a girl from the upper east side of Manhattan."

"So, you've done your homework. Oh yes, how I miss the posh east side with its fancy restaurants and designer shops! I mean, these aren't the usual digs of an east side girl, now are they?" She asked, as she carelessly pulled on the corner of her dirty t-shirt.

"Do you? Miss it, I mean? Do you miss home?"

"If I miss anything, its walking around with a coffee in hand exploring the Museum of Art or the Guggenheim - and Central Park! I miss the space - and the air in spring. As for home, no, I can't say I miss it. I wish I could call my mom sometimes, but I'm sure my family doesn't want to hear from me. Afterall, I haven't exactly lived up to my father's expectations, now have I?"

"I don't know. Did your father expect great things of you?"

"My father expected me to be a boy, I think. He had dreams of his sons following in his footsteps."

"And what were those?"

"Making it to the top of the corporate ladder. My brother at least got close by becoming a corporate lawyer, but a daughter who only had ambitions of a writing career was a double disappointment."

"Still, you were pursuing a pretty noble career. I guess I have a difficult time picturing how someone with your background ends up here." I looked around the prison to punctuate my point.

"Well, you'd be surprised what kind of women end up here. You *need* to take a deeper look around. Most of these women are young mothers who have very little opportunity except to be mules for their jackass boyfriends and pimps. I suppose you're right, I'm not the kind of girl who ends up here. I had a choice - unlike these women. I guess that makes me the stupid one."

"According to David, there's nothing stupid about you. Come on Delia. Tell me your story. Tell me how a girl who has choices ends up here. Were you set up? Were you somebody's mule?"

She tilted her head back and laughed. "Don't kid yourself! I'm no one's mule – or fool - for that matter!"

"Okay, then enlighten me! Tell me your story! Don't you want an opportunity to tell your side of things?"

"You haven't travelled much have you Scott?"

"Why do you ask that?"

"If you haven't already figured this out, you soon will. In Latin America, there are three sides to every story and you're lucky if any one of them is actually the truth. Even if I tell my story, it's doubtful you'd believe it. I can hardly believe it myself."

"Try me. Besides, maybe it needs to be told not to get to the truth, but to help others."

"Like who? Who cares about a nobody from New York who ruined her life and is going to rot away in a prison in Central America? Seriously, who?"

"Well at the very least, what about other young women like yourself who travel to these countries and need to know what can happen when -" I stopped. How was I going to finish that sentence? When you get into dealing drugs?

"When you make a bad choice?" She finished it for me.

"Yeah, exactly. That's why I'm here. I'm curious about what makes a girl who apparently had everything - and was on the path to becoming a journalist, make a choice that could ruin her life?"

"Well, that is the million-dollar question, isn't it? You really want to know? You really want to hang out in this place and hear my story?"

"Yeah, I really do."

"How much time do you have?"

"As much time as you need."

"Well as I say, you can always make more money, but you can never get back time. You better be sure you want to waste yours on a girl like me."

"I'm here, aren't I?"

"Okay, but no recordings. You can take notes, that's all."

"Fair enough. I'll call the Embassy this afternoon and ask for special permission to visit you. I don't think they normally let anyone visit more than 1-2 times per week, but David seemed to think he could pull some strings if need be. In the meantime, is there anything you could use?"

"Diapers."

"Diapers?" I looked at her in disbelief. "I know prisoners are capable of making weapons out of just about anything - combs, toothbrushes and things, but what could you possible do with diapers?"

She looked at me and smiled - the first real smile I'd seen from her. "They're not for me or for any nefarious reason. Can you bring them?"

"I'm sure I can round some up somewhere, yeah."

"Great. You bring me diapers and I'll tell you part of my story."

"Only part of it?"

"How many diapers are you going to bring?"

"How many do you need?"

"Well, Scott Harder, how much of my story do you want?"

"I'd like to hear all of it."

"Exactly! Every time you bring me something, I'll tell you more of my story."

At first, I thought Delia's request of a fair exchange each time we saw each other, was simply a tactic to get stuff brought in and benefit herself. After time, however, I realized that perhaps the girl was lonelier than she could ever admit and knowing someone was coming to visit her, gave her some glimmer of hope to hang on to. Perhaps, she wasn't the only one who was lonely – or longing for some hope. "I see you've got great bargaining skills!"

"You haven't heard anything yet, Scott Harder."

"That, I believe!" I found myself smiling for the first time since I entered that bleak, decrepit prison whose walls didn't just threaten to swallow a person, but digest every part of one's soul. If I was truthful, there was a part of me that hoped I might be able to save Delia Russell before it was too late. The irony about trying to save someone is that a person often ends up meeting their own demise.

Chapter 4: Dry Butts

I arrived at the prison two days later with a bag of diapers. Not just any nappies either. Who knew when you do research on where and what type of diapers to buy, you would discover that there's a whole environmental movement not only producing non-plastic diapers, but to help women in developing nations obtain them? Apparently, it can save them money each month and prevent disease with children not crapping in the streets.

I thought I'd like to impress Delia right from the start. It did occur to me if she wanted to use them for some other purpose than actually on babies, my efforts of finding environmental ones would be in vain. But what the hell? I figured trying to get an authentic prisoner's story was a crap shoot - don't mind the pun - and it could all blow up in my face, so why not start off right?

The good news is, she was waiting for me on the *patio* when I arrived. I wasn't able to give her the diapers myself. They had to be opened and inspected in case I was trying to smuggle some treacherous item in to help her escape or kill a fellow inmate. After all, she did have a reputation at the prison as being the only female to actually succeed - at least temporarily - at escaping.

In any case, the guards would give them to her after they'd passed inspection. I did show her the receipt at least.

She smirked a little at me trying to prove to her that I was honest. Hell, it was kind of funny, but obviously, I wanted to create good faith with her and it appeared this attempt had worked. There'd be other attempts that failed miserably.

"So, are you going to tell me what the diapers are for?" I asked as I sat down.

"What the hell do you think they're for?"

"I don't know. You tell me!"

"Dry butts! That's what they're for! Have you looked around here? It's a women's prison and many of them have children. I figured they might need some help."

"And I suppose everything you can offer has some benefit to you as well, right?"

"Well, I may not have lived up to my father's expectations, but he didn't raise a fool! When you're in a place like this, your motives can't be completely altruistic. If you can't afford things, at least you can trade. Besides, these babies and kids don't have an easy time of it in here either. Most are born here after some dumbass comes for his conjugal visit."

"They keep these children here in prison? Seriously, isn't there family members that can take them?"

"I guess they figure the children are better off with their mother, at least for the first few years. Most kids are removed around four years of age, but not all. Some of these women don't have families, that's why they're here in the first place."

"God, that's a story all its own! How many children are in here?"

"I don't know for sure. The mothers and their kids stay in a separate area - although, I've met some of the mothers."

"Well, while we're on that topic, I'd like to begin by asking you about your family."

"You start right off with the tough ones!"

"I figured talking about family might be easier than talking about why you're in here."

"How do you know the two aren't related?"

"Related? Did your family have something to do with you being in here?"

"No. Not exactly, but one's family does influence one's decisions, right? Anyway, if you think talking about family is easier than talking about prison, you obviously didn't do much homework on mine!"

"Well, I know a little about your brother James as I tried to pass myself off as him. That didn't work too well, did it? What happened between you two anyway?"

"I already told you. I'm an embarrassment to his reputation."

"I know he visited you a few times. You couldn't have always been estranged."

"No, there was a time in our childhood that we were close. He looked out for me in school, but once he went off to university, he never looked back. After he got married and had children and was finally out from under my father's thumb, he saw his chance and took it. Success seemed to take hold of him and we simply didn't see the world the same way anymore - if ever."

"How's that? How do you see the world?"

"I was the kind of kid that noticed things. I may have grown up in Manhattan, but I saw the other side of New York. While many of my school mates were into designer dresses and having things, I always felt badly for the have-nots. The streets were lined with homeless people and we were taught - more by example than anything - to just step over them. I never understood, if we had money and were living well, why we didn't do more for the poor.

"My aunt Gretta - my mom's sister - lived in the Bronx and when I would go to visit her, she would take me out with her to volunteer at food kitchens. Those experiences stayed with me, I guess. It makes you feel like you have a greater purpose when you're helping people. And if I was really being honest, I also hated the idea of ever ending up that way - without money or in the streets. Yet, here I am in a worse place!"

"Well, at least you're trying to help people in here, in some small way. That must make you well-liked by most."

"That depends. In prison, there's always people who will see what you do as being self-serving because that's all they've ever known, and then there's ones who appreciate it. My good friend, Eye, lives in here with her two boys who were born here and she's got another son on the outside. She and I get on well."

"Did you say, Eye?"

"Yeah, Scott, haven't you noticed nobody uses their real names down here! I'm not just talking about prison either. This whole country, you really never know who you're talking to. Most locals have three or four given names and most always go by a nickname they've earned. I'm surprised you're using your real name!"

"I don't have much choice but to use my real name when trying to infiltrate this place."

"Well, maybe I need to give you a nickname!"

"That would be interesting to hear!" This would probably be a good time to divulge that I changed Delia's name for this story - it only dawned on me later that the name I gave her sounded a hell of a lot like, "Deal ya" which in the end, seemed appropriate. Her last name I took from the male name that is most associated with drug crimes in the States. Again, appropriate. "So, if you had to give me a nickname, what would it be?"

"I don't know. Nicknames are earned – over time – like a reputation. It takes a while to figure it out. Did you have any siblings? Did they ever give you a nickname?"

"Speaking of not wanting to talk about family, let's change the subject." I felt very uncomfortable telling Delia anything personal about myself. Maybe it was because it was the role of the journalist to be objective and removed from the story. Besides, like Delia, I wasn't ready to talk about my family to her – or anyone. I changed the subject. "So, what's Eye in here for?"

"Interesting story! She and her husband - a former police officer - kidnapped somebody a few years ago. She got 16 years. I'm not sure what he got, but he's probably bribed his way out of prison already! Like you said, money talks. Anyway, Eye's a good mother. She runs a little tienda in here selling food and clothes to the other women. If I can help her out - and yeah, trade things with her, it all balances out."

"What does she think about you – a foreigner - being in here?"

Delia leaned back and laughed. "Well, I've never asked her. You try not to care what anybody thinks, especially about your situation. I mean, these women have seen it all and I'm sure I'm not the first gringa to end up here. You just keep your eyes and ears alert and your opinions to yourself. You definitely don't ask too many questions! You keep your window rolled up."

"What does that mean?"

"It means, you mind your own business and you try not to make any judgements. Your worst enemy can become your best friend and vice versa. It's like survivor island I guess - you gotta be smart about who you make alliances with and try not to piss off too many people along the way."

"Is that how you've survived in here?

"I wouldn't say I'm surviving. Most days I feel like I'm dying a slow death. I exist."

Delia's smile disappeared and her entire body tensed. "So, what else do you want to know? You can probably research about how things work in prison, but as you know from being a journalist, you can't research about someone's life. You've got to hear that firsthand, don't you think?"

"I agree. Again, that's why I'm here. Before we really get going, however, there are probably a few things we should talk about."

"Probably."

"Well, you know, I wouldn't even be allowed to interview you if this was in the States. As journalists, we're only allowed one inmate interview a year and that's limited to three hours. In any case, David pulled some strings at the Embassy and I have unlimited access for now, but as you know, anything down here can change at the drop of a hat. So, I thought we should establish some guidelines of our own. That okay with you?"

"Why don't you run yours by me and then I'll tell you mine."

"Fair enough! Well, I wanted to make it transparent that anything you tell me, I reserve the right to use for my story. However, I only intend to include what the Embassy and the courts already know about your incarceration. Anything else you tell me - about breaking the law, that is - is strictly between you and me. I'd like to come here every day for a couple of hours. I've got a deadline to be home before Christmas and I'd like to keep it. If I can't make it for any reason, I'll ask the Embassy to contact the prison and let you know. I'd appreciate the same courtesy. I don't really want to come all the way here, just to find out you're sick or detained for some reason."

"Okay, that's reasonable. Anything else?"

"Yeah. If anything were to happen to me, the only other person I'm forwarding your notes to is a friend in New York, just as a precaution in case I lose mine or have them confiscated by the guards here. If anything happens to you, I reserve the right to continue to write your story, even in the event of your death."

"Well, you get right to the point, don't you! Who is this *friend* you're talking about?"

"Her name is Angelica. She actually came to me and let me know that David might be able to help me contact you. She seems pretty sweet - and trustworthy."

"Beware of the sweet ones, Scott. They're the ones that can cause you the most trouble in the end!"

"Point taken! Regarding the issue of my death - or yours, I thought it better to get right to the point as we need to face the fact that shit happens down here - and in here - every day!"

"Every hour!"

"Exactly! Okay, that's about it. What are yours?"

"Everyone I talk about - they've either been my friend, still are my friend or in some cases, want me dead. I only use aliases or nicknames. Don't even try to get their real name from me. Deal?"

"Deal. Although, I may ask you questions about them, to get a sense of who they are, but I assure you, nicknames only."

"Okay."

"Let me ask you something."

"What?"

"Why are you agreeing to this? You say you've still got friends - and enemies - down here. Why risk it? I mean, I know we talked about how it might help some other young girl, but what really changed your mind?"

Delia looked at me and smiled. It was the first time I noticed that she was missing a tooth on both her upper and bottom left gum and how yellow her teeth were. What had really happened to turn this apparently stunning blonde into a woman that looked the part of a prison inmate?

"I know I'm never going to make it out of this shithole. I did once, but they're going to make sure I never see the light of day again. Part of why I got the sentence I did, was because they are making an example out of me. Then I go and escape - what kind of example will they make out of me now? Anyway, I know my sentence is only 25 years, less the almost six I've served, but I'll be dead by then. So, it's this simple: I don't want everything I went through - everything I learned - and everyone who touched my life - to die in here with me. And I figure, like you said, maybe my story can help even one girl not be stupid enough to do what I did."

"Fair enough Delia. Fair enough. Shall we begin?" The irony of my question was that I knew we'd begun from the moment I heard her name in that damn bar on 3rd street. There are just some people - and their stories - who you know are going to be a part of yours. I understood what she meant about the people she'd met who had become a part of her story. What's that expression? *Once you know someone, you can't unknow them.* You can only decide how little or how much you're going to let them affect your life. I had a strong sense, Delia was going to have an immense impact on mine.

Chapter 5: The Package

"You'd think being transported to the only women's prison in Honduras would have been the scariest moment in my life. It wasn't. Nothing could compare to the seven years of chronic pressure - by far, the highest highs and the lowest lows a human can endure that transpired between diving in the ocean for that package and ending up in this hellhole in Tamara, Honduras.

"You know, I remember as a kid walking the beach with my dad, chasing the sandpipers, always hoping for some kind of treasure. Of course, when you're a kid, a treasure could be a sand shovel or plastic toy or a coin. Little did I know, what kind of treasure - more like a curse - was going to find me that day on the coast.

"After I watched it from the beach, I didn't immediately jump in and grab it. One, because I didn't want to attract attention to it or myself, but mostly because there was some part of me that believed if it was for me to find that it would come ashore all on its own. I returned to my 3rd floor balcony - I was staying in someone's guest house at the time - and watched it slowly moving down the reef, being battered by the waves. I didn't want to lose track of it and I knew that if it made its way much further it would be in plain sight of the resort - and its guests - just up the coast.

"I knew that if I could swim to it and draw it up on the reef that it would be more difficult to spot than on the sand. The sun was going down and I knew that I didn't have much time before I lost sight of it, but still, I bade my time.

"Just before dusk I dove off the rusted ladder and swam about 30 meters. It was early November, the onset of the rainy season and the sea had begun to churn tumultuously those last few days, but I persevered and managed to grab the damn thing. It was so heavy! I honestly didn't think I could carry it. In the end, I managed to drag it up into a rain pocket on the iron shore of the reef. It still had a rope attached to it - probably ripped free from the other packages at some point, so I managed to tie it around a tall stalagmite until I could come back down later at night.

"I think back on that day and how methodical I was about the whole damn thing and yet, I was just a naive city girl with no real career and absolutely no exposure to hard drugs. I still wonder where I got my grit from - and how I was capable of making the decisions I did. Perhaps my father's influence had rubbed off on me as he always said that when you see an opportunity, you should take it. I'd like to think I saw that package as a chance to help myself get ahead - and in doing so, further my ability to help others. Or maybe that's what every drug dealer tells themselves in the beginning!

"Anyway, later that night, I dragged that big ass thing up to my third-floor room and tossed it in my hammock. It was a deadweight and swung to and fro while I paced back and forth thinking about what to do next."

"Did you ever think about reporting it?"

"Of course! I thought about it a lot. Even after I sold my first few kilos, I thought about reporting it. With every new sale or exchange, I played with the idea that perhaps it wasn't too late. Perhaps, there was still time to report it, to turn in what I hadn't *disposed* of; but with each deal where the white shark" - this was Delia's term for it - "was replaced with greenbacks, a little more of my soul was noshed away. I knew very little about drugs and corruption until I came upon that package. I learned fast.

"By then I had a few friends on the island, but I knew I couldn't share what I'd found with just anyone. I knew that when it came to drugs or money, it changed people and the safest thing for me to do was to keep it under wraps until I could figure out what the hell I was going to do."

"How the hell did you know what it was?" I asked this because something in Delia's confession about her own lack of exposure to drugs and her description of how she found the package, just didn't add up.

"I didn't know what it was, but drugs or money washing up on shore isn't a rare occurrence down here. In fact, after every hurricane, one hears rumours of the locals finding packages all over the islands. I also figured it might have been dropped off a boat by somebody who didn't want the authorities to see. Those are the kinds of packages you really have to worry about."

"Why is that?"

"They're the ones who belong to someone and eventually, they always come looking for it. You better hope you don't have it in your possession when they do! There are all kinds of crazy stories down here and all over the world of these packages washing up on shore. Have you ever heard about the story of Sao Miguel?"

"You mean the island off of Portugal?"

"Yes, that's right."

"It seems to me I heard something about cocaine washing up there."

"Yeah, it did. That was one of the first stories back in 2001 that I would have loved to write about, but one of the other guys at *The Times* got chosen to cover it. It didn't stop me from reading about it though. There was over half a ton of cocaine that washed up on the coast of that island.

"The Sicilian guy, Antonino Quinci was actually transporting it from South America across the Atlantic for some gang in Spain. Somehow, his boat was damaged while crossing the Atlantic and he wasn't going to make it to Spain, so he had the bright idea of trying to anchor near Sao Miguel temporarily, but the shores are really shallow there and the boat ended up stuck on the reef. He tried to throw most of the shipment overboard to save himself from the authorities, but in the end, all he really did was mess up an entire island of people and landed himself in prison, which he eventually escaped from.

"So, these locals of Sao Miguel started finding bricks of cocaine all over. I guess it was turning up in both the powder form and yellowish crystals and most of them had never seen it before so they didn't even know what it was. They soon figured it out though, and it basically made the entire island go crazy. There were some people consuming more than a kilo in a month and one guy even hooked himself to a drip of water and cocaine and sat in his house, getting high for days. Some of the locals became dealers and were shipping the white shark in milk bottles, tins and even socks and beer glasses. Some were selling it right out of their cars.

"So, this Quinci guy stayed on the yacht he'd thrown the shipment from and was eventually caught by the police and then sent to prison in Spain. Apparently, though, pretty much the entire time he was in there, he was allowed to be on the phone and rumour has it that he'd been arranging to rent a scooter and escape. So, one day, he wraps his arms in cloth and starts to climb the wall of the prison, over the barbed wire and apparently the guard in the tower didn't shoot him because he was afraid he might hurt someone. Obviously, he was being paid well!

"So Quinci gets away and hides out in crop fields and then in one farmer's chicken coop for almost two weeks. Eventually, he was caught and put back in prison - I think he got ten years or something."

"So, what does this have to do with you finding a package exactly?"

"Well, I guess from me having prior knowledge of the Sao Miguel story, I just assumed what it was floating up on shore. That, and I knew enough to not actually try the stuff."

"So, you're telling me this story became a cautionary tale for you to deal the contents, rather than hook yourself up to a drip?"

"Well, that's one way of looking at it. I suppose it also taught me about the pitfalls of such foolery and if one ever gets into prison how to escape it!"

I'll be honest, I'd seen and heard a lot as a *New York Times* journalist, but there was something in Delia's brash reference to things that fascinated me. Especially the part about an escape when she had been guilty of such a thing herself - which had added years to her sentence. Perhaps this is what kept me coming back for more. I had to admit, I'd lead a pretty boring life and living vicariously through her was more intoxicating than I can describe.

"So, you've got this package that you rescued from the surf and dragged it up to your room and stuck in your hammock. Then what?"

"Well, I didn't know if it was drugs or money. I hoped it was money. If it had been, things would've been a lot easier. I could have just kept it hidden for a couple of years. But, as I discovered, it was the great white shark and it got its teeth in me and wouldn't let go. Of course, it also opened up a whole new window of entrepreneurship for me. I finally had a career path."

"A career path? Is that a joke?" Again, her shameless way of referring to something that had put her away practically for life made me want to judge her - and at the same time, understand her brazen demeanor. I simply let her continue.

"I mean, if I wasn't going to hand it over to the authorities, I had to unload it slowly and methodically. If I was going to do that, I had to be smart. I had to figure out a plan. Most people I'd become friends with knew very little about me. They knew I had worked for *The Times* and most assumed I was a world traveler, so I thought what better idea than to tell people I was travelling and writing a book about drug smuggling. Obviously, I would need to do research, so I started asking questions and as most people love to share stories, they were very forthcoming with what they knew on the topic. As it turns out, everyone on the island either knows someone who does drugs, sells drugs or has been busted with drugs, so it wasn't hard to get information.

"I'd also been on the island long enough to know there was a market for what I had - and a lot of them were my closest friends who I'd been partying with for months. The trick was, how was I going to unload the white shark without getting a reputation for being a drug dealer? The truth is, you can't. Whatever you're into on the island becomes your reputation. So, I knew I had to be convincing at selling myself as a writer. People typically either believe the best in you; or the worst. Most strangers chose to be wary of me and make shit up, which was even worse. I didn't care, as long as it kept people off the scent of what I had found - and kept the police away from me. Obviously, I managed for a while, but as I've learned, either your reputation or your choices eventually catch up with you."

I had learned that a journalist was only as good as her or his questions and while I knew that Delia had grown up in a privileged home in the upper east side of New York, there was an edge about her that seemed to dispute it. I became very aware that if I was to get to the truth about this woman sitting in front of me, I had better formulate the appropriate questions.

"Looking back on it now, do you regret what you did?"

"I regret getting caught. I don't regret the experience, although there are some moments I wish never happened. I've lost a great deal of friends - and my family - because of my choices, but in the end, that package is the reason I've met some fantastic people, so how can I wish for some other outcome?"

"Don't you wish for your freedom?"

"I wish for a lot of things, but as I heard once, 'You can wish in one hand and crap in the other and see which gets filled faster.'"

"Delia, you have a wonderful way with words."

"Of course, I do! I'm a writer, remember!"

"Yes. a writer by day. A narcotics dealer by night!"

"Something like that. So, Scott Harder, what is your vice?"

"My vice? Perhaps it's seeking out stories I have no business writing."

"I'll accept that answer for now, but eventually, I'll figure it out!"

When I left the prison that day, I asked myself for the first time, what *was* my vice?   Delia would make me question a lot of things about myself - and my life - and of what I was truly capable. It would be the price I'd have to pay for getting to the truth about her and her story. It would also mean discovering the truth about myself - the good, the bad and the ugly.

Chapter 6: Chihuahua

The next conversation I had with Delia was two days later and cost me two bags of diapers. It wasn't long before I realized it was in her nature to *do business.*

"So, since we didn't really get too far the other day, I'd like to hear about after you got the package up to your room and in your hammock, what you actually did next?"

"What every girl who finds the great white shark does! I went and got drunk!"

"Okay and after that?"

"I think I stayed drunk for the next week or so. I really didn't want to face what I'd found - or what I'd done with it."

"Which was?"

"Kept it, dumbass! Sorry, it's just that I'm not used to talking about this and sometimes your questions irritate me. Anyway, I was living in a friend's guest house at the time and I knew I had to make a decision pretty quickly, so I went out and bought a suitcase - I had only brought a large knapsack - so I could transport it quickly if I needed to."

"And where were you living at the time?"

"Away from prying eyes and busybodies, thank goodness! I needed some time to think - and a quiet place to do it. I was near an area called Lawson Rock."

"That's one of the ritzier neighbourhoods on the island, isn't it?"

"That's right. Exactly where you find rich, shark-snorting people, desperate to escape from the reality of their lives and who are more than willing to buy it from an American girl, rather than have to deal with complicated - not to mention - dangerous locals."

"You knew all this when you moved up there?"

"Nope. As it turns out, I knew very little about the island at the time. I had been staying in the west end at a resort for my first few weeks. I guess if I had never relocated, I would never have found that package. Looking back on my decisions, I was either really lucky or really stupid. Sometimes, I figure I was both. But as they say, a person's luck always runs out!"

"So, what were you doing during the time before finding the package?"

"I had been hanging out in the local bar most nights, getting to know people and listening to lots of interesting stories. So, I just kept doing what I was doing - scouting out people who might *know people* and learning a whole shit load about human nature and the different areas - and cultures on the island."

"So, how did you get the nickname Chihuahua?"

"How'd you know that?"

"I've done my own asking around, getting to know people, scouting out people and learning a whole shit load myself."

"Touché! Well, I'm not going to talk about that right now."

"Why not?"

"Because I'm not!"

"Okay, then you tell me. Where - or who do we go to from here?"

"I don't want to talk about me - I told you, it's the people I've met that are important."

"Okay, fair enough! Go ahead."

"Well, I met a guy in my first few weeks - don't look at me like that - he was gay!"

"Look at you like what? No judgements here, I promise!"

"Hmmm, I saw your expression! Besides, we both know that in a southern destination like this, it only takes days - sometimes hours - for people to hook up. The problem with that is that it's a small island. I met a girl from California who told me about having three, one-night stands in her first week on the island and then a few weeks later, if she doesn't run into all three of the guys at the same restaurant! There's some bizarre shit that goes on down here and it's hard to tell if it's just coincidence or literally, a sign from the universe to smarten up. She also told me that there was a strain of herpes on the island - mostly in the younger diving community that you just can't get rid of once you get it. Turns out the only thing free on the island are STI's and herpes - and chlamydia can be picked up at any local hangout. Some refer to it as the Thanksgiving buffet! All the viruses you can get in one place! Eventually, it became my line to most guys who hit on me, if they wanted their "free dose" they could find it somewhere else!

"Anyway, hooking up wasn't my game - at least, not at first. My plan was to stay away from men and get my shit together. Of course, as you know, plans go awry! So, anyway, this guy's name was - let's call him Bernie - he was one of the few guys who I trusted, mostly because he didn't want to get in my pants and he was Canadian."

"Ah those blessed Canadians!" I refrained from mentioning to Delia that my mother was Canadian who met my father while she was on a trip to New York. We joked in my family that we were as wasp as you could come as my grandparents on both sides were from Protestant England. It didn't help that I was as white as a ghost even after days of burning in the hot sun. There were only two shades of myself I ever saw in the mirror: Casper the friendly ghost and Clifford the Red dog.

I suppose my personality could be summed up in the same caricature profile - sickeningly sweet and ever-helpful. Or at least, that's what the girls in high school always told me. Hence, I became the guy friend instead of the boyfriend. I'm sure a few thought I was gay as I never dated in high school. I knew my biggest problem was my shyness and part of why I went into journalism was to get over it. You can't remain in the shadows and get the story.

I suppose, there was still some part of me remaining in those shadows though – telling other people's stories. Like I said, I was boring and I knew it. I guess I sought out people who lived more interesting lives than I did, hoping some part of their fabric would wear off on me. It hadn't happened yet. I suppose I was hoping that Delia could somehow change that.

"So, this friend of yours – Bernie - he was a nice guy?"

"Maybe, although when you got to know him, he could swear like a trooper and you sure as hell didn't want to get on his bad side. I liked him. He was sarcastic as hell and made me laugh. He should have been a comedian. Jesus, some of the shit he said was hilarious. On the first night we met, he sat down beside me and said, 'I might not be a gynecologist, but I know a cunt when I see one!' I probably should have slapped him, but I found it pretty funny. We struck up a conversation about the island and I soon learned that he hung out with a particular party crowd - the type that liked to party on yachts and had money to throw around.

"A few months later, after I found the package, he was the one person I felt I could confide in. And, I had always wanted to party on a yacht, so I asked him if he knew anyone who would do an exchange."

"An exchange?"

"Yeah. An *exchange*. I wasn't ready to have any money pass hands yet. I thought I was being more creative than your average dealer - and perhaps, safer. Little did I know what can happen when you let your guard down even for a minute under the illusion that you're safe. You're never safe!

"Anyway, it just so happened that there was a big party - a fundraiser for an animal rescue shelter - planned for that upcoming weekend on some rich guy's yacht who had come in for about a month on holidays. He knew Bernie and some others on the island and agreed to let them use his yacht

- and well, I'm sure he was getting a few good deals out of it.

"I thought it was the perfect cover to realize my dream of spending some time on a yacht and practicing my drop off techniques. You have to remember at the time, I didn't know squat about what I was doing, but I figured if dumb-asses could deal drugs, why not a Columbia graduate?"

"I suppose that makes sense. I think."

"It doesn't matter if it makes sense. None of what I got myself into made sense. Anyway, the big night came and Bernie had made sure that I got my ticket - they weren't cheap - a 1000 G a pop. All I had to do was put on a dress, stuff my bra with the agreed upon amount of white shark and enjoy my first glitzy night on the ocean. Easy peasy!"

"So, how did you know how much a 1000 of white shark was?"

"Well, looking back on it, of course I was getting ripped off, but it was my first deal so Bernie told me they wanted a "Big Eight" which is about 125 grams for a 1000-dollar ticket. That meant they were only willing to pay me about $10 dollars a gram. I mean, I did some research and even most street dealers were asking anywhere between 20-26 bucks a gram. Little did I know, for the Colombian C I had, which wasn't what you'd call "street", I could have charged these highty-toighties a hell of a lot more. I wasn't going to argue my first-time doing business. There was plenty of time - and plenty to learn - about the trade, but I was a fast learner and I got a whole lot smarter as time - and deals - went on.

"Bernie had spent some time with me that week - at my place, but he brought his own personal stash - showing me how to measure out that amount. I worked it out that I had to carry about 60 grams in each side of my bra, which is only a few ounces, so it wouldn't be a big deal. I also figured out something else!"

"What's that?"

"Victoria's secret!"

"What? What the hell do you mean?"

"There's so much padding in those bras that if you remove it, you have a hell of a lot of room to carry other shit in there. I learned that from my mother who always told me to stuff mad money in my brassiere when I was a teenager so if a boy expected something from me - or I got pissed off at him - I'd always have cab fare to get home."

I wanted to broach the subject of Delia's mom and if she had ever called home, but didn't think this was the time to bring it up. I made a mental note to ask her later. "Okay, so you've got two Eight balls in your brassiere. So, what happened?"

"You're getting ahead of me a little! I may have made it sound all easy peasy, but have you ever opened up a package of white shark that's been drifting in the ocean from God knows where, for several weeks?"

"I can't say that I have!"

"Well, who knew when I tried to cut open the first bag that the damn shit was going to explode all over my face? I stood there stunned. I looked like I'd been in a bake-off all day. Except this wasn't flour and I was no Aunt Jemima! I had it in my eyes, my hair, up my nose - funny as that sounds

- and even in my mouth. I spent the next half hour coughing up a lung. I didn't know what to do, so I called Bernie and told him I'd gotten myself in some trouble. He didn't want the details. He just said to figure it out and that I had two hours to get my ass to the dock for embarking."

Again, I was skeptical of what Delia was telling me, but it's a strange phenomenon when you're desperate to live vicariously through someone else - you hope their crazy story is true. I suppose that's why Henry David Thoreau said, 'Don't sit down to write until you stand up and live' especially as a journalist.

I'll be the first to admit, when you have very few interesting experiences of your own, you are exponentially more vulnerable to buying into others' stories - even if there's little or no truth in them. A good journalist, this does not make! I attempted, diplomatically, to gain some form of the truth from Delia.

"Hold on just a second. Are you telling me, that was the first time you'd even opened up a bag of it? How the hell did you even know what it was?"

"Well I had opened the outer bag - it was wrapped in some kind of waterproof, heavy-duty sticky-ass duct tape or something. I could see through the smaller bags - the bricks - but I'd been too scared to open them."

"Meanwhile, you'd already lifted it from the ocean and hid it in your hammock for weeks, but you never thought to open a bag and try it, test it, make sure it was the real deal? Especially before you went off and tried to make an exchange with it - that's a new one I haven't heard before!"

"Well yeah! I told you I had a lot to learn about the whole business! I mean, I knew what it was. I wasn't that stupid and as soon as I saw the insignia on the outside of each brick, I was pretty sure where it had come from."

"Really? Even the authorities can't tell that most of the   time."

"I guess in all your digging up of shit at the *New York Times* about me, you must have overlooked the fact that one of the first stories I got asked to cover was in Colombia."

"No, I didn't know that. They wouldn't have sent you there as an intern!"

"No! That's the clincher! It was David who convinced the chief Editor to "promote" me - pay me - albeit, next to nothing besides my trip down there - to cover the story. No one else at the time wanted to do it, so I volunteered. Don't worry, I wasn't doing anything illegal down there, but I was assigned to follow a story on one of the largest drug busts in Medellin and rumour had it that it was one of the last shipments that belonged to Pablo Escobar before he was shot."

This was the 2nd time Delia lied to me. I didn't know it at the time however, and went ahead with our conversation. "I'm not worried about you doing anything illegal down there! It seems irrelevant now, anyway, doesn't it?"

"Yeah, I guess so!"

"So, what was the insignia?"

"Well, if I tell you that, I'd have to kill you!"

"Funny! So, what was it?"

"Still can't tell you. It's better you don't know. There are some things, that happened to me – and about me

- that you really are better off not knowing! In any case, when I saw what was on this package, I knew it wasn't some recent shipment - it was an old one that probably no one was looking for."

"Pablo Escobar was killed back in the 90's. There's no way it could have been drifting that long!"

"Exactly! Which meant, someone had either been hiding it for all those years and when hurricane Wilma hit, it got away from them or it had been laying somewhere for years and finally got pried loose by the winds and water. I don't know. I just know that it was a unique package, to say the least."

"I guess! So, how did the night on the yacht turn out?"

"As my initiation into the business, I don't think it turned out too badly. I was aware that if I had ingested even a little of the shark it would fuck me up for hours. Remember, I'd never done any hard shit - ever! I dusted myself off, measured out the amount I needed, got in a taxi as fast as I could and got myself over to the dock. I paced that damn thing for an hour while my mind raced about all kinds of shit. My heart was pounding and I was sweating like crazy, but I had never felt better, like I could accomplish anything. Turns out, that little accident gave me more confidence than I ever would have had if I'd been completely sober. When people started to embark, I walked that plank to the yacht like I owned the world!

"Of course, in those days, I also looked like a million bucks. I'd been running every morning on the beach; my skin was glowing and my blonde hair was so long it touched my ass - although that night I wore it up. I was wearing a royal blue, satin dress with a plunged neck and back and I looked, I'm sure, every bit the part of a girl who *should* be on a yacht!" Delia paused for a moment and something in those blue eyes of hers sparkled for the first time. "I know what you're thinking!"

"What am I thinking?" I hoped Delia didn't actually know! During the time I was interviewing her, I can't say that the majority of it was positive or that I thought she was being straight with me. I just hadn't figured out yet, if she was lying to me on purpose or she had told her story so many times, that she genuinely believed it. I can say that I grew to genuinely like the girl and as I said, I wanted to believe what she was telling me and forced myself at times to listen attentively, even when I knew in my gut that she wasn't being honest.

"I know the way I look now. I know I look like hell. I mean, I've lost most of my hair - what I have left, well, look at it, it's a stringy mess. I used to be stunning - or at least, that's what people told me."

"Did you lose your hair because of your drug habit?"

"What? What the hell? I'm not a user! I never was. I sold the shit. I never used it - except for that night. I was smart enough to know that much. No! I lost my hair from stress - stress of trying to stay out of jail for seven years! And look, I landed my ass in here anyway!"

"I'm sorry! I just assumed if you were exposed to it - and dealing it for that long, that you eventually ended up using."

"It's okay. What would you think? Sorry, I didn't used to talk like this either. I used to be a well-spoken

Columbia graduate - not a filthy-mouthed convict! I mean obviously using drugs can completely affect who you are, but it's also amazing how things - and people you hang around, can change you. It wasn't the use of drugs, but maybe the exposure to the business of it that did it to me.

"Anyway, Bernie met me at the bar on the yacht as planned. At first, he simply introduced me to a few people - probably more to get a sense of where my head was at. He had told me earlier that week if there was any moment of doubt for me, I better tell him before we lifted anchor because my ass would be off the boat. As nice as he was - and a friend - there was no way he was going to be on the hook for a grand. He also didn't really want to be blamed for ruining the night of some of his best customers.

"I told him all was well. I just tapped my boob once and he knew that was the sign for the go ahead. He nodded his head. At that point, I was supposed to go into the women's bathroom closest to the bar, lift up the back of the toilet lid and use a piece of duct tape - I had to stick it to my skin - it was a bitch yanking it off - and then attach my stash to the underside of porcelain."

"How did you know for sure you even had the right amount?"

"Well, I measured it out after I was already half-stoned so I could only hope and pray they didn't feel like I was ripping them off. As it turns out, Bernie said I'd been generous compared to most of the dealers he'd used to supply for his friends and after that, they only wanted to use me. Of course, they supposedly never knew it was me that brought it on board - or my real name - Bernie saw to that."

"So, is this where the nickname Chihuahua came in?"

"I guess, since you brought me two bags of diapers, I'd be willing to divulge that to you. It's kind of a funny story - in a sick, twisted way. Bernie loved telling stories and so one night after we were pretty sloshed, he began telling me about a guy he dated who had a little yappy chihuahua named Mickey. The dog hated him for some reason, so when his lover would go to the bathroom or leave the room, Bernie would throw the yappy thing about eight feet in the air and when he put him down, it wouldn't bark at him for the rest of the night. Of course, the next time he visited, Mickey would be right back at it again.

"So, this one night, when his lover left the room, Bernie threw the dog up in the air as usual, but got caught with him in mid-flight when his lover suddenly reappeared. He screamed and asked Bernie what the hell he thought he was doing. Distracted, he wasn't able to catch the pup on his descent and it fell to the floor and broke both its back legs! It's a horrible story really and made me wonder how I had become friends with such a person. Anyway, needless to say, that was the last night Bernie ever saw that lover!"

"No kidding! So, that still doesn't explain how it became your nickname."

"That night of my first drop, Bernie warned me that if I fucked up in anyway, he'd do to me what he did to that chihuahua."

"And so, did you fuck up? It sounds like everything went pretty well if his customers wanted to deal with you again."

"Oh yeah, in terms of the deal everything went fine. However, the rest of the night I was pretty fucked up and never stopped talking to Bernie or to anyone that would listen, so he decided to call me chihuahua anyway! God, I loved that man."

"Loved? Past tense?"

"We've grown apart, but I still miss him. Anyway, I don't want to get into that today. That's at least another bag of diapers and some chocolate."

"Chocolate too? How did I know!"

"You knew from the first day you walked in here, this wasn't going to be easy for either one of us. But isn't that what makes a great journalist - the one who gets the great stories."

"Touché, Chihuahua! Touché!"

Chapter 7: Bridgette

"As much as I want to delve into your life *after* the package, I'm really having a hard time imagining what was going on that made you think you could snatch it in the first place. I mean, tell me more about your first four months *pre-package* - or your life pre-island."

"The truth is, when I first arrived on the island, I was simply looking for peace - and a rest from the craziness of New York. I'd been busting my ass for every story - and every lead I could get, mostly because after David made way for me to do that story in Colombia, I wasn't going to disappoint him. He seemed to believe in me when very few did - even my parents. So, when I returned from researching it - and had to surrender up my notes to another *upwardly mobile* at *The Times* - I continued to work my tail off running around for others.

"I was doing just what I had done all my life - trying to prove my worth to someone - anyone - that would notice. For some reason, David noticed. I don't know if it was because he had a secret desire to get into my pants - and I didn't really care to be honest. Whatever it took to have someone in my corner, is what mattered to me. Then, after about three years, sick of running around for other people, I wanted to write my own articles. I talked to my boss, but she kept putting me off, saying I wasn't ready. I look back and I think the bitch was simply jealous of me - maybe my looks, maybe my assertiveness, I don't know. She was determined to make sure I didn't break through. David saw that. He came to me one afternoon and asked if I wanted to go for a drink. An after-work drink on a Friday night seemed pretty harmless, so I went."

As Delia was talking, I thought about what I would think if a female co-worker asked me for an after-work drink on a Friday night – not that it ever happened.   Maybe guys and girls think differently, but I certainly would have secretly hoped she was looking for more. Had Delia really been this naïve? Was she really this needy for attention? The inmate in a dirty t-shirt and ripped jeans didn't appear to me that way, but I suppose years of drug dealing and being in prison can truly change a person. I wondered how much Delia really had changed or was there still some semblance of that needy, naïve girl still lurking behind those blue eyes? I let her continue her story without interrupting.

"You know, maybe it was our wacky sense of humour - sarcastic wit really - but David and I really hit it off. He was so worldly, so charming and incredibly smart and funny. I thought of him as a father figure and a mentor. Someone to learn the ropes from. I still remember that conversation."

***

"Young lady, what would you like to drink? It's on me."

"Oh, that's okay. I can get it."

"Don't be absurd! It's on me. I insist. And no, I'm not trying to get you drunk so I can take advantage of you. What I'm fascinated with is your mind."

I smirked of course and he caught on right away. "Yeah, yeah, maybe you've heard that before and think I'm shooting the shit, but I mean it. I've been watching you at the paper for over five years now and I saw what a great job you did researching that Colombia story three years ago. You should have been promoted by now. A girl with ambition and a mind like yours should be on the way to the top by now."

"Well, thank you for saying that. I knew when I graduated from Columbia it would take a few years to get my feet wet, but yes, I'd like to see something happening by now. It's a little frustrating."

"A little? It's incredibly infuriating and I'm just watching from the outside. I mean, if you look around at most columnists and editors, they're predominantly male, so it's no surprise that it's tougher for you. Although I would have thought Sofie, with things being the same way for her, would have been more likely to promote you by now. I just don't get it. You know, I can talk to her if you like?"

"No. It's okay. Probably not a good idea. I've tried - and maybe she's right, I'm just not ready. Anyway, I know if you try to push her into anything, she can dig in her heels, so you talking to her might make it worse."

"I suppose you're right. Well, in the meantime, we can have a drink and talk about whatever you like. Where did you grow up?"

"Born and raised right here in Manhattan. That's partly why I really want to make it on my own with no strings being pulled. I want to show my parents that I can be successful like my brother - all on my own."

"And what does your brother do?"

"James? He's a lawyer in New Jersey. Married with two boys - Christian and Ollie - Oliver. They're cute. I mean, I don't see them very much, but he sends photos to curb his guilt."

"Are you not close?"

"There's a few years difference in age and well, he's one to keep to himself. His wife and family have kind of taken over his life. You know how it is."

"I imagine he's quite busy as a lawyer in Jersey as well."

"He keeps busy, for sure."

"And what about your love life? Any prospects?"

"Not really. I dated a guy in my first two years of college, but we grew apart."

"He cheated?"

"No. We just didn't have a lot in common. He wanted to get engaged and settle down as soon as we graduated and I had bigger plans. You know, becoming a famous journalist or something."

"Did you ever want to do anything else?"

"Yeah, I wanted to join the Peace Corp when I was a kid. I used to sit on my bed with all of my stuffed animals and pretend that we were flying around the world saving animals and children from poverty and abuse. Kind of stupid, right?"

"Stupid? Absolutely not! You know what I wanted to be when I was a kid?"

"No, what?"

"A priest! Can you believe that? I was an altar boy and I used to watch the priests - I never had any bad experiences with them - do their work in the streets around our neighbourhood in the Bronx and I used to think, that's what I want to do. Of course, as you get older and realize that they had to take some vows that weren't that appealing - celibacy being one of them and I really didn't like the poverty one, either - I decided to revamp my career goals. I soon realized that having a successful career and making money can also allow you to help others. So, I totally get your altruistic goals. Don't lose sight of those, no matter where you end up. Helping others is a noble ambition!"

"Thank you. I haven't really shared that with anyone before. It was my aunt who lives in the Bronx who first exposed me to the *other side* of New York, so I understand what you're saying."

"Well, here's to noble ambitions!"

***

"There was just something about David that seemed genuine to me. The kind of person that despite his success and wealth, was really grounded in reality. I liked that. Perhaps he saw that in me. What a disappointment I've become to him!"

"I didn't get that impression from him when I talked to him. He seemed to think that a girl of your intelligence probably had good reasons for doing what you did. As do I. That's why I'm trying to get a sense of who you were before you found that package. So, let's fast forward for a minute. You had this interesting conversation with David one night about noble ambitions and eventually you end up quitting the paper and moving to Central America. Then what?"

"Well, I stayed at the paper another five years - I gave that place ten years of my life. Sofie finally moved on to another department and I was finally promoted to investigative journalist, which I thought I'd love. As it turns out, I began to hate it. Then when I saw the aftermath of Hurricane Wilma and heard about the devastation in Honduras - and a number of other places - I decided it was time for me to take a sabbatical from the rat race for a while. Initially, when I first planned my trip, I was hoping to do some aid work for a few months.

"Who knew, I'd end up spending my life here! I always thought I'd return to New York after I had a chance to get the last bad guy out of my heart - and the urban craziness out of my system. Maybe I would have if I hadn't come across that package. Or maybe that package was my destiny. I don't know. Ancient history now, I guess!

"Life here was great at first. I spent a lot of days lying on the beach, snorkeling - submerging myself in a quieter, more scenic environment. My nights, I spent at Luna Subiendo drinking and conversing with people, mostly trying to mind my own business. That was until I met Bridgette."

"Who's Bridgette?"

"Who is Bridgette? Good question! She was this strange woman who just came up to me out of the blue at the bar, put her arm around me, introduced herself and said, 'I have something for you' and handed me a pamphlet and walked away. I turned to ask her what she wanted me to do with it or if she wanted it back, but she had disappeared. I didn't really pay much attention to it at first. I looked at the front cover which was a photo of what looked like a garbage dump with children in the middle of it. It wasn't until later when I took it home to read it, that I realized what she had given me. It was an opportunity."

"An opportunity?"

"Remember the conversation I had with David about wanting to join the Peace Corp as a kid? Well, this was a chance to do that - to make a difference. So, I got in touch with the organization and found out more about what they did. Essentially, many Hondurans - mostly children, live at or near the dump and every day they scour it for food or items to resell for money to feed their families. Meanwhile, like most expats and visitors, I'm sitting in the luxury of my little apartment with Wi-Fi and air conditioning, complaining if I don't make it out snorkeling or to the beach one day.

"These kids don't even get fed properly on a daily basis and I have to throw food out because I can't eat it before it goes bad. I realized that I hadn't just been looking for peace - I was looking for a purpose and I found it. There was a group of volunteers that went out every 2nd day to the dump to offer proper food and water to the kids who lived there. Some were short-term tourists that simply wanted to drop off clothes and school supplies to the kids.

"I can't tell you how that impacted me. I'd seen a great deal in my travels already, but when you're watching young children down in the rubbish - essentially what wealthier people toss away - looking for something - anything - to survive on, it takes your breath away and makes your heart ache. I hadn't been affected like that in a long time. My heart needed something else to focus on besides my latest ex."

"Speaking of that, you've mentioned him twice now. Anyone of importance? Should he be mentioned in this story?"

"Importance? Well, there's far more important people that came into my life because I was running away from him – but I suppose he should get an honourable mention."

"Do tell!"

"I think we've hit our two-hour limit, haven't we? I guess if you want to hear about my love life, you're going to have to come back tomorrow."

"Well Delia, this is slowly becoming like a soap opera where I'm left in suspense every day."

"Hold on to your hat, Scott. You haven't heard anything yet!"

"That's what you keep telling me! Can I at least know if you ever saw this Bridgette again?"

"No, but I did find out why she approached me in the first place with that pamphlet."

"And why was that?"

"I'll tell you another day!"

"We'll leave it there, then. So, what will it be tomorrow? More diapers? Chocolate?"

"An hourglass."

"Okay, I have no idea where I'm going to find one of those, but okay. I can't wait to hear about what that signifies."

"Well, in the song, *Breathe,* there's this great line that says, 'life's like an hourglass glued to the table."

"That is a great line. I guess we all have a finite time on this planet. That's why we as journalists tell others' stories while we can."

"That's why I need you to tell mine, before my sand runs out."

I got the sense that Delia knew something I didn't. I mean, I knew she thought she might die in prison, but essentially, she was still a young woman in her forties and had a lot of life ahead of her. It wouldn't be until much later that I finally understood her words that day - and finally figured out the significance of that damn hourglass.

Chapter 8: Muttonhead

So, the only hourglass I could find was a plastic one that came from a Boggle game – it seemed appropriate somehow - that I happened to find in a second hand store where expats left their crap behind when returning home from their vacation. Delia hadn't specified what kind of hourglass or if she needed a fancy one, so I thought it better to show up with something if I wanted to hear more of her story.

As it turns out, the guard had to pop off the top of the damn thing and double check that its contents were actually sand, so I was just as glad I hadn't brought a glass one. They would have had to smash it or would have simply taken it away from me. The plastic one has a rubber top that snapped back on, although I'm pretty sure they lost a few grains when fooling with it. Did it even matter? Turns out, after my next conversation with Delia, I got the answer to that question!

I was allowed to take it in with me. I suppose this was because they had checked its contents and it was very tiny - only about two inches high. It sat between us almost the entire duration of our conversation which spoke volumes regarding the situation we were in. We did in fact, have a limited amount of time together. And yet, because of her situation, she technically had all the time in the world to sit within the harrowing walls of prison, while life went on without her. It made me sad to see her in there, but I would never have voiced that to her. I knew she didn't want my pity. I, in truth, didn't want to give it to her - not at least until I heard her whole story.

"So, are you going to give up the goods on the hourglass thing? First David's reference to it and now you're asking for one in prison. What's the beef?"

"Have you ever asked yourself who gets to decide how many grains of sand are in an hourglass?"

"I haven't really given it any thought to be honest. Although, I did do some research on them last night in my hotel room."

"Of course, you did!"

"Well, what else am I going to do with my time?"

"Scott, I'm the one in prison, not you. You're free to leave your hotel room and go have a good time. All that freedom and you still choose to sit and do research."

"You know the life of a journalist - the search for knowledge and information is what drives us. I can't just switch that off. Besides, when I'm not here, I'm pretty much thinking about you and your story anyway, so it intrigues me to find out stuff - especially if it means something to you."

"So, in reality, you were trying to figure out what David meant by it."

"Well, if I'm completely honest, yeah. It would be a lot simpler if you just told me."

"It might be a lot simpler, but like I said before, you're better off not knowing everything about my story. So, what did you discover?"

"It's actually quite interesting. Did you know that hourglasses first showed up in a fresco painting in 1338, but there was something similar called a clepsydra, which is a water clock and it's believed to have existed in Babylon and Egypt as far back as the 16th century BC? I guess our fascination with time has been around a long time! And of course, the hourglass has been used as a symbol for the finite human existence. Pirates even used them on their flags to symbolize that time was running out for their enemies. I thought you might like that part! And we can't forget the hourglass figure of a woman."

"Oh! Here we go. I knew it wouldn't take you long to get to that part."

"How'd you know that?"

"Because I know men!"

"Well, it wasn't just about the figure of a woman but how they symbolize feminine energy, albeit as time goes by, the sand - or her feminine wiles drain away because of gravity. You know what? Never mind that part! It's not important. What is important is what it means to you."

"Actually, what's important to remember about an hourglass is that it's timing is directly reliant on a number of factors all coming together at the same time."

"You mean, like the number of grains of sand, the size of the hole in which it's allowed to drain, those kinds of things?"

"Yeah, those kinds of things."

Sometimes Delia talked to me like I was a simpleton and I hated her for it; like she was superior to me in some way. I understood that she'd seen a whole other world in which I was pretty innocent about and that she'd certainly been exposed to things I couldn't even imagine before and after she was incarcerated, but who was she to think she was smarter than me? The more time I spent with her, the more it pissed me off. I always tried to be one step ahead of her, but I felt like I could never really catch her. This feeling, as it would turn out, would haunt me most of my life.

"Okay, let's put this hourglass aside for a moment," I moved it from between us, "and come back to this love life of yours?"

"Some love life! It's been more like a tragedy - or comedy depending on how you look at it. I guess you'll have to decide after hearing my story. I will tell you though that when people say everything happens for a reason, it does make me wonder why my path crossed with this particular individual considering where he'd been - and where I was going to end up. I met him on the night I'd been out for that first drink with David. In fact, David introduced me to him as an acquaintance of his. Let's call him Muttonhead."

"Muttonhead?"

"Yeah. The reason will become apparent as I tell my story."

"Okay, go on!"

"When I first laid eyes on him, I felt an instant attraction - like the kind of electricity they describe in movies, but you don't really believe it exists. He was tall, dark and had an incredible head of hair - long, black, silky curls. Well dressed, articulate, funny - all the things a girl from the Upper East side is supposed to be attracted to, you know. The kind of guy you could bring home to dad.

"David had to get home, so he left us there and we closed down the place with great conversation. When he walked me to the subway, I was already smitten. He simply kissed me on the cheek, took my number which I gave up gladly and backed away from me slowly as if he too was smitten. He knew all the right moves.

"We dated for the next three months and by the fourth month, I'd already given him a key to my shoddy, cramped apartment. I mean, what could go wrong, right? I made next to nothing at the paper and I didn't have anything to steal - or so I thought! The funny thing is, I couldn't get rid of this gut feeling he wasn't telling me something. I broached the subject a few times, actually asking him if there was something he needed to tell me, but he brushed me off repeatedly.

"That was until one night, the feeling became so intense I came right out and accused him - of course the bottle of red wine didn't help - of either lying to me about something or keeping something from me. At that point, he flipped out, told me I was nothing but a 'jealous, paranoid bitch looking to ruin a good thing.' His words exactly. So, I didn't find out *what* he was hiding - but I certainly got a glimpse into his real personality for the first time.

"He stomped out of the restaurant and walked ten feet ahead of me, got in his Porsche and left me standing there on the street with no way home. It's a good thing I still always listened to my mother and had some mad money."

"In your bra, right?"

"No, I actually carry money in my purse in New York. Although, come to think of it, it would probably be safer in my bra! Anyway, I made it home and sure enough, there were already six apologetic messages on my voicemail asking me to call him back. He said there *was* something he needed to tell me if I would just see him one more time. You know, no matter what you expect, like maybe he's a got a girlfriend or a wife, or he's gay, you're never really prepared to hear the truth."

"So, what was his deep, dark secret?"

"He sat me down the next evening and told me that twenty-four years earlier, he had stabbed his girlfriend in the throat outside her university and he'd been charged with attempted murder and sentenced to thirteen years in federal prison."

"Wow! That's a deathblow to a new relationship! No wonder he didn't want to tell you."

"Those were his words exactly: 'How do you tell someone you were in jail for attempted murder when you're dating them? How do you broach that subject?' I mean, he had a point. I don't think there's ever a good time to tell someone news like that. However, I just couldn't look at him the same, you know?"

"Yeah, I get that. So, what did you do?"

"I broke up with him that night. I mean, how do you trust a guy who has already been so violent?"

"So, this is the guy that you were so broken hearted over? I mean, didn't that help you get over him?"

"That's not the end of the story."

"I should have known. With you Delia, I have a feeling there might never be an end to the stories!"

"Aren't you lucky! Anyway, the stupid, naive girl that I was, after spending two weeks missing him - or perhaps longing for that electricity I had with him, I thought to myself, 'Listen, he did a stupid thing twenty-four years ago when he was young and passionate - and his girlfriend had been cheating on him for six years with her boss' - at least that's what he told me - 'I wouldn't want anyone to hold against me, something I did that many years ago, so isn't it fair that instead of basing my opinion of him on that, I should take the time to get know him better?'"

"So, how'd that work out for you?"

"It took exactly two weeks until his violent temper flared again because I didn't want to go to a work event - he was a marketing director - with him. We had a horrible fight and he ended up standing over me, spitting in my face and calling me all kinds of horrible names. It's like something else took over his entire being. This handsome, charming guy turned into a hideously cruel person in a matter of seconds. I knew then that it was only a matter of time before he became physically violent. I told him to get out and he left. The clincher is, I forgot to get my key back from him."

"I don't like where this is going."

"No. I went to work the next day and when I got home, I knew something wasn't right. Things in my apartment were moved, but I couldn't figure out exactly what he'd done until I walked into my closet. I always prided myself on my style and my dresses - that's where most of my money went. When I opened my closet door, half of my dresses were missing and the empty hangers in between the ones he had left, looked so odd. It was truly bizarre why he chose to take certain dresses and not others. It seemed so random. Then I started looking all over my apartment and for some reason - I guess because we had just been grocery shopping together the week before - I opened my freezer."

"And what? God, don't tell me, he'd hacked up your dog and stuffed it in there!"

"No, where did you get that from?"

"Hey, you should know, as a journalist, we see some strange shit."

"No dogs, but my entire freezer of meat was cleaned out. He had taken all of it. Chicken, pork roast, a big slab of ham and a leg of lamb. And it wasn't until I discovered that he'd also taken the Swiss army knife my father had given to me on one of the few camping trips we ever took together, that I finally decided to call the police."

"I guess! The combination of your dresses, a knife and slabs of meat scream something's definitely not right with this guy's head. Like a *Silence of the Lambs,* kind of 'not right.'

"Right? Yeah, so the police went to his place, but of course, he'd been smart enough – probably from experience – to get rid of anything incriminating. They couldn't press charges. I had to change my locks, but I never really felt safe in that apartment again. You know, it was weeks after that I kept finding - or discovering the absence of things - he had taken. He took my camera's memory card that had over 500 photos on it - some of Colombia - and weird items like a brush I never saw again and bottles of perfume. It totally freaked me out. It was like he wanted to take items to remember me by."

"That's pretty fucked up. Did you ever see him again?"

"No! Not exactly, but it wasn't the last time I heard from him."

"Are you going to tell me about that?"

"Not now. I'd like to forget about him altogether! There are just some people in your life you only need to meet once, you know?"

"Has there been a lot of people in your life like that?"

"You could say that! There are people on that island who I hope to never see again - and some that are barely worth mentioning, like -25!"

"Another lover?"

"No - it never got that far! He was a guy who was as sweet as pie when I met him, but I always had that same intuitive sense about him as Muttonhead - that there was just something not right about him. In the few weeks we spent together, he was always bugging me about whether I'd figured him out or not - if I finally "had his number". He was harder to figure out because unlike other guys, he was always telling me if I never ended up sleeping with him, he wouldn't care because he valued me so much as a person.

"So, one night, I told him how I was feeling and that I knew for sure that sex was off the table. That was the night he stopped speaking to me. I did happen to see him again, as he was a bartender at one of the bars I hung out at - and so took that as my opportunity to tell him that I'd finally *gotten* his number. That it was Minus 25 - so low and cold that it didn't even factor on the scale and that became his nickname from then on. He didn't like that very much and eventually, he just faded into the abyss of uneventful people I've met along the way."

"So, I guess Muttonhead wasn't exactly uneventful then?"

"No! And in fact, the most significant impact he had on me are the things he told me about being in prison. During those last two weeks we had together, he said to me, 'you know, prison doesn't make you a better person. It makes you do things you never thought possible, just to survive.' I asked him what he meant by that and he told me that he had been involved - directly or indirectly - in eight other murders while he was behind bars. He and a group of other inmates, when they heard about a potential hit being put on one of them, would stuff their shirts with books they'd taken from the library trolley to protect themselves and attack the guy in a group. That way, officials could never charge any one of them with murder. They all kept their silence   for   each   other."

"You're kidding right? And you still continued to date the guy? It didn't occur to you at any point to get your bloody key back from him? Sorry, no pun intended there!"

"That's the funny thing. He knew just how to tell you the story so that you almost felt sorry for him. He told me that in prison in order to stay alive you either had to *off* someone or you'd be the one to get a backdoor parole."

"Backdoor parole? What does that mean?"

"Basically, you leave prison in a body bag."

"Oh! So, this guy is telling you all of this, after keeping the whole thing a secret from you for almost four months?"

"I guess he felt like once it was finally out in the open, he could just be free to tell me all of it. I guess he trusted me to never tell anyone."

"Well, I guess he was the dumb one, eh?"

"Hence the name, muttonhead! That and stealing the lamb from my freezer! Hey, at least I can take some solace in the fact that inadvertently, he was preparing me for my future!"

"Well, there's that! I'll give you one thing Delia, you have the ability to put a positive spin on things - that's something, considering where you are! I guess we should end here for today, but believe me, we're going to revisit the hourglass thing! Shall we meet tomorrow, same time, same place?"

"Ha! You're funny. I'll be here."

"Until tomorrow then. Anything I need to research tonight or bring you tomorrow?"

"Yes, could you bring me some pads and some toilet paper?"

"What? You have to provide those for yourselves as well?"

"You're kidding right? I'm telling you; they give you nothing in here. A lot of the women depend on their family members to bring them stuff like that. Pretty much you're on your own in here - and you either hope someone brings it for you or you've got some money or items to trade in order to get it."

"You know I heard once that you don't know you really love a girl until she asks you to buy pads for her and you do it. If I were you, I wouldn't really trust me to get the right things, but I'll try!"

"Well, let's not call it love. Let's call it a mutual exchange!"

"Okay! Your wish is my command!"

"Time will tell!" Delia looked at me in a way she hadn't before. There was something in her eyes - a longing maybe - but as per usual, she was too far ahead of me and had already turned her back on me before I could decipher her expression. As it turns out, time did tell.

Chapter 9: Velvet

I turned up with some sanitary napkins and toilet paper, all of which were confiscated from me at the prison's front desk. Turns out anything with padding or chemicals in it can be filled with other substances. I got the feeling because it was a women's prison and specifically where mothers and children reside, they didn't get too uptight about contraband that was pretty harmless. It was, for the most part the only way women could trade or get things for themselves or their children. Nonetheless, they still had to seize it, check it and give it to the inmate later. Delia didn't doubt I'd brought it. I guess she was starting to trust me. Or so I thought!

"So, my friend, where do we go from here?" I asked her, after we both took our lovely seats on the patio. It was a good thing our visits were limited to a couple of hours, because it was incredibly uncomfortable to sit on those metal chairs for any length of time. I didn't want to complain in front of Delia. She didn't have much choice as to her surroundings or the lack of comfort. I, on the other hand, could return to my hotel room and experience luxury compared to what she and the other women were enduring.

"Where do *you* want to go from here? And by the way, I'm not your friend." While Delia's countenance towards me had never been what I'd call warm, I had hoped we were making some progress in terms of building a rapport. I wondered if something had happened since my last visit.

"Everything okay? I didn't mean to presume anything by calling you friend. It was more of an expression really."

"Well, if you knew what happened to most people that become my friend, you'd be wise to keep your distance."

"Duly noted." I thought this was a perfect segway to delve into the people who had been in Delia's life. "Do you want to talk to me about some of those people?"

"Perhaps. I laid awake thinking about a lot of things last night. It's amazing how much you can think about while staring at a concrete ceiling, you know! I think I'd like to talk about Velvet. She was one of the ladies I met in my first few months on the island and I'd like to think she was my friend."

"Okay, fire away."

"Well, I liked her right away. She was stunning! The kind that turns heads when she walks into a room. The type who other women either long to get to know or hate immediately. It wasn't even that she was beautiful in a traditional sense of the word. Striking is perhaps a better description of her. She had raven-coloured hair and wore ruby-red lipstick. She looked like she had walked out of one of those classic black and white films - but she was all colour!

"She was also a woman with money - she'd been married to some oil guy from Texas, but he'd died and left her a fortune. The thing about her was that money didn't matter to her - maybe because she had so much of it. What did matter, was helping others. She was out at that dump every run they made to bring food and water and clothes to the families who needed it.

"Of course, I knew none of this when I first met her. She was a friend of Bernie's - I guess since her husband died, she'd taken up hanging out with the gay community. I mean, every woman needs a *walker,* but she took it to a whole new level. Almost every party she hosted, the predominant guest list consisted of the best looking, most extravagant, well-off gay men on the island."

"Hold on a sec! A *walker*?"

"Yeah, you know - gay men who escort straight females to parties and events."

"I guess I've heard the term, but never registered its meaning before."

"You're the most sheltered NYC journalist I've ever met, you know that! Anyway, Velvet could have gone into business hooking up straight women looking for gay friends. In fact, inadvertently, I think that's what she was best at.

"She owned a home in the Lawson Rock area. It was spectacular. Three stories overlooking the ocean, a pool on the third floor and everything bathed in white alabaster and marble and accented with the most amazing aqua and terra cotta. It was like walking into an aquarium of colour. Of course, I would've never seen the inside of her house except that Bernie invited me to a party at her home about two months into my arrival.

"So, at this point, you weren't doing any *exchanges* for party invitations yet?"

"No. This was two months before the package came floating into my life. At that point, I was still trying to get my bearings, being just social enough to not completely isolate myself. There was part of me after Muttonhead, that wanted to crawl under a rock and hide away forever - not simply because of what he had done, but because I felt like such a fool to have fallen for him in the first place. It's like *tomando vuelo* against yourself, every day."

"Sorry? *Tomando vuelo*? What does that mean?"

"Oh, it's a prison term – in English it translates to 'taking flight.'" It's when someone punches someone into oblivion."

"I guess I have a lot of terms to learn from you!"

"I suspect! Anyway, I spent months beating myself up over that relationship. I had to force myself to get out and be social, so I agreed to go. Bernie, of course, assured me I was going to have a great time and the good news was that most of the men would be gay and wouldn't be hitting on me.

"He thought it would be fun to travel by water, so we arrived by boat taxi just before sunset. Great fun, but not for one's hair!" Delia looked at me like she had on my prior visit when she had referred to her looks, almost as if she was embarrassed about how she appeared now. I didn't say a word – and the fact is, I wouldn't have known what to say anyway. My experience with women was limited and while I may have been a good friend to many a girl, it was primarily because I was a good listener and not a talker. I preferred it that way. Delia continued without needing any response from me.

"There was a time when I worried about such things, like my hair, you know! I actually felt really good that night. I hadn't been out anywhere fancy in ages and was looking forward to it. I wore a halter top blouse. The kind that shows off your shoulders, you know. It was ivory and against my bronze skin, I'm sure I looked fabulous. I even remember the shoes I wore. Isn't that funny?" Delia looked at me and I saw that same sparkle appear in her eyes as if memories of a better time ignited something within her. "They were blue sapphire with zirconia diamonds on the straps." She shook her head. "Looking back on it, I can't believe I even travelled with all that shit from New York - and in a knapsack of all things!

"I mean I also packed some jean shorts and bikinis, but I made sure I brought down at least five of my best dresses - the ones Muttonhead hadn't stolen! Of course, after I found the *package*, there were a few occasions I still needed to go out looking like a million bucks. It just all seems so ludicrous now."

Delia bowed her head and was lost in thought for a minute or two. I didn't interrupt. She had a strange little smile on her face and I thought whatever it was she was remembering, it had to be better than where she was right now. A few moments later, she lifted her head, looked at me and continued.

"When we arrived in the huge foyer of her house, Velvet came out to greet us personally. She looked amazing. Her raven hair was pulled back tightly off her face which highlighted her high forehead and largely arched eyebrows. She was wearing a silk one-piece outfit - the kind you'd see from the 70's - of the most spectacular turquoise, green and orange design. It's funny, the last few years in here have done a real number on my brain, but I can remember details of those first days on the island as if they were yesterday.

"Well, stories need details!"

"Yes, I suppose you're right. Anyway, back to Velvet. She was tall - as tall or taller than me - and she had on flat diamond – not zirconia - encrusted sandals and earrings to match. Every part of her sparkled. I guessed she would have been in her late forties, early fifties, but her skin was youthful and glowed like she might have been the happiest woman in the world. Perhaps, it was because her husband had dropped dead and left her money. I don't know.

"I just know that I was drawn to her from the moment I met her. Then she spoke and it was like her words were velvet themselves. Or melted chocolate that drizzled so lovely and smoothly out of her mouth, I could listen to her for hours. She had a French accent - as it turns out, she had met her husband while he was on a business trip to Paris. They'd only been married ten years before he died. Bernie told me later that she'd been married five times, surviving three of her husbands. A common theme it would seem, among women on the island who married older, overweight American men who drank and worked themselves to death.

"After we were introduced, she grabbed my hand and asked Bernie where he'd been hiding me. She led me into the dining room and gestured to one of the waiters to come and bring me some champagne. 'Delia, you are so lovely. I'm sad I haven't met you before now. Bernie is un tete de noeud!' It means dumb ass – or something similar to that. Her English needed some work, but I loved hearing her speak French. Of course, insults were the first of many French words she taught me. She seemed very interested in what I was doing on the island. 'Delia, how you doing in this island? How long you will be here?' I told her I was simply vacationing and had no set plans. 'In that case, you must come and with me, stay for a weekend, no? We pass a bon time together, no? Bernie!' She waved to him from the bar to join us. 'Serious, you must arrange for Delia to come and stay with me.' She turned to me and whispered, 'it gets lonely here all by myself. It would be lovely to have your company.' She tapped me gently on the arm and left us as quickly as she had appeared, waving to the next guests that were arriving."

"So, what do you think of Velvet?" Bernie leaned over to ask me.

"I think she's lovely."

"Oh, she is lovely - and rich."

"That's all that's important to you, no?" I mimicked her accent.

"Honey, having rich friends is very important! They can open doors for you that you'd be knocking on for years!"

***

"At the time, I wasn't exactly sure what Bernie meant, but I certainly learned fast once that package appeared in my life. I spent the next two weekends in Velvet's guest house. Turns out, she loved to celebrate life and the next Friday, she threw one hell of a party. She had a famous singer - I can't divulge names here - who lived in the area who came over and performed a few songs for her guests later in the evening. Oddly enough, he and I had an interesting conversation about dating and marriage, and he told me, 'My wife said a man will never be the whole package until he gets his shit together!' Then he laughed and walked away. I've given his words a lot of thought since then, especially after I found what some would call the "whole package" of great white shark. Perhaps that's the only "whole package" I'm ever going to have in my life. Of course, at that time, I still had hope of meeting Mr. Right."

"And did you?"

"Did I what?"

"Meet a guy - Mr. Right? I just get the sense, there's a guy about to enter the picture. I mean, you said yourself that you looked fabulous and if you're hanging out in that kind of social circle - they couldn't have all been gay - and you mentioned you stayed with her the next *two* weekends - there had to be a guy! You must have had a reason to return."

"You mean, other than the rooftop pool, the ocean view and the tennis court, sauna and gym within ten feet of the guesthouse? Well, aren't you clever! It may be true that someone - a guy - happened to walk into her party on that Friday night. He may have been playing the sax earlier in the night and got my attention. He may have been rather good-looking with olive skin and a great smile. He may have come to me while I was standing on her large marble patio looking out at the ocean and handed me a glass of champagne."

"Yup, that sounds about right. He wasn't exactly what I pictured."

"Oh yeah, what kind of guy did you picture me going for? This ought to be good!"

"I don't know. Maybe the older, salt and pepper type - he certainly has to be tall - or at least as tall as you and he has to have a brain in his head."

"Well, this one was younger, completely bald, at least half a foot shorter than me, but he most certainly had a brain and *his package* wasn't bad either!"

"Oh, come on! I didn't need to hear that part, but great pun by the way! Seriously, I knew it was just a matter of time before one of us made that joke!"

"Listen, you asked about *the* guy. Ask me no questions, I'll tell you no lies!"

"I would have appreciated a lie - or at least an omission - on that one!"

"Sorry! Full disclosure is my motto."

"Yeah, I'll believe that when I hear it! So…?"

"So what?"

"Come on, don't be obtuse with me. What happened with him?"

"Well, he didn't turn out to be Mr. Right, obviously. More like Mr. Right now. Although, I suppose I did learn to like his company. He was different than most on the island."

"How so?"

"He was from Spain originally, but had lived and went to school in the states. He had dual citizenship and was, I don't know, exotic if you will. And well educated. He mentioned something about having an engineering degree. Of course, I was trying to stay away from men and in particular, anyone who could complicate my life on the island."

"What does that mean, complicate your life?"

"The island is small and getting involved with anyone, you run the risk of God knows what - a free dose of Herpes or getting known for being a certain type of woman. It just brings more attention to you for some reason. I was trying to stay under the radar, you know."

"Okay, so you didn't sleep with him that night, but I assume if you know about his package that it came to pass eventually."

"Well, I saw him again a few weeks later and he took me to one of the best diving places on the island. Then, I slept with him."

"Okay! There it is!"

"You made a deal with me, no judgements, right?"

"Oh, did that sound like a judgement? Sorry! My bad! Am I going to have to hear the details of his package now too?"

"Isn't journalism in the details?"

"Ha! Touché! So?"

"So, I decided to let down my guard a little and have some fun. We spent a lot of time together over the next few weeks, hanging out at Luna Subiendo at night and snorkeling by day. Some mornings we were out running before dawn in the rain; and others we were making love until he had to get up for work. What can I say? He was handsome and funny and extremely generous even though he probably didn't make much as a dive instructor or bartender. That always seemed odd to me."

"What's that?"

"That he always seemed to have access to money – and a lot of it. He took me away a few times to some pretty nice places and cash never seemed to be an issue. There were things I should have picked up on, but didn't."

"What kind of things?"

"Just things that didn't add up, but hey, isn't that always the way with relationships?"

"I wouldn't know! I haven't had much luck with women!"

"Oh no? And why is that?"

"Look at me! Do I look like I'm the kind of guy who has much luck? Hence, I became a journalist! I write about other people's lives! Anyway, enough about me! Does this guy have a name? Or how should I refer to him?"

"How about, Don Juan?"

"Seriously? That's what we're going to name him? He must have had a very special package!"

Delia threw her head back and laughed out loud and for the first time, I caught a glimpse of how stunning and exuberant of a woman she must have been in those early days of her arrival. She was fascinating in every sense of the word even now, because she was a walking dichotomy. Once a stunning, classy blonde journalist from New York turned drug dealer with a weathered-face who was crass and could probably swear with the best of them. Not to mention, she was an inmate in a federal prison in Central America. It boggles the mind.

"Well, he did have quite the special package! How I miss it sometimes!"

I'm sure my cheeks flushed red at her comment. "Don Juan it is then. God help me, no one is going to take this story seriously!"

"Don't you think it's already serious enough? When you really think about it, it's so unbelievable that I'm sitting here in a Honduran prison - even to me - there has to be something funny about it. If I don't laugh, I'll end up crying."

I looked at Delia and I could see the tears well up in her eyes. I wondered if it was sadness - or perhaps, that part of her that missed the life she'd once had. Whatever it was - it was the first raw emotion I'd witnessed from her. She wiped away the one tear she let escape and then it was back to business as usual. "Let's go back to Velvet, shall we?"

"Sure!" I was just an uncomfortable - maybe more - with her display of emotion because the truth was, I had no idea how to help her. I couldn't really make things better for her, save for the few items I could bring to her on my visits. The only thing I could really do was tell her story in a way that brought her some air of dignity - and perhaps restore some semblance of pride to her life. I guess that's why I wanted to hear everything - the good, the bad and the ugly, so that in the end, no matter how ugly it - or she - became, I could still expose the benevolence I sensed she possessed – even if it was well hidden.

"So yeah, I soon realized how generous of a person Velvet was and that she had a huge heart. In truth, the thing I came to admire most about her was that she had already realized my dream of helping others. I longed to be in that position myself."

"How did you find out about her helping others - and the dump runs?"

"It was during the second weekend staying in her guesthouse. She came one morning and rapped on my door and asked me if I wanted to see another side of the island. I didn't realize she actually meant the *hidden* component – not only of the tourism industry, but of a culture - that no one wants you to see. Ironically, she was a part of the organization I had read about in that pamphlet. I began to believe that things were happening for a reason, you know. That there were signs that I was on the right track. Little did I know how sideways a turn my life was going to take in only a matter of weeks.

"Anyway, as soon as I visited the dump with her and I witnessed children - seriously, no older than four or five years old - picking through that smelly, disgusting mess just to survive, I knew I had to do something. I ended up going on the dump runs with her and some others once a week. To be honest, I couldn't have gone every two days like she did. It was far too upsetting for me to watch. That's basically how our friendship blossomed; and I began to learn how things really work in Central America.

"To get to the dump, we had to drive by the only electrical company on the island - RECO - it should have been called RICO - which means rich in Spanish - as that's what a few Americans we're becoming on the backs of Hondurans and expats alike. The owner of the company - a guy from Texas - was charging over four times the rate we pay in the States for electricity.

"He had support from some expats on the island because he had volunteered to pay for the dump to be moved to another area. Turns out - and it was clear to me when Velvet took me to the dump that first Saturday - the real reason he was doing it, was because the current dump was rotting away on prime oceanfront real estate. I wonder who had to gain from moving it to a less desirable spot on the island?

"Be sure to write that in this story, will you? People need to be aware. You know, it's one thing for locals, in their desperate attempt to become rich like Americans, to do business in this way. It is entirely different when a foreigner who has the means and the knowledge - unfortunately, not the wisdom or compassion - and should be contributing to a developing country, but instead is making money off the back of it."

"Why do people not stand up against it? Surely foreigners can speak out against it, if not the locals?"

"Fear. The island is small and everyone knows everyone. Truth be told, no one wants to piss off one of the richest guys on the island - they might want - or need something from him one day. I have nothing to lose by speaking out. Everything that ever mattered to me has already been taken away."

"I'm sorry about that. That you've lost your freedom."

"I wasn't talking about my freedom. I was talking about Ghost."

"Whose Ghost? You didn't mention this person before."

"He's not a person."

"Is he passed away? Is that why you call him Ghost?"

"No! He's my dog."

"Your dog? I didn't realize you even had a dog. I was only joking when I asked if Muttonhead had killed your dog, you know!"

"I know. I didn't have a dog in New York. My apartment was way too small. I met Ghost on one of my dump-runs."

"I'd love to hear about him, but I think we're past our two-hour limit already. Can we begin with Ghost on my next visit?" I was busily writing down a few last notes, but when I looked up, there were tears in Delia's eyes again. I knew it was probably a good time to stop - as much for me as for her. "I'll be back tomorrow, okay? And we can carry on where we left off. Anything else I can bring you?"

"No. I'm alright. Thanks. I'll see you tomorrow." Delia got up and left our table more abruptly than she ever had and I saw her reach up and wipe her face a few times before disappearing behind the gate that separated the patio from the inmate entrance. I can only imagine how badly she didn't want me to see the tears, that despite her best efforts, escaped anyway. She couldn't have known how badly *I didn't* want to see them. I hadn't, up to that point, felt as awful about leaving her behind in that place as I did that day.

Chapter 10: A New York Minute

The hourglass became an appropriate symbol for the time – or lack of it – Delia and I were able to spend together. It would be a week - not just a few days - before I could see her again. The well-known phrase, *in a New York minute* signifies how fast something can happen - or how quickly a minute can pass. As a journalist, we always seem to have time constraints and deadlines, but I had never before been so aware of time passing after I met Delia.

The real significance of her question about who gets to decide how many sand grains are in an hourglass, finally dawned on me. She wasn't talking about the science behind it, she was talking about our lives and who - or what - decides our fate of how much time we each get on this planet. Why do some of us get a lifetime and other's lives begin and end in a New York minute? Why do some of us sit around our entire lives and waste the time we're given and others choose to suck the marrow out of life?

What really awoke me to the awareness of how I was passing my own allotted time was other people determining how much time I could or couldn't spend with Delia. It turns out, someone at the prison was concerned about the number of visits I was making and the amount of items I was bringing in to one inmate. I would learn later how both came to impact Delia in regard to how the other inmates related to her. At the time, it seemed that someone put up a stink about it and I was denied access on my next visit.

All I could imagine was that Delia was sitting on that concrete slab waiting for me and I let her down. I hoped she wouldn't wait too long and that someone would send word to her that I wouldn't be coming for a while. I did get the Embassy to call on my behalf, but who knows if messages are truly delivered to inmates.

In the meantime, I made a call to David Fisher in New York to see what he could do. The truth was, I was becoming more and more suspicious that something more had been going on between the two of them and this hourglass message had something to do with it.

"David, do you mind me asking if you and Delia were more than friends? Was there - is there - something more going on that I should know about?"

"Well, Scott, you get right to it, don't you? I'm sure if there's something else Delia thinks you should know, she'll tell you. Our relationship was strictly professional, I can assure you of that. Although, I will admit I came to think quite highly of her and her work at the paper. One might call us friends, I suppose."

"And this hourglass thing? What significance does that have?"

"That? That's just an inside joke between friends. It doesn't mean anything important."

"She asked for an hourglass to be brought to the prison, David. It has to mean something." There was silence on the other end of the line. "Hello?"

"Yeah, I'm still here. Listen, Scott, I've got a deadline to meet. I'll make a call to the Embassy to see if they can lift the embargo against your visits. Until then, stay well and say hello to Delia for me."

The line went dead. The son of a bitch hung up on me. The next phone call I made was to Woody in New York. I asked him to do some digging on our *friend,* David Fisher. I had learned that sometimes as a journalist you've got to take a step back from what you've been focusing on and shine a light on the things around it, to truly get the whole picture.

It took about two days for Woody to get back to me. He discovered that David himself, had spent some time in Colombia back in the early 90's reporting on the drug trade going in and out of Medellin. David had taken – or was granted - a six-month leave from the paper - a strange thing for a columnist based in New York and reporting on its city's infrastructure to do in my estimation. As it turns out, he apparently had been kidnapped about two weeks into his stay in Colombia and held for ransom in the Andes jungle for four months. Reports were that he managed to escape on his own, following the Cauca river down to a nearby village.

There were photographs taken of him after he emerged from the jungle and while he looked much slimmer in the photos than when I met him, he didn't appear to be abused or harmed in anyway. He was asked about their treatment of him and other than mentioning his captors, while trying to get information, pistol-whipped him a few times, he hadn't been treated that badly.

I knew I had to do some more investigating of this *friend* of Delia's, but it would have to wait. My focus was still on her and her story. It took a few more days for the prison to allow me access again and when I arrived this time, I had three bags of diapers.

I figured I needed to make up for a week's worth of visits and I knew that I needed to do whatever it took to get Delia to trust me and to really begin opening up about things. During our last visit, I felt like she was letting down her guard with me and allowing me to see the other - more vulnerable - side of her nature. When I saw her sitting on the patio, I could tell that even a week without visits had caused her to close back up again.

"Hey you! How have you been?"

"Just great!" The sarcasm was heavy in her tone.

"Look, I'm sorry! We did talk about this - and how at some point, things could get difficult."

"Yeah, we did talk about it. It doesn't mean putting off my own things to come and wait for you, isn't a bother."

"What things? I mean, you're in prison. Where have you got to go or get done?" Well, that did it! My stupidity and insensitivity were like bullets firing at her and she got up, called for the guard and was gone before I could even utter an apology. I wasn't even sure why I was so abrupt with her. I mean, I didn't appreciate her tone after everything I had done in order to get back in to see her again, but it wasn't as if she'd really owed me anything, least of all, her life story.

I guess being in Honduras and visiting the dank, dark prison was getting to me too. I was frustrated with her - with David - and with myself because I felt like every bit of information she shared with me, while it gave me small glimpses into her life, I was still literally and figuratively on the outside looking in. What was I missing? Who was this woman who I was spending all this time and energy on when I could have been enjoying autumn in New York?

When I left the prison that day, I was ready to pack it in and return home. I didn't figure Delia would ever talk to me again anyway. It had been difficult to get her to finally open up as much as she had. I figured she was a closed book now. That was until I received a phone call the next morning at my hotel. It was David.

"Look Scott, you need to get back into that prison. I got a phone call last night that something happened to Delia."

"What do you mean, something happened?"

"Look, they won't tell me any real details over the phone. They told me she was in the infirmary. I don't know what the hell is going on down there, but she needs your help."

"What the fuck? I just saw her yesterday. I mean, she was pissed at me, but otherwise, she seemed fine."

"Well, obviously, she's not fine. I'd fly down there myself but I'm up to my neck in work right now." The funny thing is that the last thing I wanted was David turning up. There was some part of me that felt – or maybe wanted to believe that I was one hundred percent responsible for Delia. Who knows, maybe there was a part of me that didn't want him coming between us - between whatever rapport we had built already.

As soon as I got off the phone with him, I made a call to the Embassy and found out that Delia had been transferred to the infirmary within the prison and not taken to the hospital. I had a sigh of relief because I figured if it had been anything really serious, she would have been taken elsewhere. Of course, I also knew because of her prior escape, she had been a high alert inmate. God only knew if she would get proper care within the prison with its deplorable conditions. I made my way there that same day.

When I entered the infirmary, which reeked of alcohol and sweet-smelling cleaning fluid, my heart sank. It consisted of two beds practically side by side. The walls were an ugly mint-green colour void of any windows or pictures. Delia was lying in one of the beds asleep. I had only been told that she tried to hurt herself the previous night after lights went out. I didn't really believe it – and I'm not sure why. Perhaps, it was because she seemed like such a tough cookie to me incapable of giving up on life – or perhaps, it was because I didn't want to believe that something I had done had caused her to give up. When I saw that her wrists were bandaged and she looked as pale as a ghost, the reality of her situation began to sink in for me.

I felt responsible for what she had done. I don't think I realized how truly vulnerable she was and I suspected that my visits, while she might have pretended were bothersome had in some way become something to look forward to and so when I missed an entire week and then dismissed that her life in prison had any meaning, it had put her over the edge.

The truth is, I had never asked her about her daily life in prison. What did she do all day? What kind of interactions did she have with the other women? Did she ever have the opportunity to see the children or the mothers her diapers might have been helping? The truth was, I was so fixated on getting her story - of how she became a drug dealer - that I completely missed the point that prison life had become her new story and was every bit as important - and real for her.

As I stood there looking over her fragile frame - no longer hidden behind that tough exterior - I made a promise to myself that I would pay more attention to all aspects of her life, not only the ones I thought would make a good story. That was the moment that I realized I had a choice about how I was going to spend my time with her.

I needed to begin asking questions to not only understand why she had made a decision that landed her in prison, but also about her other choices while being incarcerated. It seemed to me that by helping others on the inside, she was attempting to make up the time she'd wasted on the outside. I realized too, that I was no longer in Honduras to get a story - I was there because a fellow human being needed my help.

Chapter 11: Ghost

Two days after Delia came out of the infirmary, she was permitted a visitor. The Embassy contacted me on her behalf and relayed to me that she would like to see me. The day I had visited her after her suicide attempt, she had never woken up, so as far as I knew, she had no idea I had come to see her. I hadn't wanted to wake her, but I was secretly hoping one of the nurses would tell her that she'd had a visitor so she would be comforted knowing that someone cared about what happened to her.

When I arrived on the patio and saw her for the first time since the infirmary, the colour was back in her face. Her wrists were still bandaged and as hard as I tried not to look in that direction, I knew I had failed because she immediately pulled her sleeves down. It was the first time I had ever seen her wear a long-sleeved shirt. The truth, it was so stinking hot, most of us foreigners couldn't handle wearing a lot of clothes. I was always amazed at how the locals could walk around in jeans and long-sleeve shirts. I guess they had just become accustomed to the heat. I preferred the cool air of autumn and I missed my city. New York was a fabulous place to hang out in the fall. Nonetheless, here we were again - just Delia and I - on our concrete slab they called a patio and the blasted metal chairs, staring at each other. "Listen, I just want to say-"

"It's not your fault!" She cut me off. "Really. I've been going through some dark times in this head of mine and

I think talking about all this shit just stirred things up for me. Maybe reality sank in that I really am never going to get out of here alive. I don't know, but I don't want you to think that you had something to do with it."

"Listen, I appreciate you telling me that, but the truth is, I was a shit to you that last day, insinuating that just because you're in here your time or anything you do, doesn't matter. It does matter. I know, even if you're using those diapers to trade stuff, that you're still helping those mothers and kids out. You could have asked for anything from me. You didn't. I just wanted to say, I'm sorry for never asking you about your life in here - and what you must go through on a daily basis. Like most journalists, I was too busy trying to get the story and forgot that there's a human being sitting in front of me."

"Thanks! It's nice to be seen as a human being. In here, you're just a number. So, have you figured out why you're helping me yet? And don't tell me, it's just about getting a story. I sense there's more to it than that!"

"I suppose there might be. I haven't really shared much about my life with you – as a journalist, you're supposed to stay objective – separate from your story, you know? There are some things about me – about my life – that I'm still figuring out."

"Yeah, like what? What are you still figuring out?"

"I lost my sister a couple of years ago."

"What do you mean, lost?"

"She um, she committed suicide."

"Hey, I'm sorry! I didn't know or I wouldn't have been so abrupt."

"That's fine. It's hard to know what to say about these things."

"Were you close?"

"Yeah, I guess. I mean, she was three years younger than me and I probably wasn't as close – or as nice – as I could have been. You know, big brothers can be stupid when it comes to their sisters! I thought she was happy. She was married and had a little boy – Joshua – my nephew. I knew she was dealing with post-partum depression when he was first born, but we all thought she was improving. In any case, he was about two when she – when she decided to take her life. She was just about to return to work – she was a teacher. I got a call from my parents labour day weekend that she'd slit her wrists in the bathtub. It's something that you just can't get out of your mind after you hear it, you know? All I could think about was her poor husband finding her like that and her little boy who was never going to see her again."

"And what about you? How did you deal with it?"

"I'm not sure I did! I just threw myself into my work and followed every lead for every story I could to forget about it – to forget about her. Isn't that crazy? Thinking you could forget about your own sister? Who does that?"

"Lots of people! Lots of people do exactly that – go on with their lives and bury every ounce of feeling they can't face. I remember my own mother's words to me, after one of my good friends in high school was killed in a car accident. I had just come home from his funeral and I was sitting in our upper east side penthouse, staring at the window. She came over to me and put her hand on my shoulder. I thought she was going to say something of comfort to me, but instead she asked me what was wrong. I was a little dazed of course and over-reactive and looked up at her and said, 'what do you mean, what's wrong? I just buried one of my best friends.' And she didn't miss a beat and replied, 'Well, honey, you can't dwell on these things!' Can you imagine that? Your own mother saying you shouldn't dwell on a person's death minutes after they're put in the ground forever! And unfortunately, that was my lesson on how to deal with pain and loss, so I totally understand how easy it is to try and forget about people. My mother was right about one thing – it's easier than feeling the heartbreak of it. At least, for a while! The thing is, you can never really outrun your pain! One day, just like now, it catches up to you and you do things in reaction to it and you don't even know you're doing them. Like, you being here – trying to save me – is no doubt some subconscious desire to make up for not being able to save your sister."

"That's your psycho-analysis is it, Dr. Russel?"

"Tell me I'm wrong!"

"I can't! I don't know. Maybe you're right. One thing I do know, is that I am here and so are you, thank God! And I can be of some help to you. So, no more bullshit. You can talk to me about anything, even if it's just what you did yesterday."

Delia let out a little chuckle. "Do you want to hear about my daily constitutions too?"

"Okay, maybe not that much detail. So, what is your daily life like? What do you do in here every day?"

"I try to keep busy, mostly. Most days, if I can muster up the energy, I try to do a little exercise in my cell. I know that sounds funny, but running was such a part of my life before I was in here that any kind of exercise I can get, grounds me. After breakfast, I'm on laundry duty for a couple of hours, washing bedding and stuff. I volunteered to work at that because you get to have conversations with the other women and no one bothers you. Of course, I've had to brush up on my Spanish. Most of the women in here, don't speak English. Most don't even have a high school education, which is sad. Their children probably won't either.

"Anyway, it's a great way to keep apprised of things going on in here. Who's selling what. Who's got what to trade. Who's newly pregnant or found out their man is cheating on them on the outside - that's pretty much a daily occurrence! We call the laundry detail, *El Periodico - the newspaper,* where everyone gets the daily news. We even have a comic section where the girls tell dirty jokes to keep us entertained - they loved my gynecologist joke - or at least, I think I told it properly in Spanish!

"We've got a horoscope section where we tell each other's futures, like, 'yeah, you're in here, for life! You're probably going to get a knife in your back one day. You're going to be pregnant by the new year!' At least, that's usually the fortune for the girls who partake in the conjugal visits on a regular basis. We even have an economic section where we exchange bids on items and make deals. Ironically, even in prison, I'm still working in a crazy newsroom! Anyway, it makes me a little money for snacks and chocolate. Fuck, I never realized how much I loved chocolate until I couldn't get it when I want it.

"You really take the everyday stuff for granted, you know? That is of course, until it isn't at your fingertips. In the afternoon, we're allowed out into the grounds - the guards call them "the gardens", but that's a joke! I've barely seen a blade of grass growing, let alone a flower! And the sand fleas are horrible. They don't just bite - they take chunks out of you and leave big swollen bumps all over your ankles. Of course, bug spray is nonexistent in here, so if we stay out there for any length of time, they drive us crazy. Some of the girls' bites have got so infected from their scratching, they've got scars all over their legs. Anyway, that's our *garden*! I sure miss flowers too. Their colours - the smell of them. Hell, I miss a whole lot of things. Mostly, I miss Ghost."

"You mentioned him the last time we talked. Did you want to tell me about him?"

"Ghost? I think he's my Mr. Right. I miss him terribly." She breathed in a deep inhalation of air and let it go. "I remember the first day I saw him - it was at the dump that Saturday that Velvet and I first went out there together. We were busy handing out water and some pre-packaged grocery bags to some people when I saw something run past us and behind a mound of garbage. At first it scared me. It looked like the size of a wolf - way too big to be a dog.

"I stopped what I was doing and slowly walked around that mound of stinking, pile of rubbish and there he was, his snout buried in a pile of trash. I watched him for a good minute. He was huge - truly, the size of a wolf. He was completely white, but a dirty-white like he'd been out there awhile. His head was the size of a small dog and he had a long white tail like a husky or something. I think he's mostly German Shepherd - I'd never seen a white German Shepherd before. Anyway, there's some mix of something else in that boy.

"One minute, he was fixated on the garbage looking for his next meal and then his head was up and he was staring right at me. No kidding, I thought for sure I was going to *be* his next meal. He raised his ears and just stood there staring back at me. This sounds strange, but there was a kindness in his face and I knew he wasn't going to hurt me. He looked at me for a few more seconds and then ran by me and was gone down the next mountain of garbage.

"Our meetings went on like that for a good month. He would appear and then disappear just as abruptly, like a god-damned ghost. So that's what I started calling him. One of the locals - Osito - who came to help us give out items, came up beside me one day while I was watching Ghost scour for goodies. 'You know, sweetheart' - he called everyone that and I had to admit, coming from him, it was kind of endearing, not a sleazy pick-up line like most guys - 'that dog's got no home. He sure would love to go home with you!'

I turned to Osito for just a minute and gave him *the look* - he called it that because when he'd say something inappropriate to a woman - especially 'those gringas' as he referred to us - they'd always give him the look. Apparently, I gave it to him that day. Not only because I got the sense he was insinuating *he'd* like to go home with me, but also because anyone suggesting that I adopt a dog when I was already in a small apartment - and in a foreign country, was a horrible idea. I told him so. "Don't you just love horrible ideas?" He retorted and walked away.

It didn't take long for Velvet to broach the same subject with me - probably on the promptings of Osito. "You know Delia, there's many expats that adopt dogs down here - and even take them home when they go. It's not impossible, you know!"

"Not impossible, but highly improbable."

"What is the difference? Remember, my English is not good at times."

"It means, no. I can't have a dog that size in my little apartment."

"No! But if you move into my guest house, you could! It's plus grande, no?"

"Velvet, I can't afford to rent your guest house."

"How do you know! You don't even know what I charge!"

"Okay, what do you charge?"

"What are you paying now?"

"$850 a month and even that's high for my budget."

"Then I charge only $800!"

"What, are you kidding? Why would you do that?"

"Why? Because I can! You are mon amie, no? And I think not only that dog needs you, but you need him!"

"You think so?"

"I think, yes! Your lover will disappear as they all do, but that dog will be loyal pour toujours, no?"

"Perhaps!"

"Then that settles it! We will have Osito go out tomorrow with the other boys and capture your beast. I will pay for all the veterinarian bills!"

"No Velvet! I can't ask you to do that!"   "You're not asking me! I'm telling you! Darling, look at my life - how much money do I need? Seriously, let me do this act of kindness for you - for my sake and the dog - what do you call him?"

"Ghost."

"Oui! Ghost - what an appropriate name! He's like, how do you say in English, an apparition! Like most of my husbands! Here today, gone tomorrow! Ha!" Velvet threw her lovely head back and laughed. The woman kept me entertained, that's for sure.

"So, the next week, I was the proud owner of a half dog - half wolf creature. Of course, the first order of business was to give him a bath. The only way I could think to get him in water was to throw some sticks into the ocean and it seemed to work. He loved it! He seemed to take to domestic life better than any man I'd dated, so perhaps Velvet was right. It wasn't long before he graduated from the floor to my bed - without my permission of course - and he became my bed mate from that time on.

"My lover came and went, just as Velvet said and I was back to being single, except for my new Mr. Right. We were inseparable after that. He even went back to the dump with me on occasion to see his old friends, but when it was time to pack up and leave, he never disappeared. He was right there waiting by the truck, ready to go. He knew what side his bread was buttered on!

"Life was pretty good for a while. I was getting into a routine of running in the mornings, having coffee with

Velvet and relaxing by the pool or playing in the ocean with Ghost. However, as with most things, it didn't last. I was only in Velvet's guest house about a month when I came home one night to find it ransacked. My passport and my money were gone and I couldn't find Ghost anywhere. I was devastated. The police were called, but didn't really do anything. They told me it was likely that they had poisoned my dog so that they could rob the place and so they wouldn't be looking for him either. They just assumed he was already dead or if the perps had taken him, they would have already tried to sell him.

"Velvet had me move into her house for a while until I felt safe again and she stepped up security. She tried to reassure me that Ghost was alive and that we would find him, but it didn't help. I just couldn't accept that he was gone. I nearly drove myself mad looking everywhere for him. We even spent days at the dump looking for him thinking he might just naturally find his way back there if they'd let him out that night.

"Then there was some rumours flying around that there had been a couple of guys breaking into that area of the island and they'd been bragging about it around town. There was also some rumours - I called them rumours because I didn't want to hold out hope that maybe, just maybe, Ghost was still alive - that some kind of giant white wolf had been spotted in a certain local neighbourhood. Even though I had heard about island justice, how was a girl like me going to go into some local neighbourhood and demand my dog back? As it turned out, the universe offered up a solution."

"And what was that?"

"A Machete!"

"Wow! Talk about taking things into your own hands."

"Machete wasn't a knife. He was a man - a great big hulk of a man."

"Well, I can't wait to hear about him, but it'll have to wait until tomorrow. I've got some errands I have to run this afternoon before the stores close. Can we meet tomorrow? Do you feel up to it?"

"Yeah, that would be alright."

I didn't ask Delia if she wanted me to bring her anything at the end of our meeting. I already knew what I needed to do. "I'll see you tomorrow then. Oh, and Delia" - I tried to catch her before she disappeared. "Thanks for sharing about Ghost today - and your life in here. It means a lot to me." I didn't just say those words to be nice - for maybe the first time since I started hearing her story, I truly meant them.

"Hey!" She caught me on my way out.

"Yeah?"

"Thanks for sharing about your sister today."

"Thanks for listening."

"You didn't tell me her name."

"It was Sarah."

"Wow! That is ironic isn't it!"

I nodded and smiled. "It sure is!"

Chapter 12: Machete

The next day I was more excited than I had ever been to see Delia. I felt as giddy as a school boy after his first kiss – of course, I never experienced a schoolyard kiss myself. I decided to make my dismissiveness up to Delia in the way of gifts. This kind of gesture was not my usual method of operation - and I didn't want to give her the wrong impression, but I didn't care. I had run out the day before and got her flowers - Stargazer lilies because I knew when they blossomed, they'd provide the most beautiful scent of any flower - and of course, chocolate. I had an assortment of dark, milk and white chocolate. I wanted to make sure that she had something of pleasure and hoped either the flowers or chocolate would lift her spirits.

Of course, what I didn't recognize at the time was that one day my visits would cease and so too would my gifts and that absence might be too much for her to bear. Not because my presence was something special, but because I was her only link to the outside world and when I had my story and was ready to go back home to my comfortable life, where did that leave her? Alone in a Central American prison!

I wish I'd had more wisdom in those first few weeks of getting to know her. I wish I'd exercised more restraint and common sense about the reality of her situation. I just got so caught up in being her hero, I didn't think about the future. Looking back on it, I wish I'd done a lot of things differently, but hindsight is 20/20.

When I arrived at the prison, they inspected the flowers but since the chocolate was already pre-wrapped, they let it by. I was already waiting for her when she came out to the patio.

"What's all this?"

"I wanted to surprise you – to bring you something you didn't ask for."

"Scott, this is really sweet, but seriously, I told you, Ghost is my Mr. Right!"

"I thought you might be worried about that. Listen, this is not a romantic gesture - or not the typical kind. I simply wanted you to have the things you've been missing. You've been through a lot lately and you deserve some happiness - even if it's just a small thing."

"This is not a small thing. It's a big thing. I haven't seen anything so beautiful in a long time. She leaned over and smelled one of the half-opened blossoms. "God, they smell so good! Are these for me too?" She tapped the box of chocolates.

"They are."

"Okay, but I'm not sharing or trading these. Well, maybe the milk chocolate ones - not my favourite - but not the dark or the white." She looked up at me and smiled. Although her teeth were yellowed from lack of care and attention, she still had a beautiful smile.

"I'm glad I could bring you some happiness."

"You did. Thank you. You know, there have been a lot of things - and people - along the way to help me get through some dark times - even in those first few weeks after Ghost's disappearance - that sounds kind of funny, doesn't it? Maybe I should have known with a name like that, that I wouldn't have him long! Anyway, one of those people, was Machete."

"Yes, with a nickname like that, I can't wait to hear about him."

"Well, I couldn't have survived this long without him. Ironically, he became my weapon of choice soon after Ghost disappeared. I already knew his reputation before I met him. He was a local artist on the island who made his living at painting panoramic ocean scenes and photos that gringos would bring down of their kids or pets they wanted transferred from a picture to a painting. He was extremely talented and because of it, probably better off than most Hondurans in the West Bay area. Unfortunately, with popularity with the ex-pats, also comes notoriety with other not so well-off locals.

"I had first heard about him from another guy - Kenny - who'd been on the island for about eight years. He was a redneck from Ripon, Wisconsin - which seemed appropriate somehow - and always wore a neon green hat so you could see him coming. That green hat became like a beacon on the island - and in the bars - for women to take flight!

"He was bad news, but worth talking to if you wanted to infiltrate a community of *bad news* kind of people! He was also an alcoholic, so he was in everybody's business - but forgot a lot of the details and usually filled in the blanks for himself. That's the thing on an island of that size -

everybody knows everybody's business and just like a small town in the States, if they don't, they make it up.

"The first night I met Kenny, his pick-up tactic was to stare incessantly from across the bar and then if I happened - believe me, I tried not to - to look his way, he'd smile this creepy grin at me. For the next hour, I watched him methodically make his way around the bar towards me. He finally passed me and then swiftly came back around from the pillar and leaned over to me.

***

"Hey Chica! Mind if I sit down?"

"If you want." I didn't know who he was - but every cell in my body, told me *he* was bad news! I'm pretty sure, I felt the hairs on the back of my neck stand up as soon as he spoke.

"How long you on the island for? What you doing here? Where you staying?"

"That's a lot of questions for a girl to answer before she's even had a drink!" I tried to avoid answering, but I should have known that what I said, he would take as some kind of an invitation. I was naive in those first few months on that island!

"Well, if you don't want to answer my questions or talk to me, that's fine. I'll go away!" Of course, he didn't. After a few minutes and another drink, he tried again. "You wanna go get a bite to eat?"

I didn't know anything about him at the time, but I figured out pretty quickly that he was either a drunk or the kind of guy you'd never get rid of. "I appreciate your offer, but I think I'm just going to eat here."

"What the fuck? You can't even go for dinner with someone? Fine! If you want to eat the crap at this bar, go ahead. I tried to do ya a favour."

I was trying to be polite - not make any enemies on the island - and avoid confrontation of any kind, so I appeased him by at least inviting him to sit beside me. I asked him where he was from and what he'd been doing on the island. 'A little bit of this. A little bit of that,' was his response.

"You know, when I originally arrived on the island, all I wanted was peace and to just hang out at night, have some conversations and then go back to my apartment. I soon realized that the local bar – Luna Subiendo was not the place to hang out if you didn't want to end up hearing the details of someone's life - or some story somebody wanted to share with you.

"So, Kenny went on about a whole lot of shit that night and began telling me a lot of stories and he just happened to mention Machete. So, I asked him what had happened to give him that nickname.

"Machete? He's a fucking crazy guy, man! Blew a guy away, just cuz he cut his face. Stay away from him, man! He's bad news!"

***

"This was the common nickname most expats gave to local guys on the island. What I always found ironic, was that a lot of expats were into just as bad shit or worse, than any local. Kenny himself - I found out later - had a habit of hitting on underage girls and God help the woman or girl who rejected his come-ons. I suspect, he'll get his just rewards in the end. You can't keep that behavior up on that island and not piss the wrong person off.

"In any case, he wasn't the only one. There were a lot of expats like that. I remember two guys from Texas sitting down beside me one night and when I asked them - asking questions became my thing in order to establish I was a writer - why they lived on the island if their climate back home was basically the same, they told me everything I needed to know!

"The one guy leaned over the other guy as if it was some big secret he was about to tell me. 'Cuz there's no rules down here - or at least nobody gives a shit about them. The States has too many rules, you know what I mean? Life's so much better when you don't have the government breathing down your neck! Am I right, friend?' He sat upright again and the two of them clanked glasses in agreement.

"I knew exactly what he meant. I'd already heard enough stories of American men who came to live on Honduran soil to avoid paying taxes and to save their money for more unsavoury things, like hiring prostitutes and putting young Honduran girls up in shitty apartments in exchange for sex.

"One woman I met - Karen - after spending months building her dream house with her husband, she discovered that while she was in the States working, he was down on the island using their dream house for a nightly rendezvous with numerous prostitutes and hosting cocaine parties. Ironically, his name was John. Eventually, which often happens to these blokes, the girl's pimp extorted him for money to not tell his wife about his dirty secret. In the end, he was too cheap to pay and soon enough, she found out. She kicked his ass out and she still lives in her dream house. I put that guy's name in my hat for later. He'd become one of my regular using customers.

"There were things on that island that I wish I'd never witnessed! Of course, back then, I was still full of just enough self-righteousness that I felt justified in judging others. Or perhaps, it comes with the territory of being a journalist. Let's face it, while we're supposed to remain objective, the bottom line is, we are constantly judging society and sizing up people.

"I remember one evening on my way to Luna Subiendo I had caught a collectivo – I'm not sure if you've been in one yet – they're the taxis where people share fares with other travelers because it's a lot cheaper. Anyway, I was already in the taxi when it stopped at the Pirate's Den Motel on the way down the mountain and a 70-year-old gentleman – I use that term loosely – that frequented Luna Subiendo most nights – got in after the teenage girl he'd obviously just spent an hour or two with. I think I felt my skin crawl when he slid his hand between her thighs. She was sitting in the middle between the two of us. Ironically – and as a writer this wasn't lost on me – we got behind an old beat up truck with a huge sow on the back of it. No kidding, this pig was so large, the truck couldn't go more than a few miles an hour or the thing would have rolled right over or worse – out of the truck! This 70-year-old man leans towards his young conquest and asks in Spanish, 'Como tu dices Pig en Espanol?'

"You know in life, when a door just opens up for you and you know you'll never get another opportunity to walk through it? Well, I leaned forward and took it upon myself to answer his question: "I'm pretty sure it would have your picture beside the word in the dictionary! It's *cerdo*, by the way!"

"I don't think the girl spoke enough English to understand my comment, but he certainly did.
I suppose after everything I've been through and things I've done, I can't really judge others the way I used to. Although, I don't think I'll ever get used to some of things that go on down here. You know?"

"I do understand. It's hard to keep objective about things sometimes." I wasn't just referring to what Delia was talking about. I knew that I was losing some of my own objectivity regarding her – and I surmised I hadn't even heard the worse yet! On one hand, as a journalist, I knew how dangerous that could be and on the other hand, I knew that if I didn't allow myself to be more open and human regarding her, I would never hear the rest of her story. It's a difficult line to walk. I hoped I had the wisdom to figure it out. "So, why don't you get back to Machete?"

"Yeah! I'd rather talk about him anyway! I knew as soon as I heard his story - at least Kenny was good for something - that he was someone who I wanted to know. Apparently, he had come home one night and discovered someone - another local - ransacking his place and when he began yelling at him to get out, the guy pulled out a machete and slashed him from stem to stern - or in this case, forehead to jaw - and left him for dead. It was a neighbour who heard the ruckus and got him to the local hospital. Luckily, he survived.

"The guy who broke into his house was well known on the island for doing shit like that and of course, Machete found out who he was and where his local hangout was. He simply went over there one evening, walked up to him with his mutilated face, giving the guy just enough time to recognize who was about to take his life, aimed his gun and shot him in the face. The Honduran police arrived, decided that that dispute was over and simply walked away.

"You know when you first arrive to the island and you hear about the crime and these kinds of things, you think, Jesus, is there no justice here? And then after a couple of months, you soon realize, that *is* justice. A no fuss, no muss kind of justice that doesn't cost tax dollars or make big shot lawyers richer. It's just two people - or families or gangs working their shit out.

"Anyway, I figured that's the kind of guy you want as your *friend* – certainly not your enemy - if you want to stay safe on the island. So, when he finally walked into the bar one night a few weeks after I'd heard his story, I made sure I made my way around to where he was at. The funny thing was, I hadn't even found the package yet. Little did I know the level of protection I was going to need in the future. I just figured if he was a friend, he could scare off any assholes I didn't want near me. Of course, in the back of my mind, I also thought he might be able to help me get my dog back.

"What struck me first was his size. He was massively built and stood a foot above everyone else. The second thing - okay, maybe it was the first thing, but who wants to admit it - was the serrated scar that ran from his forehead over his right eye diagonally down to his left jawbone. Hence the nickname, Machete. When I wandered up beside him, he was ordering a tequila and simply ordered a second one - with lime - and when the bartender put it in front of me, he turned to me, nodded and swigged back his shot.

"There was something grand in that small gesture of ordering a lime for me. Perhaps it was because I was female - or a gringa - and he assumed I preferred it that way. I thought it was kind of chivalrous. It wouldn't be until much later when I actually had a chance to ask him why he did that.

"In any case, we were *friends* from that moment on. I don't even know why. I always sensed he meant me no harm and would become my protector. Many nights after that - although I realize now, it could have seemed creepy - he just sat at the back of the bar and drank quietly and I think, kept an eye on me. Kind of like a big brother does for his sister. Well, some big brothers!"

I didn't mention anything to Delia at the time, but something in her words made my stomach contract. There were things that I suppose I would have liked to share with her as I got to know her, but again, as a journalist, you're supposed to keep yourself out of the story and your feet well-placed behind that invisible line. I wondered if it was already becoming a little too blurred for my liking. I simply let her continue and kept my thoughts to myself.

"Eventually over the next few weeks, Machete and I finally had a conversation about his paintings.

***

"What made you begin painting?"

"You don't want to hear that boring story!"

"Yes, I do!"

"Entonces, mi tia – my aunt Clara bought me a paint set when I was twelve years old. I had to wait a few weeks until my pops came home from fishing and brought me a canvas. I guess I just started from there. Never stopped until this happened." He pointed to his scar.

"I looked at him - it's funny - I really didn't see the scar anymore. I saw past it to his kind, dark eyes and heavy brow. He had striking features - like I said, he was huge and so was everything about him. His cheekbones protruded further than they should, his nose was red and bulbous and his smile - which he rarely showed - was as broad as his face.

"I went on to ask him if one day, when he was feeling better, if maybe he could paint something for me. It took him a few weeks to come around - and maybe he wasn't doing it for himself at all - but he agreed to begin working on a painting for me, for 1000 lempiras. I didn't know at the time, but he'd never have a chance to finish it.

"Anyway, I ended up paying him a hell of a lot more than that over the years I knew him - and not for anything as beautiful as one of his paintings. So, when Ghost went missing, I thought who better to know about any rumours going on in local neighbourhoods. I waited at Luna

Subiendo every night for a week hoping he would grace its doors.

"He finally came in on a Thursday night - Ghost had been missing for about two weeks by then and I was losing hope of ever getting him back. I told Machete what had happened and I asked him if he might be able to help. I didn't care so much about my passport - that could be replaced - but I wanted my dog back.

"I fretted and stewed the entire weekend that perhaps I had forced Machete's hand into doing something dangerous. Velvet tried to distract me from my own thoughts, but still I paced her halls for days until we heard a knock at her door late Monday evening. Velvet came to get me on the patio where I was staring out into the star-filled sky, listening to the ocean waves.

"Darling, you need to come downstairs."

When I descended the stairs, standing there in her front foyer was Machete – and beside him, sitting as well behaved as he could, was Ghost. The second I moved, Ghost leapt towards me and he was standing on his back legs licking my face. When we had finally had enough of our own reunion, I turned to Machete and although my head only came to his chest, I gave him the biggest hug I possibly could. He didn't hug me back, but I felt his large hand on my shoulder. Ghost was still on his hind legs trying to get in between us to lick my face. There is an indescribable reverberation in your soul when someone does something that selfless for you for no reason at all, except that he is your friend. From that day on, I felt like I owed him my life.

"He didn't get my passport or my money back, but I did hear that those two thieves lost a lot of teeth that night and one wasn't able to walk for weeks. After that, I began to believe very strongly in what all the locals referred to as *island justice*. For the first night in weeks, Ghost and I slept in the guesthouse together.

"Machete was just one of the many people I met on that island that in some form or another, touched - or tried to destroy - my life. Some of those encounters were well-timed and mutually beneficial and some were downright horrible."

"Well, that's quite a story. I'm glad you were reunited with Ghost and this Machete character was there to protect you. Heaven knows, we could all use that. Well, that's all the time for us today. Is there anything you need me to bring tomorrow?"

"No. I think these" – she looked at the flowers and box of chocolates – "will keep me going for a few days." She got up to leave and as I packed up my notes, she leaned across the table – even though it was against prison rules and touched my hand. "Thank you."

"You're welcome. I'll see you soon."

"Okay."

Chapter 13: Petero

"So, you've talked a lot about the people you've met, but not how you got in here, in the first place. Do you want to tell me what happened? I mean, you were down here for seven years without too much trouble, right?"

"That depends on your definition of trouble! I saw lots of trouble in those seven years, but managed to avoid the authorities for the most part. My biggest enemy, as it turns out, wasn't them. It was my own lawyer - Petero."

"Peter? Is that his name?"

"Look up what Petero means - it's Argentinian slang - it describes him accurately enough! My father used to tell me, 'keep your friends close and your enemies closer.' The thing is, you don't even know who your true friends - or enemies are until you've either got shitloads of money - or you run out of it. You know in the movie, *Shawshank Redemption* when Andy is joking about how he ended up in prison and he says, 'Me? My lawyer fucked me!' Well, no word of a lie, that's exactly what happened to me. God! When I think about how stupid I was in those first few months, I could slap myself.

"I was working on the assumption that just about everyone I met could be trusted. I wanted to believe that the Honduran people especially, were great and some were. And a lot weren't! Just like the foreigners I met. It seemed that everyone - locals, expats and tourists alike had some kind of personal agenda. Some just wanted to get ahead or out of their miserable existence; some wanted to forget about the life they'd left or make a new one - and others were just out to get laid or feel better about themselves. Whichever objective it was, you wanted to be damn sure you didn't get in their way of achieving it.

"If a local wanted to make money off of you for some service, you better damn well comply. If an expat wanted to believe something about themselves, even if you knew it wasn't true, you better not compromise their illusion. And if a tourist wanted something from their vacation, it was better to never let them believe they could get it from you. That includes a good time, sex, drugs or anything else they might be hoping for!

"Of course, I learned all of this through experience and so within those first few months, I made a lot of *friends* and acquaintances. Some of those relationships turned out just fine - usually with the people who were on and off the island within 1-2 weeks. I came to realize, the longer someone was on the island, the more they expected of those connections.

"In any case, I met up with some Europeans - I always found them to be just a little more sophisticated and intelligent than most travelers from the U.S. and Canada. They seemed to have a worldliness about them that was lacking from people - probably myself included - from the western world. There was a lovely girl from Switzerland - let's call her Susie Q. She was on the island to dive and had helped out on the mainland at a children's center and was going back there to visit when she left the island. We hit it off right away and spent a lot of nights at Luna Subiendo having drinks and chatting about life. I had introduced her to another really nice couple who I had met earlier that week. Their story was a crazy one!

"He was from the States and she was from Russia. One night, after a few drinks, I happened to ask how they met. They proceed to tell me that she was his mail-order bride. He had been through a nasty divorce and was feeling pretty low when one of his friends suggested that he try the site. Funny enough, they connected almost immediately and wrote back and forth for a few months until he finally flew to Russia to meet her. According to them, as soon as they saw each other, it was love at first sight and they've been together ever since.

"A lot of people - including myself, up until that point - have judgements about people meeting in this way - especially men who technically "order" their brides in this fashion, but hell, if they both find happiness - that mutually beneficial connection I was talking about - then why not? It's no crazier than thinking you can meet someone at a bar one night and end up together for life, is it?

"Anyway, the same night they told me that story, we ended up eating at a place that delivers your pizza to you right in the street. It reminded me of New York when we'd leave the nightclub and enjoy some street meat. God, I miss those knackwursts with tonnes of sauerkraut, don't you?"

"Now I do!"

"Yeah, sometimes I have to admit, I miss New York! Anyway, I was already half in the bag when this tall, dark, long-haired guy - what the hell is it with me and guys with long hair - who was holding a book under his arm just turned up beside me. He just looked smart. Little did I know how street smart he was!

"He told me he was a lawyer and at the time I found that extremely attractive - who would have known I'd need one some day? Well, seven years later, he was instrumental in my arrest. It was him who sold me out. Of course, it wasn't until months later when my case was about to go to trial that I discovered this. It was Osito - another one of the locals that the expats called *bad news* - even though he got his ass out to the dump to help kids every week and I rarely ever saw expats do that.

"Anyway, he managed to get a message to me which wasn't easy thanks to the new "iron fist" policy implemented by the Hernandez administration that from the moment you're arrested for drug trafficking, you're put in jail with no chance for bond."

"Well, that's ironic!" I was trying not to interrupt Delia when she was on a roll, but I couldn't help myself since everyone in New York had been awaiting the trial of none other than President Hernandez's brother who had just been charged with drug trafficking. "Honduras' own president's brother – one of the biggest kingpin dealers in Central America! I would have liked to sit in on that trial, but my schedule just wouldn't permit it."

"Well, how do you think his brother got away with it as long as he did? I heard that at his trial, he and other drug traffickers testified that, in exchange for them supplementing Hernandez's political campaigns for years, he just turned a blind eye to their dealings.

"I think about the small scale that I was involved in the trade - and here I am in prison for years because of a policy implemented by the very man who benefited the most from the larger trafficking rings, including his own brother's. I'm glad I didn't know all of this at the time of my trial! This stupid policy of his has caused Honduran prisons to be two hundred percent over their capacity, which you can imagine leads to all kinds of problems.

"Anyway, one of the guards slipped me a small piece of paper one day while I was out in the garden. It said three words: 'Abogado - trato hecho.' I knew what it meant immediately and I did what I had avoided doing since I was charged - I called the U.S. Embassy - they had made some suggestions regarding lawyers when they were first apprised of my arrest, but I had declined help from them. This time however, I asked them to call David at *The Times* and have him contact me."

"So, why did your lawyer rat you out?"

"I can only guess that it was to make money from me. He knew I'd been making money hand over fist and he wanted part of the cut. He wasn't going to risk his career getting into drugs on any level, so he saw his opportunity - Central America brings new meaning to the 'land of opportunity' - and he took it. What better way to make money from me - he asked for a $10, 000 retainer - partly because lawyers are killed here in Honduras more than any other country in the world and it's become an extremely dangerous profession, and partly because he knew I had it and that I was desperate. What a great plan, right? Befriend me. Gain my trust. Rat me out so you can become my lawyer and make shitloads of money off me. Son of a bitch!

"I heard later that not only did he make money off of being my lawyer, but that he had made a deal with El Negro's lawyer - after he was arrested - that if he gave my name to authorities, El Negro might not be extradited to the States. I got arrested and El Negro got extradited anyway. I figure we got fucked and both of our lawyers made a lot of money.

"After I got that note, I was desperately hoping to hear from David before I made any move. I couldn't just fire my lawyer and be left without one. I took some solace in the fact that he would at least have to go through the motions of trying to get me off or get a lighter sentence for me. Maybe he was genuinely making an effort - let's be honest, I was more beneficial to him on the outside than I would be trapped in a Honduran prison. You know, at the beginning of my trial he had 'absentmindedly' suggested to me that I might want to let him - or someone - know where the rest of the drugs were and where I was hiding my money in case something happened to me.

"I look back on that conversation now and I realize that's exactly what he was hoping for. Thank God, I never gave him that information. I was stupid in those days, but experience was teaching me a great deal. Not enough, apparently that I let my guard down where he was concerned.

"Anyway, imagine my surprise when I got notice one day that I had a visitor. It wasn't David as I had hoped. It was my brother, James. I guess David had called him and, on his urging, - and that of my father's - who had already had a heart attack when he found out about my arrest - James had finally come to see me. I'll never forget that conversation. It was the last one I ever had with my brother."

***

"Well, Delia, you've surely made our parents proud this time. It wasn't bad enough you quit your job and just had to come down here to this God-forsaken place, you had to wind up in the foulness of its jaws!" My brother had a great way with words and I suspect it helped him a great deal in court!

"Well James, it's really nice to see you too!"

"Look Delia, I'm down here because our father is dying and he pleaded with me to come, but let's face it, I'm not a Honduran lawyer. I have no jurisdiction or ability to practice here, so all I can do is offer you some sound advice."

"I'm all ears!" I said, while secretly wanting to punch him in the face. I just sat there and prepared myself for the older brother's advice that he had always felt compelled to spew onto me over the years. I knew nothing good would come from his visit, but I bit my tongue because I knew it would be the last time I would ever lay eyes on him - and I also knew he was my only link to the outside world and to my dying father.

"Fire this lawyer. Give him no reason. David can arrange to provide money for you through the U.S. Embassy - dad was willing to take a mortgage out on their condo in New York to pay for your lawyer bills, but there was no way mom or I would let him do that. I just thought you should know, he at least wanted to help. In any case, let the Embassy help set you up with a lawyer they've already got on their roster. Most of them have had background checks - unlike the sleazy guy you chose to hire - and they'll do the best job they can for you."

"Is that it? Any other advice, big brother?"

"Yeah, if you ever manage to get out of here, don't come home. Hide away in some remote place and live out your days peacefully. Let mom and dad think you've died or just disappeared. They've already had enough disappointment, don't you think?"

"That's great advice James. I appreciate it." I wanted to spit in his face, but held back. "Do you think, since you came all this way to give me such great advice that you could relay a message to dad for me?"

"I can do that. What is it?"

"Tell him I love him and that I'm sorry."

"Too little, too late, but I'll tell him. Just so you know, he probably won't live until Christmas. You've put him in an early grave and you're going to have to live with that for the rest of your life - wherever you end up spending it. I left a little package from mom with the guards." He stood up to go, but before he walked away, he looked me right in the eyes and while I could see how angry he was, there was also pity. The funny thing was, that made me feel worse than his words had. I wish he'd just turned his back to me. I sat here, on this same concrete slab and watched him walk away and knew that that part of my life that I left behind in New York was over.

"The next day I was visited by a representative from the U.S. Embassy who offered to go over the list of lawyers with me. I declined once again. Why run the risk of being fucked twice? I thought I might as well just stay in bed with the same devil I'd already been sleeping with."

"You weren't sleeping with this no-good lawyer, were you?"

"No, Scott, it's just a figure of speech."

It's funny, but I knew that was the third time Delia had lied to me. I wondered, in that moment, what else wasn't she telling me? Hadn't I given her permission to lie or omit certain things she thought I didn't want to hear? I wish now I'd never made that deal with her. Perhaps if I hadn't chosen to remain deliberately obtuse in some things, I could have helped her more. Perhaps not. Maybe her brother had been right. Perhaps, she had chosen a path that no one, not even her own family could help her escape from.

"By the way, what was in the package your mother sent?"

"This. She pointed to a diamond studded brooch pinned to her hat. I had noticed her wearing it before, sometimes on her shirt pocket, sometimes on the hat she'd chosen to wear that day. "It's not real. They're just zirconias. I've been asked to trade it a few times for cigarettes or chocolate - tempting - but I haven't yet. Perhaps, it's got some sentimental value as my mom sent it. Maybe I'll trade it one day." She smirked.

That was Delia's fourth lie. No one in prison was allowed to possess or wear anything of true value - more for their protection than anything. No one in a Honduran prison

- not even the guards - would believe that an inmate would ever possess, let alone, wear real diamonds anywhere in plain sight, so they never questioned it. As with many things in Central America, sometimes they're more undetectable when they're right out in the open. I never voiced my suspicions about any of Delia's lies. I simply smiled and thought David was right. This woman was either exceptionally brave or extremely stupid. I was betting on the former.

Chapter 14: The Queen

"Can we talk about three years ago - about your escape?"

"Just to clarify, it wasn't *my* escape! It was an escape that came more out of opportunity than anything."

"Okay. Why don't you tell me what really happened!"

"What really happened? You mean the truth as I know it?"

"Okay!"

"The truth is, drugs - and the trade - make people do crazy shit - and eventually, even the smart dealers end up in here. I always remembered that story about Sao Miguel island from when I first started at *The Times* and I suppose when our bus got ran off the road -"

"Hold on, did you say run off the road? I thought it was reported as an accident - a mudslide or something?"

"A mudslide in the dry season? Really? We were hit by another large vehicle - I didn't really see it except out of the corner of my eye. Our bus - it was just a small minivan really - after it was hit, veered off the road and into the ditch. I think the driver was killed instantly and I could hear the guard in the passenger side moaning, but none of us girls stuck around to help.

"I suppose, on some level, I still feel badly about it, but when you see an opportunity to get out of this hellhole, you take it. You run and hide and don't ever look back. So that's what I did. I ran and hid in the middle of the jungle. I was hurt - I broke my wrist in the accident and I had nowhere to go - and I knew no one on the mainland, but I thought maybe just maybe, if I could make it to the coast undetected, I might be able to get a boat taxi to one of the islands."

"So, who hit the bus?"

"Well, the only two other female inmates on it were some no name girl I'd never met and the other was rumoured to be none other than "The Queen" - one of many of El Negro's girlfriends he had running cocaine for him. They never found her. The other girl was caught within a few hours hiding out in an outhouse."

"It took them three days to find me. I almost made it to the coast. I was in La Ceiba in a gas station's bathroom, trying to clean myself up, when the police broke in and arrested me. Someone must have snitched on me. I can tell you one thing, had it actually been planned, I would have had money with me and been able to pay off people for their silence. Money buys you everything down here - including your freedom. So, just like Quinci, they caught up with me, but if I ever get another-" Delia pounded her fist against the table, "Nevermind!"

I knew enough not to pursue that conversation and where it might go, at least while we were sitting on the patio in a Honduran prison. We both knew that she was now considered a high-risk inmate and while they were never made to wear handcuffs or anything like that, the guards were on high alert when it came to Chihuahua. I was surprised sometimes, that she was as candid as she was about everything, but I guess she figured she'd never get out and really had nothing to lose. In any case, I was grateful for her honesty when she actually told it to me.

Chapter 15: Chacarron

"So now that we've established how your lawyer fucked you, and how you managed to escape three years ago, I think I'd like to hear more about the seven years before you ended up in this hellhole. What happened after your first exchange - the yacht party? That's where you earned the name Chihuahua - and I guess it stuck."

"You could say that. Bernie never introduced me as that, but whenever he was making a deal for me with some of his friends, that's how he referred to me. No one had any idea - at least I didn't think they did at the time - to whom he was referring. He also had another guy - Chacarron -"

"Chacarron? What does mean?"

"Bernie had a lot of friends that had a habit of talking too much and there's no shortage of Spanish nicknames for people like that. Chacarron's namesake was actually a parrot from one of the famous yacht clubs on the North side of the island. I'd spent some time there on a sailboat - another story for later - and there was this damn, annoying parrot that every day would talk and incessantly mimic just about anything a person would say. Most people loved that parrot and apparently the guy who ran the place - it was actually owned by part of the Kennedy family - said that the parrot had more friends than he did. In any case, for the three days I spent there, I watched the parrot entertain the visitors and sailors alike. I knew the bird had some sense because there was this very annoying American woman that came in on a yacht with her husband and one lovely afternoon, she was trying to get that parrot to mimic her - it's questionable who was more annoying - her or the bird.

"In any case, I was sitting there reading a book - or should I say *trying* to read a book, but was so utterly distracted by the two of them, I just gave up and watched them carry on like idiots. The woman made the mistake of trying to pet the damn bird or maybe feed him, I don't know, but he latched onto her finger with his beak and wouldn't let go. Needless to say, some choice words came out of her mouth. She never bothered him again after that and apparently, that's the day the parrot learned the "f" word.

"Anyway, a few days after the yacht party, Bernie introduced me to a "friend" of his who was helping him out with acquiring some needed "items". Bernie thought this guy - who I later named after that parrot - Chacarron - could help me to unload my *stuff*. He was a local who was pretty *connected* on the island - 'I know people' was one of his favourite sayings. As it turned out, he did in fact know a lot of people that were interested in using what I was selling. Probably, if I had known his reputation with the locals, I would have been wise to avoid him, but at the time, I wanted to unload the whole package as fast as I could and saw him as a viable option.

"You know, you just can't unload that much white shark in a hurry, especially if you don't want to get caught doing it. Chacarron was the guy who many of the expats went to the "grocery store" for their parties. He arranged my first official drop. I had already told Bernie that I would be charging $30 a pop. He didn't argue. The purity of the stuff I acquired was what they refer to as *white gold* - the best you can get.

"No one used real names and no one met anywhere near where you lived or frequently hung out. Technically, I as the dealer should never know the client and vice versa, but Chacarron was true to his name and couldn't help but tell me who was benefiting from my white gold. Turns out it was a well-known actor who owned property on the island. He usually always turned up alone - left his wife in the States - apparently, she hated the island - and threw crazy parties in her absence.

"When he told me who the guy was, I was just as glad I'd bumped up my price. I was to arrange a drop off and separate pick up spot that were neutral to both parties. I thought what better place than a fuse box closet situated on a nearby dock where I could watch from a distance? I had, during my initial days in the west end, watched the comings and goings of boaters. I knew that those fuse boxes never got checked until the end of the month. Otherwise, there was no reason to pop the latches and open them. Late one night when I was sure I was alone; I dropped the item - about 10k worth - inside the second fuse box. Each box was directly related to whomever owned the boat slip. I watched the number 2 slip for a week and there was no boat coming or going from it. It must have been an expat who was away or a slip that wasn't in use. Either way, I figured it was the safest to use.

"Chacarron was to make the pick-up at midnight and drop the cash off in another pre-arranged place. I liked to pick my money up in the strangest of places. Chacarron said I was the crazy bitch on the island that made him climb trees and structures that he would never have been caught dead on otherwise. Turned out, he had a terrible fear of heights! It's amazing what a punk will do for money. After I found out about his fear, I took great pride in finding the highest structures I could to make him drop off my money. He hated me for it - or that's what Bernie always told me.

"You know, when I first began, I thought I *was* crazy - I wondered if maybe I'd lost my mind thinking that I could do this kind of thing. After the first few successful drops, it really makes you feel confident. Like gambling, after you win a few times - even if it's just a small amount - it convinces you somehow that you've got the greatest luck and you just keep going. You become numb to the fear after a while and you're so excited about the next deal and your money that it literally takes over everything else you think about.

"I was still living at Velvet's guesthouse with Ghost, but as I started to make more and more money, I decided that I should either rent - or even buy - a place of my own. Bernie put the kibosh to that, however. He told me that whatever I do, don't bring attention to myself. Rent a higher end place maybe, but sit on purchasing anything if I wanted to stay under the radar. So that's what I did.

"I also had to find places to stash the money. I couldn't just walk into a bank and deposit large sums into my American account. Turns out, you become creative at laundering your money. There was a couple who I met who was opening up a new business and were looking for investors. I decided to loan them some money at 18% interest which of course, was highway robbery, but the more I did it, the less guilty I felt about it. Like I said, just like cocaine, greed numbs you to most things.

"I suppose I ran the risk of never seeing my money again with these risky ventures, but my customers knew that behind every business deal I made, stood - literally and figuratively - my trusted friend, Machete. No one was willing to take the chance at pissing him off - or any of the number of people he knew and was related to on the island. That first investment made me quite a bit of money as it turns out and that couple are still in business today doing really well for themselves. I liked them. They were kind and deserved success. I can't say that about everyone with whom I did business.

"It was only a matter of time before either my luck ran out - or I met up with some unsavoury, deceitful people. There's just as many of them - or more - on that island than good people - I can tell you that. Chacarron set up a deal with a couple of American men who wanted a shipment - I call it that because it was larger than any I'd been asked to deliver before - 2 kilos - for a two week long yachting trip they were planning. The deal was supposed to go down just like always. I drop off the *material* - I came up with all sorts of names for it - and Chacarron would be getting the money from them and then delivering it to another pre-arranged place.

"I didn't make him climb any high structures this time. It was too important that it all went well. As it turns out, when I went to pick up my money by boat - I had arranged to have it put in a place in the mangroves over by St. Helena the next day, it wasn't there and Chacarron was nowhere to be found. I was pissed and about ready to send Machete on the chase, but Bernie insisted that I just give him some time to round up his "friend" and for me, to stay put and wait. I listened to him yet again.

"Soon enough, the local authorities got a report of a half-drowned man clambering up the iron shore, on the northside of the island. Bernie told me later that these Americans guys after Chacarron had dropped off their bricks, got him drunk - roofied him, raped him and threw him overboard. They had taken off a day early on their yachting trip and no one had seen them since.

"I knew all I could do was bide my time until they returned. It's not like I could report them to the police. As it was, Chacarron was threatened within an inch of his life - and probably beaten by the local police - to give up the name of the person he was working for. For the first time since I'd met him, he never squawked or opened his mouth. He also never did another run for me again.

"Bernie told me it was more likely to do with the humiliation of being raped by two American guys - and everyone on the island knowing about it - that did him in. I always felt badly about what happened to him, but I guess this was what they call collateral damage in this game. I never saw him again after that deal, but I felt like I owed him something, you know, for not ratting me out. Who knows, maybe one day I'll be able to make it up to him.

"So, should I ask what happened to the American guys?"

"Let's just say, their two-million-dollar yacht had an accident about a month later and I'm pretty sure its pieces are still all over the coast of the north shore. They weren't on it at the time. I've no idea who did it and I never did recuperate my $60, 000."

This was Delia's fifth lie.

"I lost a lot on that deal, but Chacarron was the biggest loss I took. I had to find myself another runner and Bernie wasn't keen on using anymore of his friends to help me out. My deals were becoming larger - and more dangerous - and I wasn't about to cut back. I wanted to go bigger. I wanted to get rid of the stuff quick. This was my first mistake, but it wouldn't be my last.

"The funny thing is, I never gave it any thought to what I would do after I had actually unloaded my stash. I could only think ahead to my next deal. That was until I met a man named Captain Rufus. He was an interesting character who'd been on the island for over 10 years at that time. He put down roots and made a life for himself. He'd seen it all!

"I always thought, he should write a book about his life. Rumour has it that he finally started one. He didn't drink - or at least, he'd take long reprieves from tipping up the bottle. He told me that the day he quit drinking, he began the day seeing if he could wait until the afternoon to take his first drink. Then it hit 5 o'clock and he thought, 'I wonder how much longer I can go' and he just kept playing that game with himself until he realized he never did give in. He hadn't taken a drink since 1975. Now that's will power!

"I admired him right away. He had an adventurous spirit and he had turned up on the island, in his own words, 'by accident. I got on the wrong plane, ended up here and never left.' I loved spending time at the bar with him hearing his adventurous stories and learning about the history of the island from him.

"He asked me once, what my plans were and if I was going to stay on the island like he had. 'You might want to put down some roots here, young lady. Find yourself a good place to live - and then do it.'"

"Do what?" I asked.

"Live!" He walked away soon after he said that, but not before introducing me to a Canadian couple who had come to the island ten years earlier with a dream of owning property and building their own treehouse. I thought a treehouse was an amazing concept and when they invited me to theirs one afternoon to see it, I fell in love. I felt my heart soar for the first time in a long time.

"The delight of wandering up those steps high into the trees was exhilarating. In that moment, I finally knew what I wanted to do with my money. I was going to begin searching out property and planning my own tree-house where Ghost and I would go to live one day after I was finished with my *business*. It's funny, with all the money I made during those seven years, I never longed for anything more than just that - my treehouse in the mountains overlooking the ocean with my best friend beside me. The interesting thing is, once you get a dream in your heart like that, it never goes away. I still sometimes lie in my bunk at night and imagine Ghost and I up high above the world."

"That's a lovely dream if you ask me. Perhaps, it could still happen."

"Well, just like in *Shawshank Redemption*, Red says to Andy, "Hope is a dangerous thing. You're in here and your dream is way out there.""

"Ah, but don't forget how Andy replies: 'Remember Red, hope is a good thing. Maybe the best of things. And no good thing ever dies.'"

"Yes, he does say that, doesn't he!" Well, I could call you Red, but you're no Morgan Freeman. In fact, I don't think I've seen a whiter, white man than you! You're as white as powder - or the great white. Do you ever get out in the sun?"

"No, I'm too busy working - or interviewing people in prison!"

"Touché! And just for that comment, I think I'm going to call you Pancake from now on!"

"Nice! Just what I've always wanted for a nickname."

"Well, it's fitting! So, maybe Pancake, someday you'll go looking under a big tree and find a box from me." Delia said this as she smiled and winked at me. She never called me Scott again after that day.

My nickname had become Pancake. I felt honoured that she'd *named* me - like I'd become some part of her story from that day on. I think from the first time I heard about her, that's what I longed for - to be a genuine part of someone's story, not just a reporter on the outside getting information. I'll remember that day as one of the best visits I had with Delia. Perhaps because of my new nickname and perhaps because it was the first time she shared her dream with me and somewhere deep down, I began to truly believe it might come true one day and that was a much better feeling than the dreaded guilt I always felt when I left her after our visits. Yes, it was a good day indeed.

Chapter 16: Osito

"What I've learned from being in here is that it's just as important to have friends on the *inside* as the outside - maybe more so. Hence, I learned to keep my head down, my mouth shut and my ears and eyes open. The only other thing you can hope for is to have friends - and family - on the outside that supply you with things to trade. Because I've had access to things - and some money here and there - I was able to make some connections - and I guess, you'd call them friends - here on the inside.

"It certainly hasn't always been easy with the other inmates, although compared to some, I've had it pretty good. It wasn't that I was never bothered. When I first got here, I was the new fish and meaner, bigger girls can smell you out. The other thing I had against me was that I'm white. Spanish girls have a hatred on for white girls, especially when their Honduran men think we're some kind of exotic item on the market and will try to hit on us right in front of their faces.

"I had a number of obstacles to overcome when I first arrived on the block. Lucky for me, a lot of the girls had heard about me - and my array of *friends* I had on the outside and knew enough not to bother with me too much. The girls who hadn't heard of Chihuahua were warned pretty quickly. They also knew that I was smart and had a good heart and because of my work with kids at the dump - some of which were either the children of or related to the girls in here - I had a reputation for being one of the gringas that actually gave a shit about people down here. I was beaten up a few times - when you saw me in the infirmary it wasn't my first visit."

"What do you mean? Do you mean you'd-"

"No, I'd never put myself in there before, but other girls had."

"Wait a minute, how'd you know about my visit to the infirmary?"

"You can't keep secrets in this prison!"

"Well, I was kind of hoping the nurses would be good enough to tell you that you had a visitor."

"Good enough to tell me? What they told me was someone had come in to see me, but made me pay up to find out who it was. Good thing I still had some diapers. Turns out, even the guards and nurses are dirt poor and can barely afford things on the outside."

"Don't they check their purses and bags when they come and go from the prison? Isn't it dangerous for them if they get caught?"

"Wow, you really don't understand how things work down here, do you? Who do you think are doing the inspections every day? Other guards who need things - favours. Everybody, inmates and employees alike, are dealing and doing business just to survive most of the time."

"Didn't you figure it was me? I mean, I'd been here the day before? You probably didn't need to trade diapers for that information, did you?"

Delia put her head down for a split second, removed her hat and smoothed back her dirty, blonde hair. As soon as she did this, I understood it was a sign of embarrassment. She was hoping it was someone else - someone else who cared enough to actually show up after she tried to off herself. I didn't know if it was David or James - or someone I hadn't heard about yet - and I wasn't about to ask. I figured that eventually, I'd hear that story too. I changed the subject back to her inside connections as quickly as I could and we were both thankful that the moment of awkwardness had passed.

"Yeah, there's Eye, who helped me trade with other mothers as she saw more of them than I did, except for those days I worked in the laundry room. There are a few other girls that have come to my rescue. When I first arrived, there were two girls in particular - let's call them Drucilla and Anastasia who were pretty nasty and wanted to take me on as their bitch. I wasn't that desperate yet.

"They caught me a couple of times in the can and in the garden and threatened if I didn't become their *bicho*, I'd get a good beating. Lucky for me, my friend Osito, who was originally from the mainland, had a sister and a cousin in here. They'd been doing some hard time, one for kidnapping and the other for murder. They heard about my troubles and took care of the evil step-sisters one night in the yard. I don't know what they did exactly, but those sisters never bothered me again.

"I can't count the times I've just been plain lucky in here - and even during those seven years I was dealing. I could have - and probably should have - been shot or just disappeared like so many have. I guess the worst didn't happen, even though there was a time when I thought being incarcerated in a Central American prison was the worst that could happen. I was wrong.

"Osito's sister, Mava and his cousin, Azul kept a pretty close vigil on me. That is, until Azul was stabbed to death a couple of years ago. Apparently, the fight was over some cigarettes that she didn't pay for. Mava is still here, but keeps to herself a lot more now.

"After Azul was killed, I decided it was time to get my own cell. I'd been sharing one with another girl - Azelia - who kept to herself most of the time, but got really edgy after Azul was off'd. I think she was paranoid that anyone who knew me had a target on their backs. Either way, if you wanted a cell to yourself, you had to pay about $300 American. Even though I didn't want to bring that much attention to myself - or my financial ability - I decided it was safer - and more peaceful to just cough up the dough for it."

"You can just order your own cell in here?"

"You can order - and get - just about anything, if you've got the means and the money for it. You can try to pay for protection too, but you run the risk of getting extorted for more each time. I found it easier to just gain protection from my own reputation as a Chihuahua and from my actual connections I had on the outside. I guess from doing so many dump-runs, Osito and I had become what I would actually call friends - and that made his family, my family.

"He also became my negotiator after Chacarron. He took some pretty big risks for me in the years he worked for me, but I paid him well and I suppose he felt he owed me his loyalty. Unlike Chacarron, he was tight-lipped about everything that went on - and I never actually knew who I was supplying except a few minor details. I also never lost another dollar again. Osito saw to that.

"He wasn't the kind of guy to fall for some dumb-ass Americans trying to get him drunk. And I doubt very much anyone would want to roofie or rape him. He was a pretty ugly looking dude. He was missing most of his teeth and had some mean scars on his face. I guess he'd been quite the fighter when he was young and used to get paid for street fighting.

"Young boys on the street who have no place to go are often picked up by fighting pimps. These pimps give these boys a home and get them high on drugs and then tell them that they owe them. The only way these kids can pay these pimps back are to fight. Basically, they're pulled into cock fighting for humans. What a brutal life!

"Anyway, Osito told me the reason he finally made it off the streets was because of a girl - Lolita - he met at one of his fights. She came and wiped away the blood from his face and took care of him and after that, she never left his side. He told me the reason he finally fell in love with her was because she told him she loved his tooth - the one big molar he still had. I'm not sure if she was right in the head or not, but he referred to her as his *muneca* - his doll - and said he'd never loved anyone the way he loved her. I guess when a person loves you for the one good tooth you've got in your head, what more can you ask?"

"Can we talk about David's visits down here for a minute?"

"What do you want to know?"

"Well, I guess I'm wondering how many times he's been down here and what he's been doing to help you. I'm curious if that was by bringing you stuff or helping you financially? I wanted to ask you how you've had access to things in here? Was it David or other people that have helped you out?"

"David was instrumental in the first couple of years as he made sure there was a trust fund set up for me with the U.S. Embassy and that I had access to it when I needed it. I mean, he brought me a few things on the couple of visits he made here, but as you know, they limit what you can bring in. I've had some other visitors - and some help - over the years, but eventually, as with everything when you're in this hellhole for years, finances dwindle and friends lose touch - or simply don't want to come here. I've made do, but it hasn't been easy. You always seem to be so fascinated with David? Why is that?"

"Well, to be honest, my private investigator found out some interesting things about his past and I've been curious since I first discovered you two knew each other, what is the connection you have. I mean I came right out and asked David in one of our conversations and he told me that your relationship was purely professional, but that you had become friends."

"Well, then what more do you need to know?"

"Delia, he spent almost six months in Colombia. The very place he fought for you to be allowed to cover a story. Don't you find that more than coincidental?"

"Well, considering I didn't know he'd spent time in Colombia until just this minute, I guess I do find it somewhat strange."

This was lie number six.

"You had no idea he spent time in Colombia or that he'd been allegedly kidnapped in the early 90's?"

"Why do you say allegedly?"

"Well, since he decided to go there of his own volition, then get himself kidnapped, but manage to escape all on his own and a few years later, he's instrumental in supporting you to go down and cover a story on Pablo Escobar's drug cartel - all of it seems a bit too coincidental if you ask me."

"So why haven't you asked David about all of this? Why ask me? What could I possibly know about his past or his motives?"

"I tried to ask him about these things, but he hung up on me and then, the next thing I knew, I was getting a phone call from him about you, and I - well, I haven't had a chance to ask him again. I suppose when I hear you talk about your connections inside and outside of prison and I know he came down here at least on two occasions to visit you, I wouldn't be a good journalist if I didn't delve more into this whole situation."

"I suppose you're right. Maybe he's come to visit out of guilt. Perhaps he felt responsible for introducing me to the whole drug trade in Colombia in the first place. Or maybe he thought I took his words to heart - that it was easier to help people if you had money - and he believes that's why I decided to start dealing once I found that package, rather than just turn it into the police."

"That all sounds feasible, but I just get the sense, there's more to it than that. I mean, when he came to visit, what did he say to you? What did he bring?"

"You know what? I'm really tired. The heat is sweltering today. I think I want to end here."

"Come on Delia, tell me something!"

"I was. I was telling you about my life in here - and you switched subjects on me. I'm just tired. Let's talk again tomorrow?"

I didn't push the topic anymore that day. I knew Delia - and David - were hiding something. I figured I'd go back to my hotel room and give Woody a call and see if he could dig up anything more. As it was, I was extremely tired as well. Mostly of feeling like I was going around in circles regarding the topic of David - and how he really fit into Delia's story. Maybe I'd never figure it out - but I was hell bent on giving it my best shot, whether Delia Russell wanted me to or not. I said my goodbyes, asked her if there was anything she wanted - her request this time was a little odd, but I told her I'd do my best - and I left, feeling a little less guilty about leaving her behind that day.

Chapter 17: Pablo

After I scoured the neighbourhood near my hotel looking for the item Delia requested, I headed back to take a rest. When I reached the front desk, there was a fax that had come in from Woody. I wasn't sure what I was looking at until I got back to my room and read it carefully. It was a record of deposits made to David Fisher's bank account - I had no idea how Woody obtained it, nor was I going to ask - over the span of one month in 1991. It was nine months before Pablo Escobar was arrested for narco-terrorism charges and three months after David had returned from his harrowing - I use this term lightly - kidnapping within the Colombian jungle.

There were seven deposits to his account in the span of one month, each for over $10,000 American. I suspected that Woody only felt comfortable sending one page and if I had my hands on David's bank records before and after that, there would be many more deposits. I called Woody a few minutes later.

"So, the media - at least the article in the *New York Times* would have us believe this guy was kidnapped and escaped on his own. My sources in Colombia -" again, I wasn't going to ask Woody how he knew people in Colombia - "tell me that he wasn't kidnapped at all, but had asked to be escorted in by "tour guides" to meet with the Colombian cartel working under Escobar. I suppose on the surface one might believe he was just after a story and got in way over his head and ended up being a pawn in their game. Looking at his bank records however, tells me there's way more to it than that."

"What do you think? This guy was doing deals or trafficking for Escobar's cartel?"

"Hey, the amount of cocaine that was being transported into the States at that time was monumental. It's possible he was working for the cartel. Maybe the guy didn't make much at the time when he was working for the paper."

"Well, I can attest to that. A lot of us work on commission for our stories which is hardly enough to live on in New York. But still, risk your life, your family, your freedom for it?"

"Money talks, brother. Money talks. Do you want me to keep digging?"

"Yeah, see what other records you can find and how long these deals went on for? I mean, wasn't Escobar killed in 1992?"

"That's right about the time, Fisher's deposits stop. I guess even while Escobar was in prison in 1991, he had guys working all over for him."

"No doubt. Apparently, from what I'm learning, prison doesn't stop inmates from criminal activity, it just transforms it into other methods. You don't suppose sending Delia down in the mid 90's to cover that story about the last drug shipment was just a ruse, do you?"

"Anything's possible. I don't make assumptions in my job. I just dig and try to find facts. What my clients do with those facts, is up to them."

"So, you're not going to voice your opinion about this one then?"

"Not over an open line while you're in Honduras, man.   There   is   something   else."

"What is it?"

"I know you didn't ask me to look into it, but when we spoke last, you happened to mention there was a guy that Delia dated who apparently was an acquaintance of David's?"

"Yeah, Muttonhead, what about him?"

"Can you see if you can get his real name from Delia?"

"Why?"

"There's a guy by the name of Peter Manning whose name keeps coming up. When I traced David's bank records to who was making those deposits, this guy's name was on them. Perhaps this guy that David introduced to Delia was more than just an acquaintance?"

"I'll see if I can get her to tell me his real name, but it's doubtful. One of the rules we made when we started this was that she'd only use nicknames. Who knows, maybe she hates the guy enough after what he did to her, to tell me. I'll see what I can do. How's New York doing without me, by the way?"

"It's not the same, man! Speaking of which, when are you getting your ass back here? I thought you wanted to be back before the holidays."

"That was my plan. I'll be here at least until after Thanksgiving. We'll see after that. Thanks for the info buddy. Keep me posted on anything else you find."

"Will do. Over and out."

Woody might not be willing to form any opinions out loud, but I had already made up my mind that David Fisher had somehow had been trafficking drugs out of Colombia and when he saw Delia's naivete as a journalist wanting to make her way up the ladder, he saw another opportunity. Just what that opportunity was, I didn't know yet. Is it possible when she went to Colombia, he had asked her to do some trafficking? Had she agreed? Was this why it was so easy for her to keep the package she found? I didn't know if I should broach this subject with her or not. I ran the risk of pissing her off permanently and never getting any answers. I figured I'd take another approach and this particular item she had asked me to pick up for her might just help me do it.

The next day when I went to see her, I emptied all of my pockets just as I had always done on my previous visits. This time, however, I had worn a hat. I had to remove it as well and the guard quickly inspected it and handed it back to me. They knew it was extremely hot out on the patio and that it wasn't unusual for Delia or the other inmates to wear hats for protection from the sun. She had actually given me the idea. It was the first thing Delia noticed when she sat down with me that afternoon.

"Finally, had enough of the sun, huh? I noticed how red you were getting in the face sitting out here every day. So, did you find one?"

"I did."

"Do you have it?"

"I do."

"Okay, why so curt?"

"I can't give it to you until you give me some information."

"Isn't that all I've ever given you?"

"You've told me lots of stories, yes. But I want some information."

"Okay. About what?"

"About what you were really doing on that trip down to Colombia."

"I see." Delia sat back and looked at me. "Maybe I don't need that item that bad."

"I'm banking on the fact that you do."

She breathed in deeply and took off her hat and placed it close to where I had my hands folded. She turned so that her back was directly to the officer on guard. "Okay. David asked me to travel to Colombia for something other than to cover a story. He needed my help!"

"I presumed that much. What did he ask you to do?"

"He was being threatened by Escobar's cartel. He hadn't been back in over four years because the last time he came through customs, he was cavity searched and detained for four hours and questioned about his frequent visits to Colombia. Why someone didn't get suspicious earlier than that, heaven only knows. What guy, who was kidnapped and held for months, would honestly go back to that country ever again?"

"So, you did know about his kidnapping?"

"Of course! How could I work for *The Times* and not know? Anyway, he wasn't about to return there - he was scared he'd never make it back out alive."

"So, he sent you? What the hell?"

"I had an investment in going."

"He paid you?"

"He paid me half before I went and said he'd pay me the other half when I returned."

"What was it that he wanted you to do?"

"There was a shipment that went awry. It was supposed to be dropped off to him near the hotel where he was staying. He was supposed to smuggle it into the States and arrange for payment. Except when he went to get it, it wasn't there or that's what he told the cartel."

"So, he was lying? He actually had the balls to steal from Escobar's cartel?"

"He was sick of smuggling shit for them. He realized that once he was in, he could never get out. He was never going to be free of them, as long as Escobar was free. Instead of bringing it back to the U.S. he hid it. He had heard through the journalistic grapevine that the authorities were about to arrest Escobar and he figured once he was out of commission, any drugs, especially smaller shipments, wouldn't be missed."

"And he sent you down there to get what he'd left behind? How did he even know that after all those years, it would still be where he left it?"

"Let's just say it was in a secure place and only he had the key. Until he passed it to me."

"So, you went down there under the guise of covering the story -"

"That part was true. I did cover the story. I wanted to prove myself at *The Times*. The money he was paying me would help me pay my rent for a few months, but it wasn't going to last forever and I knew that."

"So, you just got the shipment and came back with it? Just like that? No questions asked? No search? Nothing?"

"Just like that! It was a time when things had settled down. Escobar had been killed by the military police in 1992 and the cartel had shifted its focus from Medellin to Bogota. Any girl doing a story on drugs surely wouldn't be trafficking them, right? I mean, don't get me wrong, I was scared shitless, but David always had a way of convincing me that things would work out. And it did for the most part."

"Until now."

"Until now."

"And this time, in Honduras - did David have a hand in this too?"

"Of course not! Partly why I left New York was because seeing him every day reminded me of what I'd done. I wanted to get away and forget about those past few years - and I had the money to travel for once in my life. Down here, I got involved with bigger fish than David. That was after I was down here for about three years, and it turned out to be very lucrative. After my own package started to dwindle, I was approached by someone at one of the local bars I hung out at, who they call *El Negro*.

"You're talking about El Negro - Los Cachiros's henchman? Jesus, woman, it's a wonder you're still alive!"

"Well, I guess my own reputation preceded me, because he'd heard about Chihuahua and that she was running a good business. He wasn't a man who liked competition of any kind and wanted to know if I wanted to up the ante, so to speak, to the big wheel. I wasn't sure who he was at the time, but I had my suspicions.

"It's difficult to keep a low profile - I was discovering this about myself - on an island of that size. His connections were wide and large and rather than having him see me as any kind of competition, I decided to work with him. I knew that any time you chose to run deals from Colombia on your own - which is what I had started to do after three years of selling the shit I'd found - it would eventually piss someone off."

"So, you're telling me this package that you found wasn't the beginning and end of your 'innocent' unloading? You kept going?"

"Scott, how long do you think 20 kilos will last you? I easily unloaded that in the first three years."

"And you're telling me that David had no part in this and wasn't having you deal for him during all this time?"

"I already told you, David had nothing to do with what I was doing in Honduras."

I wouldn't realize this was lie number seven until much later. I guess, despite the fact that I knew she had lied to me already, I wanted to believe her - and to believe that she trusted me enough to confide in me. This desire, as it turned out, was more about my own ego than recognizing Delia's need to protect herself. How could she really trust anyone - including me? This is why I didn't bring up the subject of Muttonhead at that moment. I guess I just wanted to believe a little while longer that Delia trusted me to tell me everything. It wouldn't be long before I had to face the truth myself.

"Well, that's ironic that drug money you made to travel, landed you here in prison!"

"Yeah, that's the universal joke, right?"

"So, I guess now I understand why David has felt responsible for helping you out - it also explains why he hasn't made too many visits here."

"So, now that you have the rest of that story, can we move on to what's really important?"

"And what's that?"

"Let's see your hat for a second. You don't look half bad in a hat." She ran her fingers across the rim and the insignia. "A Yankees cap, no less!"

"I thought you might appreciate that."

"I do. Thanks!" A few moments later, she handed it back to me and slowly placed hers back on her head. "I better cover up this mop - I look like Pebbles, except without the bone!"

We both thought that was a good place to end the conversation. I'd gotten the information I'd wanted; and she got the item she needed. It was, in her words, a mutually beneficial meeting. The story of Delia Russell was for once, starting to make a lot more sense to me. I didn't realize however, that there were still many missing pieces of the puzzle and I had no idea what the bigger picture was. Nor could I have known that not only would I not be making it home in time for the holidays, I wouldn't see our beloved city again until the next autumn.

Chapter 18: Bam Bam

I didn't get the reference to Pebbles that Delia had made at the end of our conversation until I looked back into my notes I'd taken on one of my visits with her. There were some details about places, events and people that she didn't go into a lot of detail about so I put them on a separate list of things to ask about - or refer back to at a later time.

This was one of those times. She and I had made an exchange two days before without the guard noticing - or so I hoped. The day before that, she hadn't actually asked for an item, she simply pointed at the brooch she'd been wearing on her hat every day for the past week.

I had somehow figured out Delia's sign language - call it a very lucky guess - and realized that she needed money and the best way to get it was to have me bring in a brooch that looked almost identical to the one she had so that she could pass the real one to me without drawing any attention to herself.

I wondered if her mother had known all along that one day, the brooch would be worth much more to Delia financially than any sentimental value. Perhaps, the apple didn't fall far from the tree. Perhaps too, it was her mother's way of providing for her daughter in prison, without the judgement from her son.

In any case, Delia could never have gotten its worth in prison. After I returned to my hotel that day, I vaguely remembered some reference she'd made to another friend she had met during her time on the outside. As soon as I read the name, it became apparent who I was supposed to find in order to pawn her diamond broach. He was a local guy who lived on the island of Roatan, who she had nicknamed Bam Bam because despite being Honduran, he was an albino. He also, as it turned out, was good at using a club on people if they owed him money.

When I got a hold of him - on behalf of Chihuahua, he agreed to meet me in a place called French Harbour. It required me to spend a day travelling off the mainland to Roatan, which was a pain in the ass, but since I had never been there - and it had been where most of Delia's story had taken place, I figured it was time we became acquainted. Little did I know, how many more times I would revisit its shores.

As for Bam Bam, besides some work he'd done for her during the seven years she was dealing, he also ran a water taxi to and from the two quaint little islands - Big Cay and Little Cay off Roatan's coast. It was known for a number of other things, like its sloth and monkey reserve and the caged tigers its owner kept at the smaller of the two islands. The place was a wonderland of fun where one could snorkel, paddle board, float around and drink or catapult oneself off a rope into the ocean.

It was also well known for its nefarious owner - Kaveh Lahijana - who was originally from Iran, but had gained his American citizenship, but had been living in Honduras. He'd been arrested just months before I arrived, for money laundering, as well as a number of other illegal acts, leaving behind his tigers and animals to be cared for by his Honduran girlfriend who was still running the place. For a journalist or a storyteller, there was no shortage of characters on and around the island to use for inspiration.

In any case, Bam Bam owed Delia a few favours and when I showed him the broach, he had no problem coughing up quite a bit of money for it. I figured it was more of a payback than an exchange. I doubted any pawn shop would have paid that much.

Either way, once I had the money for it, I was to await my next sign in order to know who to give it to. At the time, I did think it odd that Delia didn't want me to give it to the U.S. Embassy which usually kept money in trust for American inmates and made sure that they had access to it whenever they needed something on the inside.

Looking back, I should have asked a lot more questions than I did. Or perhaps, there was a part of me that didn't want to know the truth. Wasn't it Delia herself that told me it was better - and safer - if I didn't know everything? As it turns out, it wouldn't be long until a few more pieces of the puzzle fell into place. And as the pieces were falling, little did I know that the key piece to this story was about to disappear forever.

Chapter 19: Guatusso

My next visit to Delia was odd to say the least. When I arrived, I was taken into one of the detainment rooms and asked to wait. I was then asked to take off my shirt - they apparently wanted to make sure I wasn't wearing a wire, which was odd since I could have carried in a tape recorder had I wanted to. I'm not sure if they got wind of our exchange or what the hell was going on. I was asked to leave all personal items in a bin and was only allowed to take in a pen and my notebook - which they had also taken from me for a good half hour. They returned it to me, said nothing more and then ushered me out to the patio.

When Delia came out, she wasn't wearing her hat and carried nothing with her either. I waited for her to sit down.

"What the hell is going on?"

"I don't know. There was a cell search yesterday and a bunch of shit was confiscated from us. I lost a few things, but I'd already traded all the diapers so they didn't get those."

"Do you think they suspect something?"

"They always suspect something, but usually it's just an excuse for the guards to steal from the inmates. I don't know. I do know that there's been word that a number of girls in here are starting to hate me because I've had a daily visitor and they know you've brought me stuff. I try to trade most of it, although I kept the flowers and the dark chocolate. If you can trade most of it, then most of them don't get too jealous. They're just glad they can get their hands on stuff from the outside.

"Tensions are high in here anyway. There's too much overcrowding and prices for things - even at the canteen are going up. It puts the inmates on edge and then the guards get jittery about fights breaking out and shit. Who knows? Anyway, did you find my *boyfriend*?"

"Bam Bam? Yeah, I found him. The deal is done."

"Good. you're getting really good at this undercover stuff, reading my signs and stuff. I could have used you in those seven years on the outside!"

"Well, thanks for the compliment - I think!"

"How much was the gift?"

"One grand."

"Not bad. Bam Bam must be feeling generous these days. So, I need you to find another friend. I haven't mentioned him before - and he needs to be protected, which means you need to make sure no one is following you."

"Following me? Who would be following me?"

"Listen, there are eyes and ears everywhere. Word gets out. There are some people who are more than willing to pay the guards to see the visitors list about who comes in and out of here. Be sure, there are already people watching you."

"Well thanks for telling me this now, after I did an exchange for you."

"We just need to be careful is all I'm saying."

"And what about Muttonhead?"

"What about him?"

"Do you need to be careful about him?"

"Why are you bringing him up?"

"You tell me! You tell me what connection he had to David's little drug running business?"

"Why would you think-"

"Delia, this isn't the time to play dumb! We both know you met him on the same night David asked you for a drink. We both know what the chump did to you – that he was a thief and had violent tendencies, so I find it hard to believe that you meeting him was a coincidence."

"Do you have to be such a thorough journalist, for Christ's sake? Maybe I just don't want to get into everything that happened."

"Well, if you're going to tell your story, don't you want it to be accurate?"

"Well, that's funny!"

"Why? Why is that funny?"

"Because we both know that every story is never truly accurate, nor are the details."

"Well, maybe this one should be, considering this schmuck should be behind bars – and so should David!"

"Okay, I didn't know Muttonhead-"

"Can we cut the bullshit and call him by his real name?"

"I told you, no real names."

"Delia, this guy was horrible to you. Why are you protecting him?"

"I'm not."

"Really? It doesn't look like that!"

"Listen to me, this guy is not someone who you want to fuck with."

"He sounds like he needs to be fucked with!"

"Well, that may be true, but he's a lot smarter than I thought.   He   was   blackmailing   me."

"What? When?"

"It started after David-"

"After David what?"

"Okay, David did ask me to do some dealing for him between Colombia and Honduras. I refused at first. I was happy doing my own thing on my own terms. I didn't want to be under his thumb again."

"How did he convince you? Let me guess! He used Muttonhead to blackmail you? What did he have on you?"

"What didn't he have on me? That file I told you he took from my camera had pictures on it while I was in Colombia. There were pictures I'd taken of the Escobar cartel, among other things and he threatened to send them to the cartel and send them after me."

"But Escobar had been killed and his cartel had all but disbanded."

"Escobar might have been dead, but his ring leaders were still very much alive – including his body guards and assassins – Aguilera for one and I had photos of them. I could have identified quite a few had I wanted to. Muttonhead also knew what I'd been doing in Colombia and he threatened to go to the DEA if I didn't help David. He and David had been in cohorts for some time. It wasn't an accident that I met him, but it's on me for the decisions I made, including dating him in the first place."

"So, what's his name?"

"I can't tell you."

"Okay, so what if I tell you and you nod if I'm right?"

"Why do you want to know his name so badly?"

"Because his name is associated with thousands of dollars that were deposited into David's account way back in the 1990's."

"What? No! David hadn't known him that long. He couldn't have! That means that he'd been planning-"

"Exactly! He'd been planning it all – manipulating you, setting up that night for the after-work drink so you'd meet this guy seemingly coincidentally. They've both been making money hand over fist while using you as their mule for years! Was his name, Peter Manning?"

Delia looked at me, then looked past me and shook her head. The shaking of her head wasn't symbolizing no; it was symbolizing how much of a fool she felt in that moment and I could empathize with her.

"Look, someone needs to know about this. Someone needs to know that you were set up!"

"No! I wasn't set up! I mean, I may have been manipulated at first and yeah, blackmailed, but I had a choice. The truth is my decisions the last seven years have been my own, not David's and not Muttonhead's. I can't – I won't give them that much credit. I have to believe that I have been the master of my fate; otherwise, I've been a pawn in someone else's game. Sure, I might have started out that way, but I made my own game down here and my own rules and no matter what, I survived. That's got to count for something! And, there are people in my life who have been extremely good to me and I need you to focus on them for me right now! Okay?"

"Okay. Whatever you wish."

"So, this guy's name is Guatusso. He's another artist on the island - but he's also my friend. You can trust him. That you can bank on."

"How do you know that for sure?"

"If you knew this guy, you'd know why. He was someone I met early on while I was down here. He was never part of my dealing in those seven years. I mean, I guess I could have recruited him, but I thought too highly of him. Besides he'd already had enough trouble with the law during his life, but he'd finally started making some money as an artist with the expats and so didn't need - or want - to get involved in my affairs.

"He was simply a good friend. I used to love to sit at the bar and hear his stories. He was born and raised on Guanaja island and moved to Roatan when he was grown. He even remembers a time before television or radio existed there. He told me that his great grandmother, when radios were becoming the thing to have, sent her son - which would be Guatusso's great uncle, all the way around Roatan to French Harbour in a canoe to buy a radio. Her son came home with it, but when she turned it on, it only played a Spanish station - many of the locals only spoke English at that time. In any case, she was so angry, she sent her son back around the island to return it and get a radio that *spoke English!*"

"She didn't figure out she could just turn the dial?"

"I guess not! I thought that story, was so sweet, you know? About the innocence of some people. He told me a lot of stories that I treasure to this day. I remember the first time I ever met him. He walked into the bar covered from head to toe - his shirt and shorts anyway - in paint. He didn't just wear his heart on his sleeve; he wore his passion all over his clothes.

"He'd come down to the local bar and paint. There was one painting he did in black and white of the full moon and it was stunning. I always thought if I hadn't already asked Machete to paint something for me, I would have been glad to have Guatusso do it. In any case, we used to sit and chat about life and he told me he'd spent time in prison. I guess I should have listened more carefully. The first time was for lobster diving in illegal waters - somewhere off the coast of Nicaragua. The second time he was sentenced to six years for trafficking, but only served two of them thanks to someone in his family coughing up some dough and the third time, according to him, he was innocent, but charged with transporting and trafficking.

"The judge actually sentenced him to do rehab, but apparently, either his lawyer fucked him or the local police did. Instead of taking him to rehab, they threw away the judge's order and took him straight to prison. He didn't even know he'd only been sentenced to rehab until two years later. He was too afraid to report the police by the time he got out, so decided to let it go. He did tell me that his third time in prison wasn't a total waste because he met Left Eye Lisa."

"As in the singer?"

"Yeah, apparently, she was involved with his cellmate and he heard all about her work on the mainland."

"What kind of work? She wasn't in the drug business?"

"God no! She was using her music and doing concerts to fundraise in order to help the less fortunate. Apparently, she had a real heart for kids and had a dream of opening her own school here on the mainland. I love that idea! I'd love to accomplish something like that someday!"

"Who says you can't?"

"Harder, do you see where I am?"

"You'd be the first one to tell me that these bars don't stop people from doing things down here!"

"Yes, but mostly illegal things!"

"Well, there's nothing to say that you can't be the first to accomplish something positive from behind bars!"

"I suppose you're right! Anyway, I think Guatusso was really impressed by her. I probably wouldn't have believed him otherwise. I wish now I'd asked him more about his experiences so I would have been more prepared for mine! He's such a character! You kind of love and hate him at the same time. He shared about his family and how when he was a boy, his sister had fallen in love with a boy from the mainland who would send her money and things when he was apart from her. So, I guess at some point, Guatusso's entrepreneur side kicked in and he began writing letters to this boy himself, posing as his sister, even going so far as putting lipstick on and leaving lip imprints on the letter, asking this boy to send more money and gifts from the mainland. I don't know if his sister - or her boyfriend - ever found out or not. I'll give him this much; he had a real creative streak!

"Anyway, over the span of my seven years living on the island, we remained friends and he could always count on me buying him a beer or listening to his many stories and I could count on him to keep an eye on Ghost when I had to leave the bar or be away from him at times. That's the biggest reason I trust him - the way he was with animals, especially Ghost, who loved him almost as much as he loved me.

"So, now you know a little bit of his story. And now I need you to take that gift you got from Bam Bam and give it to Guatusso. He'll keep it for me until I need it."

"You mean he comes here to visit you - all the way from the island? Which is a pain to travel to, by the way! You'd think he'd want to stay as far away from prisons as he could. Why didn't you just have me drop it to him when I was already there?"

"You're asking me a lot of questions. First of all, I needed to make sure you made the exchange and all went well, before I put Guatusso in any danger. Besides, you need to wait a couple of weeks before you return to the island - or see him anyway."

"Well, yes, by all means, protect him! What about me, smuggling stuff out of here for you and doing exchanges? What about my protection?"

"I am trying to protect you. That's why I keep telling you to not ask me so many questions."

"Okay, I know that's my cue to not delve any deeper into that topic."

"As I said Pancake, you're getting really good at reading me and my "cues" as you call them. Is there anything else you're dying to know before we end today?"

"Just one thing, what ever happened to Ghost?"

Delia's head shot straight up and she looked at me, not with sadness from missing him as I had expected, but with a glimmer of hope in her eyes. "I hope, like any true love, he's waiting for me on the outside."

"Do you know where he is?"

"I know where he is."

"Are you going to tell me?"

"You'll find out soon enough." I wasn't sure what Delia meant by this or how that might come to pass, but I suspected I just needed to trust her this time - and that this time, she really was telling the truth. I left that day feeling strangely hopeful myself, like Delia had said she felt when the package was drifting up on shore. Like something was about to happen that was going to change everything, but I had no idea what it was.

Chapter 20: Eye

All hell broke loose two days later. I got a call from Woody of all people asking me if I had seen the news. It was only 9am and I hadn't even had my coffee yet. He told me to turn on the television - Honduran news - if I could. I turned on CNN and waited for them to get to international news. I felt like someone had punched me in the solar plexus when I saw the headline, flashing across the bottom of the screen:

Breaking news: American Female Escapes Honduran Federal Prison During Riot.

For just a second, in a confused state, I wondered why they were reporting on something that happened over three years ago. Then reality set in and I realized that they were talking about present day. I sat down - I had already hung up with Woody - and turned up the volume.

During a riot between disgruntled inmates and guards, the only American female in the prison had disappeared without a trace. Prison guards were being interrogated - and there was a manhunt going on throughout the mainland. Across the screen, flashed the mug shot of the same woman I'd been visiting for weeks. Besides that, was a picture of what Delia must have looked like at least ten years earlier. I had never seen a picture of what she looked like before. She was stunning, just as many had said to her. Looking at those two pictures juxtaposed with each other, it was hard to believe, they were the same woman.

Harder still, was to believe that she had managed to escape yet again. I sat there fixated on the television, long after her story had ended. My brain was trying to wrap itself around the idea that not only had she escaped, but that I might never see her again, followed by the trepidation that I might be charged with collusion.

I called the U.S. Embassy immediately to ask them what they thought I should do. They told me that I'd be wise to leave the country as soon as possible. Woody had alluded to the same thing while I was on the phone with him, without telling me what had actually happened.

"You might want to get out of that country as soon as possible, bro! Just saying. I'll let you decide. Good luck!" Then he hung up.

I realized I was on my own. I called my travel agent immediately, but just before I was about to book my emergency flight home, something stopped me. I still had Delia's money. I couldn't leave with it - and how was I supposed to get it to her now - even by way of Guatusso? I didn't have long to think about any of this, before the Honduran police showed up at my hotel door. I was hauled into the Honduran Police station and questioned for hours.

The good news is that I had couriered my notes home to the U.S. for safe keeping. Perhaps it was because the prison guards, when they had taken my notebook away from me even for half an hour, I sensed something was up - and having my most important possession as a journalist taken away so easily, didn't sit well with me. In the end, this precautionary move prevented the Honduran police from getting the names - even if they were mostly nicknames - and details of Delia's life. I'd never been so grateful that I had listened to my instincts. That was until later, when I would be faced with even more desperate situations - and decisions - in that country.

After the police finished their interrogation of me - at least for that day - I went back to the prison. I wanted to know if Delia had left anything behind - I knew I was stupid to think she might risk it - but I was desperate for a note, for anything she might have left at the prison to give me a clue of where she went or how to find her. There was nothing. Her cell had already been ransacked, first by the guards looking for clues themselves and then by looting inmates looking for treasures they could use or trade. Then a thought occurred to me. Perhaps she hadn't left a note, but maybe a message with none other than her friend, Eye.

I decided it was best to not request a visit that day - and so I waited a week. I persuaded the guards with money - and came equipped with a bag of diapers with the excuse that I thought Eye, who was a mother of two could either use them or sell them to help her out. Interestingly enough, the guards *bought* my reason and let me meet with her.

When she came out from behind the wall - the same wall that Delia had come from on every one of our visits, I felt a pang in my heart knowing that she would never be coming out again. I suppose I should have been happy that she was finally free - and that she hadn't been caught this time - at least not yet. However, there was an ache of sadness

I felt that she had left me behind without ever looking back - and that she hadn't thought to include me in her plans.

I mean, I knew that she couldn't include me - except perhaps to do some exchanges for her for money - otherwise I'd end up in the same place. I knew she'd tried to protect me, but that same familiar feeling of her being so far ahead of me that I'd never catch up to her, haunted me. I could only hope that one day, she might just come up behind me! There was a part of me that was happy for her - and proud in some way that she had managed to break out without anyone - even me - knowing about it. Although, I suspected there had to be someone else who knew - someone else who helped her get free.

I began with Eye. When she sat down, she smiled at me - which I wasn't expecting. I knew her history of how she'd helped her husband kidnap someone and that's how she landed behind bars, so I was expecting someone tougher - a more seasoned prisoner, if you will. She had a kind face - the face of a mother - and was plump and unassuming.

"Hello," I said, "I'm Scott Harder, a friend of-"

"I know who you are. What do you want?" Her tone betrayed her kind face.

"I uh,"- I had to think about what it was I did want and how to ask for it. "I uh, I spent a lot of time with Delia and now that she's gone, I've only got half her story. I just wondered if you knew anything about her - her life - or maybe where she'd go from here?"

"Ha! Well, if I knew where she was, I certainly wouldn't tell you - or anyone for that matter, but I don't know. I had no idea what she was planning."

"You speak very well in English. Did you learn here on the mainland?"

"I went to school for a few years. I had a nice English teacher. She was from the States. Delia reminded me of her. I guess that's why I liked her right away - well almost, right away."

"You didn't like her at first?"

"Nobody likes anybody at first, do they? Especially here in this place. Anyway, she grew on me. She was good to my kids - my boys. She was good to me."

"That's good to hear. I know she had a good heart - especially with kids - and dogs - helping out at the dump like she   did."

"Yeah, I heard about that. Ha! Maybe, she went back to the dump - any place has got to be better than here!"

"Yeah, maybe. That's where she found, Mr. Right."

"You mean, Ghost?"

"Yeah, you know about him?"

"Yeah, he's like her kid, you know. She loved him like I love my boys. She gave me a picture of him. In fact, I still have it. Do you want to see it?"

"Sure! I've never seen a picture of him - I just heard about how large he is. Like a wolf!"

"Yeah, Chihuahua needs a wolf to protect her!"

"Yes, maybe!" I sensed Eye had a real fondness for Delia and that made me happy and at the same time, sad for her too, as she'd lost a friend.

"Here." She pulled the creased photo out of her jean's pocket. She unfolded it and gave it to me. "She gave me that. I don't know why. You can have it if you want it, to remember her by." The photo was of the stunning Delia, sitting beside her oversized wolf-dog who was just as beautiful as she had described.

"I'd like that - very much." I took the photo from her and stared at it for a long time. Then I turned it over and there in writing on the back, was an address. I wasn't sure if Eye knew that it was there or not, but I thought it better to say nothing. If she did and she wanted me to see it, then there was no point in asking. If she didn't, I thought it better to keep her in the dark in case the address actually meant something. "I was wondering if Delia said anything to you - or left a message for me in any way."

Eye looked at me and smiled. "That photo of Ghost is her message. She said you were smart and that you'd figure it out. And that's all I got to say. I've got to get back to my boys   now."

"Okay. I left some diapers for you at the desk."

"Gracias. I appreciate that. I sure am gonna miss that girl - and all her gifts. She sure was good to me and my boys."

"She said she traded with you a lot."

"Delia? She never traded with me. She just always came with gifts - pretty smelling flowers and chocolates and stuff. She even gave me a bottle of bug spray the other day, for our lovely infested garden!"

I sat back and smiled. I had forgotten about the bottle of bug spray I had brought to her on one of my visits. It was after she mentioned about how the sand fleas chewed up their ankles. I also thought about Delia's lies. The finest one she ever told was that she'd kept those flowers and chocolates for herself, when all along they were for her friend. I felt my own tears surface. "I'm gonna miss her too!" I said and got up before Eye could see my first vulnerable moment. "Thank you so much for meeting me. Here's my card. I know it won't do you much good in here, but if I can ever be of help to you, find a way to contact me."

"Thank you. Delia was wrong - you're not such a jerk after all, Pancake!"

I just shook my head. Even after she'd disappeared, she still got the last word.

Chapter 21: Nickname

Delia would have been proud of me. I did what she instructed and I waited two weeks until I made any attempt to find this mysterious Guatusso friend of hers. Partly my hesitation was because she told me to delay my visit and the other was to wait until I felt like the heat was off me a bit - or so I hoped. I also took some time to track down a couple of her other friends.

My first visit was to an area up past Lawson Rock, near where the original dump had been. I had managed to find Velvet by way of inquiring about volunteer work on the island asking around if there was any place that I could offer my assistance. As it turned out, there was a new school that had opened up in the last couple of years and Velvet was the co-owner. When I got out of the taxi and stood on the front steps of the three story, white-stucco structure I was awestruck by its name. On the sign hovering above the front wrap-around porch were two hyphenated names followed by *Institute of Academia*. I recognized Delia's last name immediately and could only surmise that the other was Velvet's.

I slowly walked up the steps as I thought back to my conversation with Delia about Left Eye Lopez. She had been inspired by Lopez's story of trying to open a school for street kids. I wondered if Delia had any idea that her name was now on a school. When I looked around for the office or for someone to whom I could ask, I didn't have to look very far.

I recognized the raven-haired woman at the end of the hall who was every bit as graceful and tall as Delia had described.

She turned in that moment and faced me. I couldn't say for sure that she recognized me, but something told me she already knew who I was. As she sauntered down the hall towards me, I felt as if I'd been told a story and that one of the characters was coming alive before my very eyes.

"Buen dia, Senor! Como estas?"

I was expecting her to speak French, so when she greeted me in Spanish, I was taken aback for a moment.

"I'm good! Sorry, my Spanish – and my French are not so good."

"Lucky for you, I speak English as well! Can I help you?"

"Uh, yes. I was told that perhaps I could volunteer here."

"Why don't you come into my office and we can talk about that. Can I get you some tea?"

"Yes, that would be great."

"Wonderful! My office is the one on the right." She swung her arm out and pointed to the door. "I'll be with you in a moment."

The door was open so I stepped inside. The first thing I noticed was the picture on her desk. It was her and Delia embracing each other at a party. They both looked ravishing – and happy! It made me sad to think that I would never know Delia as she had been. However, I was still grateful that I had had the opportunity to know her at all. I was still staring at the photo when Velvet came into the room. "May I ask your name?"

"Yes. It's Scott. Scott Harder."

"And where are you from Scott Harder?"

"From New York. Although I've been visiting the mainland for some time now."

"Yes? Have you been volunteering there as well?"

"No. Not exactly! I've been working on a story."

"Fascinating! What kind of story?"

"A personal one. Researching really – about a person who's living there."

"Really? Who is that? A local?"

"No, someone also from New York."

"I see." Velvet dropped the pretenses and simply stared at me. The woman was brilliant and without another word, she yanked the truth from me as if she already owned it.

"I was writing your friend's story."

"My friend?"

"Yes. I believe she was a friend of yours."

"She is. Although I haven't seen her in a long time. How is she?"

"Well, she wasn't exactly living the best life up until a few days ago, but I suppose you've heard the news."

"I have. Interesting turn of events."

"I'd say!"

"So, what are you really doing here? I suspect you aren't really interested in volunteering?"

"No." I cleared my throat. "No, I'm not. I'm sorry to waste your time."

"Why don't you tell me why you're really here and I'll decide if you're wasting my time."

"Okay. If I were being honest, I don't even know why I'm really here. I suppose, especially now, there are pieces of her story that I feel like I'm missing."

"And you think I can fill in some of those pieces?"

"I was hoping."

"I see. Well, I can tell you that Delia and I hit it off right away. She was a doll, really. Kind-hearted to a fault. And a great lover of animals! Did she tell you about Ghost?"

"Yes." I smiled at the mention of him. "He was quite special to her."

"He still is."

"He's alive then?"

"Very much so."

"That's good."

"Yes. If I had to guess, he's one of the reasons that she's managed to stay alive this long."

"I'm just going to come out and ask you this and I hope you don't take offence."

"Feel free!"

"Do you know where she is? Do you know if she's alright?"

"You understand that I can't answer certain questions. What I can tell you, Mr. Harder, is that you need not worry about her. You see, Delia is a planner. Just like this school. It was her dream, you know – to open a school and help children here on the island. I may have been of some help financially and now in overseeing the administrative business of it, but she is the reason it exists. So, what I'm trying to tell you, is that trust that whatever she wanted or didn't want you to know, it was her plan all along. Whatever pieces you may feel you're missing, may have been what she didn't want you to know. And if there are pieces that still need to be filled in, they will be. In the meantime, what I can tell you is that whomever you think she is, she is so much more than what you can possibly imagine."

"I believe that. I want to trust that I will be able to discover those missing pieces, it's just been difficult to find out about her disappearance through the news instead of from her."

"Yes, well, even her most trusted friends saw it on the news first, I can assure you of that! Again, be assured that whatever Delia has planned, it will all turn out. Now, is there anything else I can help you with?"

"Yes. Just a couple of other things. The man she met at your New Year's Eve party. You wouldn't happen to remember his name would you or know if he is still on the island?"

"That I'm afraid, I can't tell you. I don't remember her meeting anyone at that party. Sorry." Of course, I knew she was lying to protect someone – I hope it was to protect Delia – and not some dumb schmuck she was dating. "Anything else, Mr. Harder?"

"I wondered if her friend, the older gentleman that she came to that party with, if you knew where I could find him?"

"Bernard, you mean?"

"Yes. She called him Bernie." I was surprised that she hadn't gone to more trouble to disguise his name.

"Unfortunately, Bernard passed away a few weeks ago. Right about the same time her other friend was killed."

"Other friend?"

"Yes, he was more of an acquaintance, I think. She had some strange nickname for him, but I can't recall what it was now. I'm sorry. I know that she would have been quite upset about their deaths."

"I see." I didn't ask anything else, but I wondered if there had been any correlation with their deaths and her attempted suicide. "Well, you've been most helpful. I'm very glad to know that one of her dreams was realized and I'm sure, many children will benefit because of it."

"That's our plan! Thank you for dropping by, Mr. Harder."

"No. Thank you!" I shook her hand and turned to walk out of her office.

"One other thing!"

"Yes?" I turned back to face her.

"Trust that if you were a friend of Sarah's, she will have had a plan for you too."

I wasn't sure what to make of Velvet's words, but they were comforting just the same. Although at the same time, I had to wonder if Delia had ever come to think of me as a friend.

"How would one know if Delia thought of you as a friend?"

"That's easy. She would have given you a nickname!"

"She gave everyone a nickname!"

"Only the people she loved – or hated. Now, all you have to do, is figure out which side you're on!" She laughed a delightful little laugh. "Goodbye, Scott."

Chapter 22: Guatusso & Ghost

I felt like I was being followed everywhere I went, just as Delia had suspected. I couldn't shake the idea that someone was about to come up behind me and unfortunately, it wouldn't be Delia. There had been no more word about her disappearance and while they were still technically looking for her, the police had only limited resources in which to do so and it wouldn't be long before Delia - at least on the mainland of Honduras - would be forgotten about.

What I didn't know was that there were other people who wanted to find her - and make an example out of her. I hoped that wherever she was, she was well hidden and planned on staying that way. In the meantime, I probably should have done the same, but having been left with only half of her story, it was driving me crazy. I also felt a responsibility to make sure that Guatusso received her money in case she needed it.

When I first landed on the island of Roatan once again, I made sure that I wasn't being followed. I had the picture of Delia and Ghost with me, but had scratched out the address on the back. I had memorized it and thought if anyone else got their hands on it, I didn't want them getting to the address before I did.

Was I secretly hoping Delia might be hiding out there when I arrived and I might be able to see her again - and know that she was okay? Yes, I was. I could hear her words in my head telling me how stupid I was for having this kind of hope and that although I might be that naive, she wasn't stupid enough to hide out on the very island where she'd been trafficking and later, arrested.

Hope does crazy things to people - it makes them believe in things that are highly improbable, which of course, sets us all up for disappointment. I hoped anyway! After I left Velvet, I caught a colectivo because I thought it was less likely that I would be followed if I was surrounded by locals, or at least I wouldn't stand out as much. Nothing stands out more than a pasty white guy who looks like a tourist. Probably no matter what I did, I still stood out like a sore thumb.

I arrived at the address on Mangrove Lane at around 2pm in the afternoon. I had no idea where I was going, until I noticed a small, wooden sign for an art gallery pointing up the hill. I thought I must be in the right place. My suspicions were confirmed when a dog the size of a wolf shoved his head over a wooden fence to my right and bared his teeth at me. I thought I actually felt the wind on my face with its every bark.

"Ghost?" I said almost instinctively. As soon as I said his name, his growling face disappeared and there was no more barking. I doubted saying his name would have such an effect on him, so I walked towards the fence. I heard a latch click and the fence opened half a foot. A dark, skinny man poked his head out.

"What can I do fo'ya, man?" He asked, in a very distinct island dialect - I discovered that many on the islands spoke either Patois or a unique form of English, not Spanish as I had always believed.

"I'm here, looking for someone - a guy named, Guatusso."

"Wat ya want wit'em?"

"I just want to chat with him. I'm a journalist from New York - well actually, I'm a friend of Delia's."

"You got some ID on you, man?"

"Yeah, sure." I fumbled trying to get out my driver's license - at the same time, thinking it was the first time I'd ever been asked for ID just to enter a fenced yard. He held it up very close to his face as if his eyesight was failing, looked at me, then turned to look at the beast behind the gate.

"You got any otter proof ya know Delia?"

"I have this." I carefully took out the creased photo of Delia and her dog and held it up. I wasn't about to hand it over. It was the only thing I had left to remember her by. At least that's what I thought at the time. I didn't realize that I had so much more of her - in my head and in my heart. I had her words, her stories and her dreams that she had shared with me.

"Whatcha wanna know, man?"

"Well, I have something for a guy named Guatusso. Would you happen to know where he is?"

"I might. Dat depends on whatcha got fo him, man."

I was starting to lose my patience. It was very hot and I was already sweating through my clothes and this guy's own obtuseness was irritating me. "Look, I'm here to deliver something on behalf of Delia to a guy named Guatusso. If you're him, open the gate. If you're not, tell me where to find him."

"Okay, okay! Don't get your knickers all tied up, man! Come in. Just don't try to pet da dog. He don't like strangers."

He didn't have to tell me twice. I wasn't about to expose my hand or any other body part to this dog. He might have looked sweet in the photo, but I saw his teeth up close and knew that any false move and I was bound to lose something. I followed the hunched over man along a muddy path - the dog sat there in all his glory glaring at me - up a set of stairs to a small wooden veranda. "Are you Guatusso?"

"Last time I checked."

"Do you have any ID?" I asked more out of frustration than seriousness.

"You wanna see my ID? Ghost! Come here, boy!" Ghost stood up from his seated position along the path and bound up the stairs and the next thing I knew, he was on his hind legs licking the man's face. I remembered Delia's story about when Machete had retrieved Ghost from the two thieves and how he had licked her face the same way. I knew then that this was the infamous Guatusso she'd been talking about and what her words meant when she told me I would find out soon enough what happened to her dog. "That good enuf fo'ya, man?"

"Yes." I sat down on one of the rickety wooden chairs and took a breath.

"You want some limonada?"

"I'd love some."

"I'll be right back. Ghost, keep an eye on our guest, boy!"

I nodded my head to signify my understanding that I wasn't supposed to move. That and I thought this guy was just playing with me a little. Trying to scare me. I could see why he and Delia got along. They had the same sense of humour. He returned in a few minutes with a large glass of cold lemonade and sat down in the chair next to me. Ghost laid down at his feet.

"I see the dog likes you."

"I think he loves me, man."

I smiled. "Maybe!"

"So, you got sometin' for me? Sometin' for Delia?"

"I do. Not to be rude or anything, but how am I supposed to know that I can trust that you will get it her?"

"It ain't fo' ya to trust me. You gotta trust Delia knows what she's doin'. You see dis dog? You tink a grand means more to dat woman dan dis dog? And whose she's left dis dog with?"

"How did you - how did you know how much I had?"

"Cause Delia told me how much she's expecting. She ain't stupid, man!"

"What? You've talked to her?" I nearly fell out of my chair I leaned so close to him. "Have you seen her since she - since she, got out?"

"Now you ask lots of questions - she warned me 'bout you - dat's not yer' concern. You need to jus do wat she told you to do and den go on your merry way."

"After everything I've been through with her - listening to her stories - and only half the story at that - and helping her - I'm supposed to just give you a grand and be *on my merry way*?"

"Firsts as all, you ain't been thoo shit wid dat girl! You wanna talk about going thoo' shit wid her, try watchin' her almost die a few times and gettin' beaten wit'in an inch o' her life for seven years. Den you talk to me 'bout everytin' you been thoo wid'er."

"I'm sorry! I didn't mean any disrespect. I'm just frustrated that I've spent all of this time down here in this country trying to get her story right - and now she's gone and I'll never know all of it."

"Is das wha's really buggin' ya, man? She told me yo might have your knickers all tied up in knots 'bout it. Jus' wait here. I got somethin' fo yo ass dat might help you feel better." He disappeared in his thatched shack and left Ghost to guard me again. The dog looked up at me - and then plopped his large head on the veranda. I wasn't convinced the dog was as vicious as Guatusso had made out - in fact, he didn't even seem to care that I was there anymore. Like mother, like dog!

Anyway, I thought I'd put my theory to the test and so I very slowly got up and began to walk past him to the front door of the house. He looked up and then put his head back down. Just as I thought! I quietly went through the open doorway and had a look around. It was just a bare minimum of a kitchen. A propane stove and old wooden countertop. There were dirty dishes in the sink and enough flies to drive a normal man crazy.

I wasn't sure where Guatusso had disappeared to, so I went a little further and pulled back a make-shift curtain and much to my surprise, the next room was filled with beautiful paintings. Some with vibrant sunsets and silhouettes of people and as soon as I saw it, I recognized the black and white painting of the full moon Delia had mentioned in one of our visits. She had been right - he was a talented artist.

There was very little light in the room and the one window had the curtain drawn. I walked towards it and slowly pulled back the material that posed as a curtain. Below the curtain was a large painted canvas - a beautiful rendition of the same photo I had in my possession - stunning Delia and her dog sitting in front of the ocean at sunset.

"You found it, eh? I shoulda known Ghost wouldn't do nuttin' to ya! That dogs got a six sense about people who loves his mama."

"I don't love her!" The words came out of my mouth so quickly that they were dripping in defense - and deceit - and we both knew it. "I'm just amazed at how you captured her photo - her likeness. Did she ask you to do this?"

"Nope. She ast'd me to finish it."

"Finish it? What do you mean?"

"Anutter man started it. I finished it."

"Another man? You mean, Machete?"

"Das right! Machete."

"Why didn't he finish it?"

"Well, you got so many questions that ha'been left unanswered, I guess dat's why Delia left dis for ya!" He handed me a leather-bound book, at least two inches thick.

"What's this?"

"It's fo' you. It's Delia's journal durin' dose seven years. She t'ought you might like to hav't."

"Really?" I took it in both my hands and opened it. There were two satin ribbons within it to mark certain pages and there, on each page, was Delia's handwriting, marked with dates and tiny drawings. "She left this with you?"

"Ain't no way she was gonna take it to prison wit' her! Anyway, I just do what I'm instructed, like you oughtta do! She told me if you turned up wid her money, I oughtta hand o'er her journal to ya."

I was rendered speechless. I could hardly believe that this woman who I thought didn't trust me at all, had left her personal journal of her years on this island, with me. In my entire writing career - having interviewed a number of prominent people and having had quite a bit of success with my articles, I had never felt so honoured in my entire life as I did that day. There was no better wish I could have asked for in that moment than to be standing in front of this beautiful portrait of Delia and her dog, while holding the rest of her story in my hands. And that's just it - her story - the telling of it - was now literally, in my hands and I knew I couldn't go home yet.

Chapter 23:   Angelica

Imagine my surprise when Angelica - David's assistant, turned up on my doorstep on the island of Roatan two weeks after I'd gone to visit Guatusso. When I first opened the door to her, I thought perhaps David had sent her to find out what happened to Delia. I hadn't spoken to him since Delia's escape - nor did I have any desire to, after I found out the truth about him using her as a mule. This is why it seemed so odd that he would send his assistant without contacting me first.

She asked if she could come in, but seemed all *business*. I offered her a drink, but she declined. "Scott, before you say anything, there's something you need to know."

"I'm listening."

"I'm with the DEA."

"What?   You mean, like the Drug Enforcement Administration in the States?"

"That's correct. I'm sure it's a bit of a shock, but-"

"What the hell? Just when I think I can't be any more surprised, there's always one just around the corner." I sat down before I passed out. I figured this was it. I was going to be put under arrest not only for collusion in Delia's escape, but God knows what? Hiding notes from the authorities - an array of possible charges against me went through my head. Meanwhile, Delia's journal of her seven years of a drug trafficker was sitting wide open on my desk by my computer. Fuck!

"Listen Scott, I'm here off the record."

"Off the record? What does that mean?"

"That means, no one else from the DEA - at the present moment anyway, knows I'm here."

"I don't get what you're telling me. Am I under arrest or   something?"

"Not right now. Is there something I need to arrest you for?"

"I don't know Angelica - or is that even your real name? You tell me!"

"It's not my real name. I'm Veronica. I've been working undercover at the *New York Times* for six months."

"Watching me?"

"No. Watching David Fisher. He's been under investigation for a few years now. However, since you came on the scene, we've been tracking you as well."

"On the scene? What does that mean? I mean, what the hell? Excuse me, if I don't know what to say! The only reason I'm involved in this is because I just happened to be at a bar one night and have a conversation with a guy who knew a girl in Honduras and that's - oh my God, wait a minute! Was that a set up? Was that guy even for real? Did you guys at the DEA set me up for this entire story?" I stood up ready to cross the room to do God knows what to this woman.

"Listen, I know this isn't going to be easy to hear, so you might want to just sit back down and hear me out, okay?"

She motioned for me to sit like I was a trained dog. I did what I was told.

"Okay, so yes, it was a set-up. I'd been watching you at *The Times* for months and knew you were ripe for a good story - and that you were restless, so I took a chance that you might bite."

"Oh, did I ever! Hook, line and sinker!" I stood up again and started to pace, racing my hands through my hair thinking that I'd like to – what was the term Delia used to beat yourself up about being stupid? Yeah, *take flight*! "Fuck! I'm an idiot! I actually thought that some greater, divine purpose sent me on this mission to tell this girl's story. Huh! And the whole time, the greater power was the fucking DEA! Unbelievable!"

"I know it seems pretty unfair, but hey, no one twisted your arm to come down here and spend the time you did with this inmate."

It really pissed me off that she referred to Delia as just an inmate, but I didn't say a word because I knew she was right. No one had twisted my arm - and let's face it, Delia *was* – or had been - an inmate. Had I made her out to be something more - some mysterious feminine hero - and for what reason? What had really been the driving force within me that I was so easily manipulated by the DEA? Was it true, what Delia had said about me? That I was wanting to make up for not being able to save my own sister? Had I become so desperate in my guilt that I jumped at the chance when I heard of another woman in distress? Could I really be that easily controlled? I turned to Veronica and glared at her. "Did you know about my sister?"

"Look Scott, I really don't want to get into that here. I-"

"Yeah, who would want to admit, even as a DEA agent that they used someone's weakness to manipulate them? Are you at least going to tell me what you were hoping to gain in using me as a pawn in your game?"

"Well, information of course. We knew the only way to get to David and figure out what he'd really been up to in Colombia - and Honduras - was to get to Delia."

"In Honduras?" I was *keeping my window rolled up* as Delia had once mentioned and not letting on that I knew anything about Delia and David's connection on the island. Little did I know, that she hadn't told me everything!

"Yes, we suspect that the package she "found," - she actually put her fingers up and used the quotation sign - "didn't wash up on shore at all."

"What? What do you mean?"

"We have reason to believe that the package was part of the same shipment David had hidden away in Colombia years earlier. Does the insignia, *hourglass* mean anything to you?"

"No! Why?" I lied, because at that moment, I realized that I'd been a pawn in everyone's game. The DEA's game, and Delia and David's game and I was done being an idiot. I wasn't telling anybody else shit about what I'd heard. I'm glad that was one of the things I knew instinctively to leave out of my notes. "What does hourglass mean?"

"Well, on one of Pablo Escobar's last shipments, his cartel changed out their regular symbol of a scorpion for an hourglass - we think - to signify that time was running out."

"Running out? For who?"

"For either the cartel - or Escobar and that they needed to be on the lookout as their operation was about to be shut down, so to speak. They may have just changed it to get the heat off of them as everyone knew it was the scorpion that was their usual insignia. Anyway, the hourglass symbol would have been on the shipment that David hid away for five years. We have reason to believe that the same symbol was on the package that Delia claims just happened to wash up on shore in Honduras. An interesting coincidence, no?"

I sat back down. The full realization that this Veronica was the only other person to whom I'd forwarded my notes from my visits with Delia, scared the hell out of me. I only did it because she had insisted as a friendly gesture from one journalist to another that perhaps it was good idea to keep my notes in a *safe place*, because one never knows what might happen in Central America. Little did I know, I had been instrumental in feeding the DEA information about Delia's life.

"I don't even know what to say. I mean, I knew that Delia didn't always tell me the truth, but I thought I could believe some of the things she told me."

"I'm sure you could - when she wasn't talking about her criminal history or anything to do with drugs or David. I suspect many of her stories were true."

"I can't believe I was feeding you information this whole time because I thought I could trust you. You sure had me fooled. You're better at your job than I am."

"Don't be so hard on yourself, Scott. I'm trained to be good at what I do - even pretending to be someone else."

"Why are you here - off the record, I mean?"

"Because we aren't after you. We're not even after Delia if you want the truth. She's been a pawn - or at least she started out that way, in Fisher's game, which is tied to much bigger fish than you or her. In fact, we believe that perhaps Fisher, if not Delia had some connections to El Negro, who was called the "Honduran bridge" between the Colombian cartel and Mexico and now that he's been extradited to the States, we think perhaps Delia - and Fisher - may have ties to Juan Hernandez, the President's brother."

"Juan Hernandez? Isn't he in prison in the States? Delia's been in prison for almost six years - how could she possibly be involved with him?"

"Scott, being in prison doesn't cut ties with these cartels as you probably know. Remember, back in 2013, before Delia was arrested, Hernandez had connections with El Chapo and promised him protection in exchange for over a million dollars towards his brother's presidential campaign. We believe, Fisher and Delia had connections to both the Colombian and the Mexican cartel at that time."

"That doesn't mean that Delia is connected now."

"No, but she has disappeared inexplicably, which means she had help from the outside."

"Maybe. I mean, how can we know for sure?"

"Well, there's something else."

"Oh God, what now?"

"We believe that Delia had help in both escapes."

"Well, that isn't hard to figure out. Obviously, she was able to pay the guards."

"No, Scott. We believe it was one of our guys who went rogue, who rigged the escape this time. We're not sure if he was involved in the first one, but he's gone off the radar and we need to find him. I need to know if there was anyone she mentioned that might have been a DEA agent or if she nicknamed someone in your notes that could possibly be this guy."

"Why on earth would a DEA agent help her escape? I don't get it." I looked at Veronica and could tell by her expression what she was suggesting. "You think he was her lover?"

"That's what we think. He disappeared at the same time of her escape. He was down here on an undercover mission during at least five of the seven years she was trafficking. Then about three years ago, he volunteered for another undercover mission investigating packages and shipments that had been thrown overboard or were reported by civilians to have washed up on shore - he was also investigating El Negro and a few other characters in the trade. Regarding his connection to Delia, we know he'd been hanging out at the same places she had, before her arrest and was here at the time of both her escapes."

I remembered when Delia had put her head down in embarrassment which had made me think she'd been hoping for another visitor when she tried to take her own life. Perhaps it was him. I couldn't think of another time she mentioned anyone - except for the lover she met at Velvet's party. Was this possibly the same guy? Hadn't he disappeared from her life as quickly as he appeared? Unless, she lied about that too! I didn't know what to believe and I certainly wasn't going to mention that there was a possible connection between the two men. I needed to get my head straight first about everything Veronica had just told me.

"Anyway, I was hoping that maybe there was something - or someone that you hadn't mentioned or simply forgotten to send to me in your notes, thinking it was inconsequential. I'm just trying to get a step ahead here and see what I can find out before I brief my colleagues."

"You know, I wish I could help you, but you've got all my notes and I don't remember her making any reference to anyone else in her life these past few years. What was this - this DEA agent's name?"

"He has a number of undercover names. He was of Spanish descent which made it easier for him to do covert missions here and in Central and South America. That's about all I can tell you about him, I'm afraid. The rest is classified. We just need to find him."

"And what about David Fisher? Have you arrested him yet?"

"Well, that's the other thing. He had a retirement party three weeks ago at *The Times* - I threw it for him - and then decided to make a quick exit. He hasn't been seen since. I suspect he figured out I was working undercover and played me, like I played you."

"Wow! It seems the DEA has a few disappearances on its hands. Now I know why you're here questioning me - all your suspects have flown the coop!"

"Yeah, we're not too happy about that, as you can imagine. We do have someone in custody however and we're hoping that he might be able to help us."

"Oh yeah? Whose that?" I asked, not believing she'd tell me anyway.

"He goes by the name of Peter Manning. Ever heard of him? Maybe Delia mentioned him?"

"No, she's never mentioned him." I felt as if someone had gripped and twisted my intestines. I didn't want Veronica to see the panic on my face, so I changed the subject. "Do you want some water or anything?"

"No, thanks. I won't keep you any further. However, I would suggest you stay put for a while so I can find you. No taking off suddenly or disappearing, right?"

"No. Actually, I rented this little place on the beach and decided to stay here through the winter and finish a project I've been working on." What I didn't tell her was that it used to be owned by none other than Delia herself. Guatusso told me about it and that it had been for rent for a couple of months since the last tenant moved out. Delia had put it in his name before her arrest in 2014 and he'd been renting it out off and on for years, making a little money on the side. I guess it was one piece of property that had some good memories for her and she hadn't wanted to part with it. For whatever reason, I was happy to be renting it as I felt closer to her there - and in some odd way, it felt right to be writing her story in the very house she had lived.

"I'll be right here if you need me!" I said, somewhat flippantly. I remembered Delia saying how she would have liked to have spit in her brother's face when he'd come to visit her for the last time and I wasn't feeling much different with this DEA agent. She was also standing less than ten feet away from Delia's journal. I just wanted her to go.

"Okay, good to know I can find you if I need you. Thank you - and thank you for all of those notes. This convict of yours certainly didn't have a boring life!"

"Yeah, she's not my convict! In fact, she's not anyone's convict anymore, right?"

"Well, she's still a convicted drug dealer who has been extremely lucky, but eventually she'll get caught. They always do, when they trip up. Although, she probably has enough money to live on, even if she disappears forever."

"What do you mean? I thought she had run out of money?"

"That's what she wanted you to believe, so you'd pawn that brooch for her."

"You knew about that too? Why? Why would she bother?"

"Maybe to throw us off the scent of what she was really planning. To send you to her friend's house to do a drop off."

"What are you talking about - a drop off?"

"That money you dropped off to her friend wasn't for Delia. It was for him - to pay him for something - or to help him out, who knows. Delia's never going to be stupid enough to show up there for money - or to have her friend try to get it to her. I guess she decided to do one last act of kindness before she disappeared. Anyway, only time will tell regarding how this all turns out."

"Yes, time will tell." I thought of my conversation with Delia about time and the hourglass. Why had she even mentioned to me about that damn symbol if it was something she didn't want me to know? There were so many unanswered questions. I wanted desperately to get back to her journal, hoping that I might find the answers to them, in its pages. "Here, I'll see you out." I said, as I ushered the DEA agent to the door.

As she walked out the door, I hoped *she* would disappear forever. I was so angry at myself for trusting her on a whim and worst yet, for sending her my notes for safe keeping. What had Delia warned me when I told her that? "Never trust the sweet ones, Scott." At least she hadn't lied about that! I was so grateful that I had never written Manning's real name down in those notes! I doubted she would make a connection between him and Muttonhead, but God help Delia if she did. Either way, it would only be a matter of time before Manning would open his trap to save himself and somehow twist the fact that Delia herself had photos of Escobar's cartel. I could only hope that somehow he'd trip up and incriminate himself and that Veronica might just be smart enough to figure out that Delia had been more of a pawn than a player in a much bigger game.

Chapter 24: Delia's Story

       This is where I remove myself from the story - at least for a time - and allow Delia's words to speak for themselves. I have not included every entry as it would be redundant to repeat some stories that she'd already shared with me. What I have chosen to include are pieces of the puzzle that our conversations weren't able to fill in - and the thoughts and feelings that this mysterious woman wasn't able to share with me, but was capable of expressing within the pages of her journal. I'll let you be the judge of what kind of woman Delia Russell truly was. Although, she wrote her real name within her own journal entries, I have inserted Delia in place of them.

Nov. 23, 2006

I've arrived on the island of Roatan - finally, after spending a few days listening to the crazy revving of engines, nearly being hit by tuk-tuks and motorbikes - and devoured by sand fleas - on the smallest of the Bay islands. What nonsense! I came here to get away from the craziness of New York and found it all over again.

Anyway, I'm excited about this trip and how it all turns out. I'm hoping to do some volunteer work soon. I was given a pamphlet from a woman - I think her name was Bridgette -

about the dump here. I hope to get there to help. In the meantime, I plan to just rest up, relax on the beach and try to recover from my ex. Here's hoping!

December 10, 2006

I can't believe I haven't written in two weeks! I've been so busy meeting people. It's been a blast. I went to a party last night at this lovely woman's house. Her name is Velvet and it suits her. She's invited me to stay at her guest house this weekend, which will be a nice change from the noise here on the west end. I've found a decent apartment to rent for a couple of months, but it's small and I can hear music most of the night. It will do for now.

The guy who invited me to Velvet's party is Bernie. Great guy! Funny as hell! We became fast friends from almost the first night I arrived on the island. Met another guy last night - not gay! Might see him again today as he's offered to take me to a great dive sight.

December 24, 2006

Missing home - the city anyway. Maybe it's because it's the holidays - although here with the sun and surf, it's hard to believe it's Christmas in New York! The last month has been interesting. I've finally made it to the dump and I can't express how sad it makes me to see such young children eating from there and looking for things to sell to feed their families. The locals and some expats try to help, but just like the piled-high garbage, the problem seems insurmountable.

We've been visited by a huge dog the last few times we've been out there. He really is something to see. He looks at me sometimes in a way that I feel like I should rescue him from there. Osito and Velvet are pressuring me to do it. What would I do with a dog that size? Besides, I'm only going to be here a few months!

January 4, 2007

Welcome to the new year! I only made one resolution this year - stay away from men! I've broken it already! Velvet's New Year's Eve party was spectacular with a great line-up of bands. I had such a lovely time and it was so nice to finally dress up and wear heels! You get in a habit here of wearing flip flops and jean shorts.

I met someone - a new guy. He's very handsome - unlike any I've dated before! He doesn't have any hair! Still, there's something about him. His name is Alex - he's from the States, but he looks Spanish. I love his olive skin. And he's funny. I'm not even sure how Velvet knows him. He isn't gay and he doesn't look like the wealthy type. In fact, he didn't really look like he fit in at the party, so we got along great. He plays the saxophone and dives. How sexy is that?

We spent most of the night on her ocean view patio talking. He went to school to be an engineer, but was too much of a free spirit to do the 9 to 5 gig. I'd like to think we're kindred spirits! He's the first guy in a long time who I actually wanted to have kiss me - and he did - right on cue - at midnight. It was nice. I hope to see him again, but I didn't give him my contact number and neither did he. Lame! Anyway, it was a nice way to bring in the New Year, even though, I promised myself to swear off men! So much for that!

January 24, 2007

I saw Alex again last night. He was at Luna Subiendo. He just showed up out of the blue after three weeks. I was glad to see him. We shared some drinks. Of course, he only drinks virgin frozen mojitos. Maybe he is gay! The one rum and coke he did drink, he had to ask for more coke. He is a self-proclaimed pussy when it comes to alcohol. I can live with that as long as he doesn't turn out to be gay! I don't need another shoe to drop!

February 14, 2007

Alex took me out for a lovely dinner and afterwards, surprised me with a few days at the Barefoot Key Resort. It was so incredibly beautiful and peaceful there – except for this bloody parrot that never shut up! And this annoying American woman who spent more time talking to the dumb bird than her own husband. The bird ended up trying to bite her finger off and I don't blame him! Other than that, we had a great time. I know I was supposed to have sworn off men, but I find him irresistible! I have another man in my life too! He's the giant dog I met at the dump. I've named him Ghost and Velvet offered up her guesthouse to me for an amazing price, so I'll be moving in there this weekend. I'm very excited as Ghost and I will have much more room - and it's on the ocean!

February 26, 2007

I can't believe I'm writing this. I should have known when everything was going so well in my life, something had to happen. The guest house was ransacked last night and Ghost is missing. They stole my passport and my money and we can't find Ghost anywhere. The police think he's dead and Velvet is beside herself with worry about me as she feels responsible for not having put enough security into place.

I guess these kinds of things happen in Honduras, but I only just found Ghost and to have lost him already is heartbreaking. Alex has been wonderful, but he is heading back to the States this week and so again, I'll be all alone. I'm feeling so depressed. I do have an idea though. I met someone - I don't want to write about him here as I'm still not sure about him yet, but he's kind of become a friend.

He's an artist and I hear he knows people. I'm thinking of asking him to help me find Ghost. We'll see.

March 10, 2007

I am so utterly, unbelievably happy! My friend found Ghost! He rescued him from the assholes who stole him from me - and apparently, beat the shit out of them. I'm writing tonight from the guest house as Ghost and I have moved back in - I was staying in the main house with Velvet the last two weeks. I have to admit, the break-in really shook me up. I felt scared for the first time in my life and I'm from New York! Anyway, Alex has returned to the States, but at least I have my other guy to keep me company! He's lying right beside me as I'm writing. Well, that's it for excitement for now. I feel so grateful!

March 29, 2007

I got a call from David out of the blue. He's heading down to Honduras this week and wants to see me. I'd be lying if I didn't say I'm worried. I'm afraid he's going to ask me to help him again. I mean, the money would be nice, but I want to put that part of my life behind me. I don't know what I'm going to do.

April 15, 2007

David has returned to the States and I feel like my life has taken a turn for the worst. I agreed to help him. I think I must be crazy. I know I shouldn't write about it here, but there's no one I can talk to about this. I'm thinking of confiding in Bernie. He seems to understand these things. David's always been so convincing - and I know he's right. I can help so many more people if I'm in a better position. I just hope he's right that it's no big deal.

April 17, 2007

Finally confided in Bernie about my problem. He says he can help me with it. The trick is to do it slowly and not let anyone else know. I've begun telling people I'm a writer and that I'm writing a story about a woman who finds a package that rolls up on shore and so I've got to do research about the drug trade. Bernie gave me the idea. He apparently experienced it himself. He and his friend were walking the beach one morning and they spotted a package. They knew instantly what it was and he confided to me that he seriously thought about dragging it out of the ocean. They even talked about hiding it somewhere until they could figure out what to do with it. In the end, they decided not to touch it. He said he had already heard too many stories about drug dealers coming to look for their packages – and making anyone who touched them, pay dearly.

I figure this was a great premise for a book so if my name gets associated with the white shark, people will just say, 'oh yeah, that girl's writing a book on the topic. Of course, she has to hang out with unsavoury people - how else will she get her research done?' Or at least, that's what I'm banking on people saying. In the meantime, Bernie is teaching me some things. He's coming over this week to help me figure out how to measure it out. I've told Velvet that he's coming to help me bake! Close enough, right?

April 29, 2007

Feeling pretty excited! Tonight, was the first night on a yacht - it was freaking beautiful! And my first night taking care of my problem. It went well, except for the baking accident I had prior to it. I think I'm still high! Maybe I'll stay up all night and count the stars! That sounds like fun. I miss Alex! I miss his kisses - and his package! He's got a nicer one than the last guy! Maybe I'll call him.

April 30, 2007

Shit! Talked to Alex last night. Can't remember a fucking word I said! God! I hope I didn't tell him anything! I'm an idiot for calling him while I was high. He told me he's coming down again - I can't remember when he said he was coming. I'll have to call him again later. I hope it's soon. I miss him terribly!

May 5, 2007

Alex has arrived on the island. He told me he can't see me right away as he's got some business to take care of. He's very aloof about what kind of business it is and of course I'm not going to ask, because I'd like the same courtesy from him! Anyway, he says that he'll be pretty busy with that, but he wants to see me. If I'm honest, I can't wait to see him. I haven't been laid in weeks!

May 8, 2007

Alex stopped by last night. We drank copious amounts of wine on the pier and fucked right there under the stars! It was great. There's nothing like making love under the stars while listening to the ocean. This morning we got up and had coffee on my balcony with Ghost. Then we fucked again in the pool. I hope Velvet didn't see us! I miss him already! He says he'll be in touch.

May 11, 2007

I haven't heard from Alex in three days! I'm so pissed. He's got my number, but I have no way of getting a hold of him. I've got other things on my mind anyway. Bernie has hooked me up with his friends on the yacht again and they want some more of my problem. Now I've got Chacarron working for me and he's driving me crazy. He literally never shuts up! He's always going on about knowing people and how he can hook me up, but I want to be choosy about who I get involved with. Anyway, he's got an actor apparently that wants to buy and few others who are interested. I hope David appreciates all the work I do for him!

May 15, 2007

Alex finally called. I didn't answer.
I'm pissed that he took so long to get back to me - and besides, he's just a complication in my life right now. I went to Luna Subiendo the other night looking for my friend, the artist - I call him Machete. I figured I needed some protection if I keep going like I am and he was so good about getting Ghost back, I think I can trust him. I also asked him to do a painting of me and Ghost. I've got a great photo of him and I at sunset in front of the ocean. He said he might do it if he feels up to it. I didn't push the subject. He did agree to be my bodyguard, for a price. I don't mind paying him. He's huge - at least a foot taller than any man I've ever met. Maybe I should get him to beat some sense into Alex!

May 17, 2007

Alex showed up at my door. I thought about letting Ghost take a chunk out of him, but I didn't. He made love to me first in my shower and then in my bed. I'm starting to really like him. Fuck! This was not in my plans! Anyway, he's headed back to the States in early June, so I guess I won't have to worry about it for a while. I don't want him to know what I'm doing. I guess that's my gage that I actually like a guy - I don't want him to know the worst sides of me.

David's kept a pretty low profile. I've only heard from him once. When he wants to put pressure on me, he always leaves me a message with just one word: Hourglass. I guess to symbolize that time is running out for me to send him his cut. I wish I had really found a package on the shore and then I would have it all to myself without all the pressure. Of course, what are the chances of that happening?

Chapter 25:
Chihuahua in Action

June 15, 2008

I've been at this for over a year and I'm growing tired of it. I really thought when I started this, it was only going to be for a bit of time. I didn't realize that David had other plans. He's upped his game now - and that means I have to as well. I've got off pretty lucky this year. No big messes except for two Americans that tried to fuck us out of our money. Poor Chacarron - he was my biggest collateral damage on that deal. He won't be back. Probably just as well. It was only a matter of time before his mouth or his carelessness cost us a lot more than money.

I've got a new kid working for me - he's a bright one and on his game. I trust him as I've been working at the dump with him on a regular basis. A good kid. He's the one who talked me into adopting Ghost - and for that, I'll forever be grateful to him. He's got some family issues - and some family members in prison on the mainland, so he needs all the help - and work - he can get. He's made a few runs for me since Chacarron left me and he's good. I hope to keep him around for a while. We've got a big one this coming July. Here's hoping it all goes well.

August 11, 2008

Alex made a surprise visit last month. He showed up at my place - I've moved out of Velvet's and got my own house on the beach. Osito and I were right in the middle of preparing a package for our next drop - with the great white shark right out on the table and Alex just walks right in. I thought I was going to crap my pants. He had no idea. He just looked at what we were doing and turned right back around again. I followed him out. I thought about saying, 'It's not what it looks like' but what would have been the point? I don't think he knew what to say, so he just stood there rubbing his face with his hands. That was worse! I needed him to say something. Eventually, he did.

"Fuck Delia! What the fuck are you into?"

"The same thing everyone is into down here. Look, I was trying to keep you away from it, not to protect me, but to protect you!"

"Really? You're going to use that line on me? Don't lie to me, Delia! I've seen this shit all my life!"

"What do you mean?"

"Delia," He grabbed me by my elbow and forcibly pulled me next to him - it was the first time he was ever rough with me. "Send your friend on his way."

"What do you mean? We have work to do." I shot back. "Let go of me!"

"Delia, will you trust me this one time? Send your friend home! You can invite him back when I leave."

I did what he asked, more because he was actually scaring me with the way he was acting. We sat down at the beach and I waited for him to talk. He let out a huge sigh. "I don't even know where to begin! I started dating you to forget about this part of my life - then I fell in love with you - and now I find out, you're a part of this life!"

"What? What are you talking about? And, did you just say, you fell in love with me?"

"Of course, that's the part you paid attention to!"

"Well, isn't that an important part?"

"Not right now. Delia, my father was an addict. Cocaine, heroine - you name it. It broke up our family - and later killed him. I promised myself I'd never get involved with any kind of drugs - or date someone who was."

"I'm speechless!"

"Well, that's a first!" He said, finding some humour in the situation.

"Look, I'm sorry! You know, I just do this to make a little extra on the side to live and help out people down here. I never meant to get in so deep. I'm sorry! I'm sorry you had to find out this way."

He sat there on the lounge, looking out towards the ocean. Then he turned to me and said the sweetest words any guy whose father died from drug abuse: "I forgive you. I know you. I know this isn't who you are! But I need you to stop. Get out of this racket right now."

I just looked at him and the only thought that came to my mind made me feel like the most horrible girlfriend in the world. It was this: 'This idiot thinks I love him enough to give up all of this - my dreams of owning a treehouse one day and of helping as many people as I can - for him! He actually thinks he means that much to me.'

The funny thing is, I did think he meant that much to me on some level, but as soon as he gave me the ultimatum of choosing, I knew what I'd choose. Not because I don't love him, but because I love my independence more. I love what the great white shark has given me: My freedom.

September 15, 2008

Alex's been gone now for over a month and the funny thing is, I don't really miss him that much. I'm not even sure what's happened to me lately. It's like I'm void of any feeling for anything. The only thing that gets me really excited - besides hanging out with Ghost of course - is the next deal. Is this what happens to people - good people - over time when they get mixed up in shit like this?

It doesn't happen overnight. It's like a slow avalanche that creeps up on you and then wham - it hits you when you're least expecting it. I got a glimpse of who I'm becoming that day Alex gave me the ultimatum. It was like I felt nothing towards him. And now, even less. Either that, or it's easier to tell myself that.

December 24, 2008

I can hardly believe I've already been here for two years. So much has happened. I don't see Bernie or Velvet much anymore, and I find during the holidays, I miss them more. Bernie still gets in touch every once in a while when he wants to hook his friends up, but I think he's scared about who I hang around with now. Machete rarely leaves my side when I'm out and my reputation as a Chihuahua has begun to precede me. Machete has been instructed to either burn this journal or get it into safe hands if I ever get arrested, but I don't really think about that much anymore.

There are scarier things to think about these days! Like my own death. Especially, with this last deal. It was worth over 100K. Osito - and two of his friends, who he swore we could trust, were to do the drop to some "fishermen" waiting on their boat over in West bay, to transport it to Belize. Osito's boys had other plans. They decided instead of taking their cut - and I'm pretty generous these days - to walk away with it to try and sell it on their own. When they didn't show up to the docks, I got a call from Osito that he was being held by the fishermen. They wanted their shipment or they were going to kill him.

It was the first time that I had been really scared for him - and for me. I told Machete that we had to go and meet with them. Machete warned me what could happen, especially if we couldn't round up the two boys who stole our goods. I told him to go and see about finding them and that I would go to the docks. It's hard to believe that these boys could be that stupid about how things work down here. Although, it would seem that there's a gender bias even within the world of drugs and when people are dealing with a woman instead of a man, they think somehow they can get away with shit that they'd never try with a man. I knew I'd have to have make examples out of them if I was ever going to be taken seriously. I also knew that Machete would take care of that for me as well. He wasn't happy about sending me out to a shack alone while he had to go on the hunt for the two boys, but I insisted. I needed at least one man to take my instructions seriously and he knew that.

I knew there was a chance that even if I showed up with another haul, that since we caused them a delay, they might just kill both of us and leave with our drugs and our money, but I had to try for Osito's sake. They told me that I was to get dropped off near La La's Art gallery and follow the dirt path just behind it to the right. When I saw a shack, come to the back and knock twice.

While I was walking along that path, I thought about turning back. Letting Osito just be the collateral damage of a lost deal, but I also knew, that wouldn't be enough for these guys. I wished, in that moment that I had listened to Machete's repeated pleas for me to get a gun. I was always afraid that if I did, it might one day be used on me.

When I got to the door, I knocked twice. It opened, one guy stuck his head out, looked both ways, and then grabbed me by my hair and dragged me inside. It was very dark and I could barely make out their silhouettes against the bright cracks of light coming from the covered windows. The darkness actually made me feel safer. I could see Osito sitting in a chair, the other guy's gun to his head.

"Hand it over, bitch!"

I took off my pack, but didn't hand it over. "First, you let him go."

"You don't do the negotiating 'round here, bitch! You tried to fuck us."

"Let him go! Nobody tried to fuck you. I've just got a couple of dumbass kids that thought they were being smart. We'll deal with them. You're getting your shipment and we want our money." I'm not sure now where I got my courage from, but I wasn't backing down. If it meant we were going to die, then so be it. If I was going to be in this racket, as Alex called it, I couldn't risk backing down.

"Just give it to her, man. We gotta get the hell out of here if we're going to make it through these waters." It was right in the middle of the rainy season and storms brewed rapidly from the East which made it treacherous to travel to Belize. I knew that they would just want to get off this island as fast as possible.

The guy smacked Osito across the face with his gun and knocked him to the floor. "There! You can drag him with you. Your money is here." He handed me a small slip of paper with a name on it. "Give us the goods."

"How am I supposed to know it's actually there?"

"Bitch, I could kill you right now. You don't have any choice but to believe us."

I knew he was right. I threw the pack to him. He quickly checked it to make sure I wasn't trying to scam him. They took their shit and left Osito - who was still lying on the floor - and me to find our way out. As soon as I knew they were gone, I went to help him up. His face was bloody and his eye was already swollen shut, probably from a few blows before I got there.

"Fuck! You said we could trust these friends of yours! What the hell? Don't ever put me in that position again!"

"Listen Chihuahua, I'm so sorry! I'm a boa! An idiota! Perdoname! Por Favor!"

"Just shut up! I'm not ready to forgive you! You've been a pain in my ass ever since I met you! I wish I'd never come out to that dump!"

"That's another thing! I never told you the truth about the dump."

"What now? More lies?"

"That girl, Bridgette that gave you the pamphlet at the bar-"

"Yeah? What about her?"

"She's my sister. I asked her to give it to you. I wanted to meet you and I thought maybe if you came to the dump to help out-"

"Jesus, Osito, is there nothing you wouldn't do to pick up a woman? Besides, how many sisters do you have? You know what, never mind! I'm not forgiving you for this or for the pamphlet! Ever! Do you hear?"

"Yeah, I hear."

"I mean it!"
"Okay."

I didn't stay mad at him forever, but he learned quickly to never trust anyone again. Unfortunately, there was still the issue of these two kids. I don't think they could have been much older than 16 or 17 and that made me sad for their families. They were never going to see their cut - and I knew Machete would get the shipment back from them, come hell or high water. They'd also never get asked to do a deal again, which could have helped them and their families out a great deal.

I never really heard what happened to them - Machete protected me from a lot of that shit - but I know that in most of the barrios around the island, most knew to never fuck with one of Chihuahua's deals again. Chihuahua also got a reputation for going out to face dealers head-on and that she must be one hell of a courageous woman. This made some locals respect me - and made others want a crack at me. I knew this wouldn't be my last encounter with death.

Chapter 26: The Reprieve

February 17, 2009

I'm laying here in the emergency hospital after getting my ass beaten again. Machete just shakes his head at me every time I decide to go to one of the barrios by myself to take care of loose ends - either another kid that's gone missing with my stash or my money - or some dumbass trying to extort me by threatening to report me.

When I first arrived on the island, I used to like it when the collectivo I was in, would take detours up into the local barrios to drop off customers. I liked experiencing the true culture of a place and seeing how the locals lived. As a foreigner, we are always either in a tourist area or hanging out with expats and remain quite sheltered. I remember seeing the hilly, one lane neighbourhoods, with piles of garbage everywhere and the street dogs running around playing or sniffing around for their next meal in the ripped open bags of rubbish.

The locals walked around as if their neighbourhood was just an ordinary neighbourhood in New York. I suppose living in squalor had for most, become a way of life. I tried not to judge because I knew I was seeing their lives through the filter of our comfortable American lifestyle. For the most part, the locals were probably content. Although, it does beg the question as to why so many feel the need to steal, kidnap, extort and kill for money as Honduras has the highest crime and murder rate in the entire world. It's no wonder I find myself in up to my eyeballs here – it's a whole new land of opportunity!

There has always been some part of me that convinced myself if I could help out a few locals by way of working for me, then at least I was doing my part. After this last bout however, I'm beginning to believe that I'm doing more harm than good. I won't go into details here, but having to go to the barrios now to collect what's mine, is very different than those earlier days when I was just an observing tourist.

This time, I lost two teeth when a local decided he'd rather beat the shit out of me than pay me what he owed me. Machete - as per usual - followed me, but kept his distance on my insistence that if I could handle things on my own, I'd prefer it. Turns out, a gringa can't really handle anything on her own when she's dealing with desperate people. He gave the guy who beat me what I've referred to as island justice, before picking me up and getting me to the hospital.

Guatusso came to visit me the other day. Instead of bringing me flowers, he created a floral arrangement from canvas and paint that he had left over. It's beautiful. I will cherish it forever.

"Wats' you doin' girl, gettin' yo'sef all beat up? Yo no' doin' somtin' right!"

"What do you know about what I'm doing?" I gave it right back to him.

"Too much. I know too much! Where's my Ghost?"

"He's with Alex."

"Ah, I sees how it is. I've been replaced by bot' of ya!"

"Ghost will never replace you. You know he loves you!"

"How I know dat? You don't come 'round and visit no more!"

"I'm sorry! You're right. I've been busy."

"Busy! I know what yo' kinda busy is. Did me gettin' my ass in prison tree times not teach ya nuttin, girl?"

"Somethings, a girl has to learn on her own I guess."

"Well girl, I hopes ya ne'er gotta learn that lesson! I jus' came to see you okay. I'm gonna go now. You take care of yo'self, ya here?"

"I will."

"Okay then. I'll be seein' ya." He leaned over and gave me a kiss on the cheek and was gone. I'm hoping he's right, that I never have to learn my lesson behind bars. I made a mental note to take Ghost and go visit him when I'm out of here.

April 12, 2009

I wrote to Alex. Before he left almost a year ago, he told me that he couldn't be a part of my life as long as I was dealing, but left me with his address and told me if I ever quit the racket, feel free to reach out to him. After the last time in the hospital, losing teeth and now losing my beautiful hair in clumps, I'm scared I'm dying. I'm worried that this so-called racket is eating away at me from the inside out - and I was lonely.

I told him that I was done with dealing - of course, I didn't use these words in my letter to him - and that I'd love to see him. He turned up a couple of weeks ago and hasn't left. He's staying with me in my beach house and it's been a nice change to live like an ordinary tourist, enjoying the beach again and feeling the sun on my skin. I'm still losing my hair, but I've put on a little weight - probably all of the dinners out and the red wine - and I'm feeling better than I have in over a year. I hate to admit it, but I think Alex is good for my spirit. We don't talk about my dealing - and I don't ask his opinion about it. Some things are just better left unsaid, especially, if you want to make a relationship work. I'm not sure how long he'll stay this time, but I'm hoping for a while.

Bernie and I have reconnected and have been hanging out a lot more. He's glad I've taken a break - that's what he called it. I think the man knows me better than I know myself! Anyway, I told him that I want to purchase property. I've waited long enough - due mostly to his words of wisdom, but it's time I put some of my money into investments - short term and long term.

He actually agreed with me and told me he'd help me find something. He wanted to know if I was thinking of purchasing here on the island - or somewhere else. I think he was hinting at the fact that should anything go down, that I have a place where I can hide out if need be. I thought his plan was brilliant. Buy a property in plain sight as the red herring - and another one that no one - not even Alex or him - would know the location.

Of course, you can't really do these things alone, but I knew Machete must know someone - a local - that wanted to sell some property in the islands. A local, whose silence I could buy. Of course, Machete knew just such a person. I wasn't going to mention any of this to Alex. He would only know of the property I was going to buy in plain sight.

I knew he loved me, but in the end, he still wasn't happy about the choices I was making. I wanted to believe I could trust him, but there was always some hesitancy within me to be completely honest with him. And the truth was, I had to be smart. I had to be one step ahead of everyone - even those closest to me, in order to protect myself. I also knew that one day, I might get caught or have to disappear and I didn't want him involved in any way. I tried to convince myself that my motives were really to protect him, but I knew the truth.

Chapter 27: Back at the Racket

October 18, 2009

Alex left and I'm back dealing. Bernie knew me too well! It wasn't like I went looking to get back in the game. As always, there were a number of factors that led up to it. One of which, was David reaching out again and letting me know that there would be a shipment coming in from Nicaragua by way of boat - ironically, they would not be coming to shore, but wanted to make a water drop off near where I was living. I wasn't really comfortable with that, but it did seem feasible considering I could easily dive or kayak to the point where it would be coming in. I'm not sure if it was the drive of finally building my dream house on the property I had just purchased - or just the love of the game, but I agreed.

It just happened that Alex had to return to the States and so I knew he wouldn't catch wind of what I was about to do. I'd just simply do this one last deal to ensure I had enough funds to last me in case I ever did need to disappear and then perhaps, we really could be together and enjoy life.

I don't know who was more delusional about our situation - him or me. What I did know was that although dealing was still exciting for me; the scales had tipped and I was actually scared of losing him. This frightened me and comforted me at the same time. I didn't want to need or desire anyone in my life - but I was glad to at least feel something again. I was worried I'd already lost my soul.

December 21, 2009

I've always loved winter solstice in New York. It is the shortest day of the year which brings promise of more light and warmer weather on the horizon. Spring still remains a long way off, but you know it's coming. I've been thinking a lot lately about my life in New York.

Perhaps by now, I would have managed to buy some tiny apartment in Manhattan or met Mr. Right and had children. The funny thing is, the idea of that never appealed to me. I suppose now, as I'm sitting at the top of my treehouse looking out over the ocean through the canopy of Kapok and Ceiba trees, that existence seems more far-fetched than being in the financial position I am now, living in the Caribbean.

While I'm extremely happy being here, it is lonely without Ghost - trying to travel with him and keep this new property under wraps is just too difficult. I've left him with my friend, Guatusso for a week while I came to oversee the completion of my house in the trees.

No one else knows where I am. I couldn't run the risk of anyone finding this place. I shouldn't even have come here myself, as there's always a chance of someone seeing me, but I had to see it for myself so I can rest in knowing that one day, I'll come here to live out my life in peace and quiet. I hope it won't be under dire circumstances with me having to hide away from the world.

My other property is almost finished and Alex, Ghost and I will be moving to an area in French Harbour, not far from the beach house I've been renting. There are new roads and hydro beginning to be put in on the island which make buying property that had always been a little too remote, much easier to access.

Alex doesn't know that I'm still dealing. I hope he never finds out! He assumed that the money I had already made, paid for the new house on the island, which it did for the most part, except that I had invested much of it in local businesses and new ventures. And of course, expanded my horizons with none other than the man known as El Negro. He owns six restaurants on the island, which helps him a great deal in his *business* and I've invested in two of them.

Sometimes I wonder if I'm just addicted to the racket itself. Maybe the excitement of it has become a part of me, more than I want to admit. And yet, I cannot deny that there is a part of me that longs for peace and quiet and to be in the arms of a man I care for while watching the sunset every night. I wonder if that longing will ever be enough to satisfy me or lure me out of this lifestyle for good.

Chapter 28: Shit Storms

March 14, 2010

The rainy season is finally over and there's been nothing but sunny days. The tourists are here in droves to dive, and I have to admit, they make for my best customers - for both the white shark and the resort that I've invested in. I know it's dangerous to be involved in such enterprises with certain people, but the money is just too good to pass up.

Alex has been living with Ghost and me for the last few months, but he seems sullen and withdrawn as of late. I'm too afraid to ask him what's wrong. Sometimes, I have this dreadful feeling that one day everything is going to blow up in our faces. How can it not? I feel constantly torn between this life I've made for myself here and what I know Alex wants for us. I suppose that's why my hair continues to fall out. I look in the mirror and don't recognize myself anymore. It's been ages since I've been out - or had any fun. I rarely have reason to get dressed up anymore.

Most of the time, I'm in cargo clothes and long sleeves to beat the incessant sun and bugs. There are nights I can't get warm, which is strange when this very climate used to suffocate me at times with its heat and humidity.

Sometimes, I think I'm going crazy or becoming paranoid. I look at Alex and wonder if he really is who he says he is. I have dreams that he's actually a cop and comes to arrest me. Some nights, I see myself in prison and see the bars shut in front of my face. Other times, I dream about finding packages that keep washing up on shore and in the dream, I can't collect all of them. I just swim around in the ocean trying to get it all. I have worse nightmares, but I'm too afraid to write them down in case they come true.

In regards to Alex, my heart wants to believe him and that all is well. My head keeps telling me to be careful. We rarely ever go out anymore - he says, because he doesn't want to attract attention to ourselves as foreigners, but I feel as if he doesn't want to be seen with me. Maybe he's embarrassed about his drug dealing girlfriend. I keep hoping that my ruse of being a writer keeps suspicions at bay, but I'm not sure anymore.

September 17, 2010

I knew it was only a matter of time before the other shoe dropped. Except this time, it wasn't Alex who dropped it. It was me.

Osito and I had another deal that went bad in June. We were supposed to arrange a shipment of over 20 kilos coming up from Colombia and get it to its transporters off the keys to be shipped up for El Negro to Mexico. The shipment went missing before it got here - a tropical storm came through and did major damage up the coast of Central America and

Mexico. Los Cachiros's cartel doesn't care about storms. They care about their shipments and their money. We've heard through the grapevine that a number of packages have rolled up on shore and we suspect they're from our shipment. However, tourists are finding them and reporting them to the local authorities so there's no way we can go anywhere near them. I'm hoping that the cartel cuts their losses, realizes that the storm was to blame and that I'm not scamming them out of their shipment.

I think about David in times like these and wonder how the hell they didn't catch on to him when his shipment just mysteriously disappeared. He was in contact with me a couple of months ago telling me he's decided to throw in the towel. Apparently, he has enough to retire comfortably and that's all he really wanted. I guess I can't blame him, except that I do. I blame him for planting a seed within me that seems to have anchored its roots and I feel like there is so escape.

Bernie has warned me repeatedly that I am in over my head and that dealing with this cartel will be the end of me. And yet, I've never made so much money in my life. I've had to open bank accounts under different names in various countries and my own properties are expanding. I keep telling myself that this will be my last deal. Then another request comes in.

The reality I have had to face was that Alex and I were going nowhere. He, like Bernie, was always worried about me, especially my health. He wanted me out of the racket - and his constant frustration with me, was driving me crazy. I asked him to move out. He did and as far as I know, he went back to the States for good. I haven't heard from him since. The funny thing is, while I do miss him, I feel like I have some of my sanity back. Trying to do business and carry on a relationship with him was too much for me to handle, especially knowing he wasn't happy about what I was doing. He always looked the other way, but he knew what was going on. I guess it's just Ghost and I on our own again.

Chapter 29: Left Eye Lisa

November 20, 2011

I had a visit from Guatusso this week. Turns out, he's worried about me. He's been hearing things on the island that Chihuahua's gone crazy. Maybe they're right. I grabbed us a couple of beers and we went down to the beach to talk. Ghost was right behind us.

"Girl, you look like shit."

"Thanks!" I could always count on Guatusso to get right to the truth. I always said, find a few honest people in your life and you'll know the truth about yourself!

"I hear lotta 'tings on dis island and I know you got yo'sef in deep. You don' wanna end up like me in some rotten prison down here!"

"I don't intend to!"

"Wats' I'm sayin' is, you gotta stop chasin' waterfalls. Stick to da rivers and da lakes dat ya know!"

"Guatusso, are you quoting a song?"

"You know it, girl! I e'er tol' ya 'bout the time I met Left Eye Lisa?"

"You did not!"

"I did so!"

"You met Lisa Lopez from TLC?"

"I did so!"

"When?"

"Way back in 2000 when I was doin' time - dat was my second arrest. I didn't e'en know dat was her 'til someone tol' me afterwards. She came to da prison to visit a guy - Asami - he was kinda my friend if you can call somebody yo friend in a place like dat. He was a real spiritual guy - like his dad, Dr. Sebi, who was a healer and had all kinds of potions to cure 'tings."

"You mean, Dr. Sebi, who was trying to heal Michael Jackson?"

"Yup! I was in prison with his son. He tol' me once dat his dad was kinda jealous of him and the girls he was hanging with and out of jealousy, his own father ratted on him for growing weed. That's how he ended up in prison in da first place. Anyway, I think Left Eye was gettin' treated by Dr. Sebi and fell for his son. I don't know fo' sure if he was her boyfrien' o' just her friend, but she went an' paid for a private cell for him, so I s'pect he was sometin' impotant to her."

"You can pay for a private cell?"

"Girl, in 'dese prisons down here, you got money, you can live not bad. You can get stuff. Hell, you can buy your way outta prison if you got enough dough."

"Well, that's good to know - I mean, if I ever end up there!"

"Don't e'en joke 'bout dat kind of stuff! What's Ghost here gonna do if you go get yoself put in the slammer?"

"You're right. It's not funny. Anyway, go on about Left Eye. I still can't believe you met her!"

"Yeah, so she spent a lot of time in Honduras. She was into all kinds of tings makin' her singin' career."

"Yeah, she became really popular after she broke away from TLC. I vaguely remember her having issues with them. I do know that song, though. I like it, but I never understood how a girl who went after her dreams told people not to. It never made any sense."

"Maybe she knew sometin' cuz she was chasin' her own waterfalls and look what happened to her! She was doin' jus' what da next lyric of her song say: 'Doin' tings her way and movin' too fast!'"

"I heard she died, but I can't remember how."

"She was a good girl I think, doin' some kind of charity work here in Honduras with her family. She even bought a piece of property dat she was plannin' on building a home or school or sometin' and help kids get off the streets. It's too bad what happened to her. So young. I saw in the news that she went off the road to miss anutter' car and went in da ditch and flew out the window. She wasn't wearin' no seatbelt. Sad ting, dat was. I hear later dat two weeks before dat happen' she was in a car dat hit and killed a ten-year-old boy. She paid for da hospital and funeral bills for his family, but da weirdest tin' is she say dat af'er he died in her arms, she felt like a spirit was followin' her and dat maybe it otta' been her who died and not dat boy. Two weeks later, she dead. I never forgot dat story. Makes ya wonder if we ain't all got a call on our heads and that we can't escape our destiny."

"Well, if that's the case, then I guess it doesn't matter what I do!"

"Dat's not da point I was tryin' to make to ya!"

"What is your point exactly, Guatusso?"

"Girl, you movin' too fast. Look at ya! You got barely no hair left and look sick!"

"You came all this way to insult me?"

"No, I'm tell' ya da truth 'bout yo'self. I came all dis way to see my friend Ghost, if I be tellin' ya da truths about dat!"

"I believe that! Well, there he is! Why don't you two play in the ocean. I'll go get us more beer."

When I came out of the house, I stood on my veranda watching the two of them, their backs to me, Ghost chasing the stick that Guatusso was throwing for him. Besides Machete, they were my two most favourite guys on the island. If I ever did have to disappear, I would miss them dearly.

I've given Guatusso's words a lot of thought, especially about Left Eye Lisa. I remember she got that nickname from some guy who walked up to her and told her, he was in love with her left eye - I think because she always covered the other one with her hair. Love does the strangest things to people!

Anyway, I wonder about that spirit she said she felt near her. What if it was meant to take her instead of that boy - and in the end, got greedy and took them both? I've never felt a spirit like that around me - but sometimes, in the dead of night, I wake up with the most dreadful feeling - and my blood runs cold - and I know that one day, I'm going to pay my dues for the things I've been doing - that there will be a price to pay for chasing my waterfalls. I just hope it doesn't involve anyone else I love.

That's partly why I sent Alex away. I'd rather him be alive somewhere on this planet - even if it means it isn't with me. I've been thinking that maybe I should do that with Ghost and everyone else I care about – maybe I should keep them as far away from me as possible.

Chapter 30: The Truth

August 14, 2012

You'll never guess who turned up on my doorstep. It's been over two years since I saw Alex and he looked great - tanned and fit. Meanwhile, I know I look like I've aged ten years. It was so good to see his face again. I know I should have sent him away, but I couldn't. I've missed him a great deal and the way he always made me feel. Selfish or not, I wanted him by my side again. He was the only thing in my life that gave me any sense of normalcy.   Is it too much to hope that it won't be taken away?

August 21, 2012

I suppose I should be happy that we had at least a week's honeymoon before Alex dropped the final shoe!   He took me down to the beach one afternoon and said that we needed to talk. I love that after a man has made love to me for over a week, then he wants to talk! Anyway, he told me I better sit down for this. I had a feeling this was where things would begin to blow up - and I'd know for certain why I always had that dreadful feeling in the pit of my stomach most nights.

"Babe," I always hate when a guy calls me babe, especially out of the blue. "I have something I've got to tell you. I don't want you to freak out or run off. I just need you to hear me out."

"For God's sake, just tell me. You're freaking me out. I reached over and clenched Ghost's fur in my fingertips. "Please, just tell me!"

"Okay, here it is. I'm not an engineer - well, at least not a practicing one. I'm not really a bar tender either, although I do dive and I do play the sax. I work for the DEA."

"What the fuck? What the fuck? What the hell are you telling me?"

"I told you not to freak out!"

"Yeah, if you were telling me you were gay or married or something, I probably wouldn't be freaking out, but you're telling me you work for the DEA. I should be freaking out!"

"You thought I was gay? Seriously?"

"Oh my God! That's what you heard in all of that? That's what you're worried about?"

"Well, yeah! What made you think I might be gay?"

"Okay, since we're going down that road - even though I'm pretty sure we need to come back to the other subject - yes, there was a part of me that thought maybe you were gay! I mean, for God's sake, you were drinking virgin frozen mojito's when I met you! Although at least now I know why they were virgin!"

"I told you I started drinking those when I was in Cuba! You knew why! I have a sensitive stomach."

"I rest my case!"

"Okay, I sound gay right now! I admit it!"

"Can we get back to the fact that you're a DEA agent after sleeping with me off and on for five years! Wait a minute! Have you been investigating me all this time?"

"Don't flatter yourself!"

"What the hell does that mean?"

"That means that the DEA only investigate big business - they weren't interested in the street shit you were selling!"

I was so pissed off at him in that moment for assuming that I'd been just a "street" dealer, I was tempted to tell him the truth, but I bit my tongue. I wasn't going to let my stupid ego put me in jail for the rest of my life.

"Look, I know how you must feel."

"Uh! No! I don't think you do."

"I'm not here to arrest you anything."

"Well, that's comforting!"

"Look Delia, I'm taking a huge risk even coming back to see you."

"Oh really? Except you've been here having sex with me for an entire week and you decide to tell me this now?"

"Okay, fair enough, but I wanted to see you. I wanted to be with you."

"What about what I want? Or what I need to know in order to keep myself safe?"

"You are safe, for now."

"What the hell does that mean?"

"I didn't just come to have some kind of romantic rendez-vouz with you. I came to warn you."

"Warn me about what?"

"The DEA - and the Honduran authorities - have been investigating El Negro for a few years now. We haven't been able to get him on anything because he's got so much protection from Los Cachiros, but that's about to change. We know he's been laundering money for years, here and on other islands. We're getting close to an arrest and I don't want you involved. Any business dealings you might have with him, you have to get out now."

"I thought I was just a street dealer?"

"Well, you started out that way, but the DEA knows you're involved in bigger ponds."

"You couldn't have told me any of this two years ago? You couldn't have warned me or told me you were a DEA agent?" I just looked at him. "No, of course, you couldn't! So, what was all of this? I guess, I was just your asset - no pun intended - in this little undercover game of yours."

"That's not true. When I met you, I didn't know what you were into."

"That's the funny thing, I wasn't into anything."

"Delia!"

"Okay, I had been doing some things in Colombia, but that was years before and I didn't come down here to get into all of this. I came down here to help people."

"And that's the girl I fell in love with. When the DEA told me you were involved in trafficking here, I almost shit my pants. Seriously! Do you know what that did to me?"

"When the DEA told you? You mean, when you walked in on Osito and I that day, you already knew?"

"I knew almost from the moment you began. The DEA has been investigating David Fisher for years, but they aren't after the little fish. They want the big ones, like Los Cachiros and Lobo."

"El Negro, you mean?"

"Right!"

"So, like I said, I'm just an asset - a little fish used to catch the bigger ones."

"Essentially, yes. That's what the DEA wanted me to do - keep seeing you - get information from you. That's why I never asked you a Goddamn thing. I didn't want to know. As long as I could go back and tell them that you were just doing a little bit of street dealing, they turned their sights elsewhere."

"So that's why you've hung in here with me so long. Otherwise, you would have left long ago."

"That's not true. I fell in love with you. I didn't want this to be a game - I certainly didn't think of you as an asset. I thought if I stayed close to you, I could protect you."

"I see! So now what?"

"You've got to extract yourself from El Negro's laundering operation. You've got to get free of it before shit goes down. His arrest is imminent."

"Alex, even if I could, it won't make any difference. I'm not a little fish anymore. I don't just sell street drugs. I've -" I wanted to tell him everything, mostly just to get it all off my chest. I wish I could have confided in him about how many properties I owned that were completely separate from El Negro's industry - how much money I had in bank accounts - how deeply I was already caught up in it, but I knew it would be like putting the noose not only around my neck, but his as well. "How much time have I got?"

"Well, many from the Los Cachiros cartel, including El Negro have been on the run for years. I don't know how much time you have. What I do know is that if the DEA - or worse, the Honduran authorities think you know something, they'll come after you first. They'll use you - and by use you, I mean threaten or torture you - to get the information they need to arrest El Negro. Have you got a lawyer down here?"

"I've got a friend who's a lawyer."

"How do you know you can trust him?"

"We've been friends for years - since I first arrived here. He defends a lot of ex-pats. I assume I can trust him."

"We were lovers and spent a great deal of time together and you didn't know I was with the DEA!"

"Yeah, you're not doing anything to help your case by the way."

"This isn't about me - or us - anymore. This is about you and your freedom. Get this lawyer - your friend - on board as soon as possible. In the meantime, do whatever you can to hide anything that can incriminate you. I'll do whatever I can to help you, but I won't be able to see you anymore."

I knew that was coming. Wham! The other shoe had dropped! I knew I had brought it on myself, but it didn't make it any easier. I let go of Ghost's fur and wrapped my arms around Alex's neck. I should have been infuriated with him, but I wasn't. I just wanted him to make love to me one last time. No matter what was going to happen, I knew that I could live on that for a long time. I'd think about tomorrow, tomorrow!

Chapter 31: "Cruising"

February 15, 2013

In light of being single again, I decided I was going to treat myself to a gourmet dinner and that's exactly what I did last night. I took Guatusso and I out for lobster. He's the best company I've had in a long time. We got talking about the cruise ships that are coming into the island left, right and center as well as other wealth that seems to be permeating the island as of late.

He told me that wealthy expats from the States and Europe, as well as some from well-known drug cartels are anchoring their yachts off the island and paying locals over a hundred American dollars just to tie up their boats and keep an eye on them while they go explore the island.

Guatusso was thinking he might go down and see if he could get in on the lucrative work, but I warned him against it. I already knew what kinds of things were going on in the harbours, mostly because Osito and I had made several deals with the crew members off the ships who were trafficking to other places they were porting in. Several tourists were also being held up at gunpoint by thieves. The harbours weren't a safe place for anyone and I didn't want to see Guatusso get into trouble - or worse, get hurt. I told him I'd just buy a few more paintings off of him if he was short on cash.

The thing about here is, that even when people are getting by okay, okay is never enough. One never knows where their next dollar is coming from and it drives people to madness - and crazy behaviour sometimes. When I first came down here, I had money to live on, but the lure of having more - and living without worry, drew me into a life I never thought I'd be living.

The funny thing is, now I have a different kind of worry - a horrible anxiety about getting caught or killed. My hair has all but fallen out and I've taken to wearing a scarf around my head. Guatusso joked with me that my new nickname is going to be Bandana. I kind of like it.

September 3, 2013

I received a letter in the mail yesterday. It wasn't actually a letter - it was an article regarding the latest seizures of El Negro's properties on the island and inquiries into the infamous Valle family that has been known to be one of the largest cocaine trafficking families in Honduras. I knew it was from Alex - and I knew it would be my last warning from him.

I stayed up all night contemplating what I should do - and where to begin. After seven years in business, you collect a lot of things - and money - and people who are working for you that are depending on you. How do you just pull the plug in an instant? How do you let go of everything you've worked - and worried - so hard for? It's a question that I know I have very little time to answer.

December 8, 2013

After one of the best - and by best - I mean the most profitable years I've ever had, I know it's finally time to extract myself from the business entirely. There is rumour that El Negro is hiding out and that they're looking for him in Europe.

I finally listened to what Alex told me over a year ago and called my lawyer friend. I had no choice but to confide in him about what I'd been doing - and at the same time, pay him very well to remain on my side of things. Even though I trust him, I also know how things work in this country. I put down a ten-thousand-dollar retainer.

In the meantime, I put my affairs in order. I made sure that my properties were unloaded - and quickly - for a bargain price, mostly to expats that loved the idea of owning on the island. I secured my finances and most importantly, I went to visit Guatusso.

I asked him, should anything happen to me that he makes sure Ghost gets a good home - and that if by any chance, they arrest me before I can get home, that my journal - which I was planning to hide in an undisclosed place - be burned or kept hidden. Guatusso warned me to burn it now, but I couldn't bring myself to do it. I guess it was for the same reason I wrote things here that I knew might incriminate me one day. Where else can one be so honest about themselves - the good, the bad and the ugly?

I figure if I'm arrested, they have enough on me already that my lame journal won't make any difference. There is another reason I don't want to burn it or for it to fall into the wrong hands. I want it - everything I've done - well, almost everything - even a girl has some secrets she keeps within her heart - and everyone I've met to go on, even if I can't.

I hope that maybe one day my family - even my brother - will read this and understand that I never meant to get in so deep and that there are people - and my dog - that I care about it. I want someone to know that I wasn't a completely vain, selfish girl from New York's Upper East side.

There is more to me - just like there's more to every person than what you see on the outside. I also hope that Alex might know one day - even though I could never bring myself to say it to him - that I love him and that it hasn't all been some game where we've been pawns - but that what we shared, meant something.

December 18, 2013

I wish I could write that this year was finishing well, but instead I'm writing the most horrible thing I've ever had to write. Machete, my longtime friend and protector, died in my arms last night. I honestly thought the man was indestructible. He was so big - larger than life - and so sweet to me and Ghost. He protected me when he should have run for his life - and right to the end, he was loyal. I'm so stupid. Despite all the warnings, I decided to do one more deal. One more kick at the cat, before I retired. I should have realized that the cat has nine lives, while the rest of us only have one!

We were supposed to meet Osito out in the mangroves to pick up our money for the last shipment. I don't usually go on any of the runs. Machete wouldn't usually allow it anyway, but I insisted. It would be my last deal - my last run and I wanted to be part of it. I also intended on paying the boys a large chunk of the proceeds and tell them it was time to pack it in and go live a good life on what we'd made.

I didn't know it would go so wrong. When we motored into the narrow canal of the mangroves, I had a bad feeling, but ignored it. I figured if anything was wrong, Machete might have picked up on it. We came out to the edge of the clearing where it opened up to the lagoon, but Osito wasn't there to meet us and there was no boat.

We waited for about fifteen minutes and were about to leave - you never stick around too long after the meeting time because you know something is usually up. Then we heard the motor of another boat coming down the next mangrove canal. Figuring it was Osito with our money, we stayed there, right out in the open.

The next thing we knew, we were being shot at. Osito wasn't in the other boat - I didn't know that they had already shot him and left him for dead in the shallow waters off the other shore. Only because of the skilled maneuverings of our boat driver - Flamingo - we were able to get turned around and under the cover of the canal we'd just come from before the boat was right on top of us.

When the firing stopped and I could finally get my bearings, I realized that Machete was down and wasn't getting up. I crawled over the wooden seat to where he was lying and slid myself over beside him. I tried to roll him over onto his back, but he was too heavy. I could only manage to turn him sideways and wrap my arms around him, holding his head close to me. He'd been shot in the chest. There was blood everywhere.

Flamingo kept motoring to the dock from where we'd left, while I tried to stop the bleeding. I looked down at his big hulk of a face and smoothed away his hair from his eyes. He was looking up at me with a shocked look on his face. I will never forget his expression - it was as if he couldn't believe it himself, that he was actually mortal and could be dying.

He reached his big paw up to my face and wiped away my tears.

"Don't be sad, little Chihuahua. I was sick of living with this scar anyway!"

"Don't be stupid! That's the sexiest part on you!"

He gave a little giggle, but it made the blood gurgle from his bullet hole and I thought I was going to be sick.

"Listen, I got nobody- "

"Don't be silly! You got me!" I cut him off, but he put his finger to my lips.

"Listen to me, Chihuahua. I got nobody. The only thing that matters is my paintings. You see they get somewhere nice, okay? Promise me?"

"Of course! But you're going to be okay!"

"No, little pup, I'm not. Now don't be sad. You hear me! You get out of this business like you were planning and go live in your treehouse and take that wolf you call a dog with you. You hear me!"

"I hear you, but you're going to be okay!" I kept repeating those same words while watching him slip away. I wanted to believe them so badly, I thought maybe that it would make them true. It didn't.

Chapter 32: The Painting

January 5, 2014

After the ceremony for Machete, we all got together at Luna Subiendo for drinks and to celebrate his life. I took my leave early, because even though I knew he would want me to celebrate, my grief was almost incapacitating. I walked along the west road until I reached the far end where the pavement gave way to gravel and began to walk up the long, dirt path to where I knew he had been living. He had had his key in his pocket that day on the boat and so I removed that from him, along with a coral necklace he was wearing and some papers that were in his pocket. I knew that if I didn't take them, they would disappear on the way to the morgue.

I approached his home very slowly. It was a tiny, wooden cottage, painted green with large red Hibiscus flowers blossoming over the front of it. It was prettier than I thought it would be. I should have known. I unlocked the door and went inside. The curtains were pulled, so I opened them to get some light. His sink was empty and his bed was made. I smiled. I thought about how interesting of a man he'd been - and how instrumental in my life he'd become - and yet, I'd never been in his home or knew about his past, except the few things he shared with me.

His dad had left his mother with five kids to raise and he'd moved out at fifteen to the streets. He longed to be free and made a living at first, by collecting bottles from the homes around the island. Later, he started collecting things people - mostly expats - would toss out or give away when they left the island. Eventually, he was able to rent his own place and after his siblings were grown, he moved back in with his mother to help her out. This is the house where they'd lived together until she died of cancer in early 2000. After her death, he apparently started painting seriously for the first time in his life and had been making his living by painting various things for people on request.

I walked through the little kitchen and pushed open a door to what I thought must be a second bedroom and inside, were numerous canvases and paintings. Some were hung up, but he'd run out of space and so some were simply standing against the walls along the floor. They were of landscapes and sunsets and a few painted faces of children and pets left over from expats that never got a chance to collect them. I turned towards the one small bed in the room and stopped in my tracks.

There was the painting I had asked him over five years earlier to paint for me. The sunset and ocean were complete, but the two figures in the painting were only outlined. It wasn't finished. He'd never asked me if I still wanted him to do it -

but he'd kept the photo of Ghost and I that I had given him. I'd never wanted to push the subject and so forgot all about it in the craziness of what we'd been up to for the past few years.

I walked towards the painting and reached out with my finger and ran it along the outline of those two figures - of me and my dog. I wondered when he'd began it - and why he never finished it - or signed it, which made me sad. I looked down and there at the bottom right was an envelope. I picked it up and opened it. There was my photo and a note addressed to me:

Little pup,

I hope you never have to read this note - or see your painting unfinished, but if you do, then that is our fate. For some reason, I could never complete it - I guess I knew if I did, I'd have to give back the photo of the two of you. Perhaps, it's because I was waiting to see how our story turned out. If you're here, then it didn't quite turn out the way I'd hoped. But if you're reading it, it means there's still time for you. Take the painting and finish your story. I hope it all works out for you and your wolf-dog!

Love your friend,

Karl (I don't think you ever knew my real name.)

March 8, 2014

I arranged for Guatusso to take Machete's paintings. It was the only thing I could think to do with them. I left the painting of Ghost and I with him as well. I was too sad to keep it with me. Every time I looked at it, it reminded me of what I'd lost - and how Machete and I never got to finish things.

There were things I would have liked to have said to him. When he told me, while on one of our adventures together why he'd ordered a lime for me the first night we met, I laughed, but never said a word. I wish now I'd said something. He told me the reason he ordered it wasn't because he was trying to be chivalrous like I thought - but because he thought I was too sweet and I needed to be *soured up* - those were his words.

He told me that in order to survive on an island - or anywhere - as a single female, I ought to put on a sour face - the kind you make when you suck on a lime, if I wanted to keep the assholes away. He joked that it would work as good as having him around. I wished I'd thanked him for teaching me that lesson and for the times that I couldn't be sour faced enough, he always stepped in to protect me. And yet, respected me enough to stand down and let me take care of things on my own, if I asked.

I miss him dearly. I told Guatusso to hold onto the painting until maybe one day the wound healed a little and it didn't hurt so much. He agreed.

April 17, 2014

I suspect this will be my last journal entry. Alex got word to me today that my arrest is imminent. They took El Negro into custody on March 26 and if I'd been smart, like Bernie and Guatusso told me, I would have disappeared then. I didn't want to leave Ghost - and I don't think I really thought it would happen. Maybe I was hoping that Alex would swoop in and save me - or tell me he could get me a deal. Maybe if I had turned myself in before El Negro got arrested and made a deal for information, I could have saved myself. Either way, I figured that would have got me killed.

I called Guatusso and told him to come for Ghost and my journal. I tied Ghost - which I absolutely hated doing, as I've never had him leashed before - to a large tree about a quarter mile down the beach. I could hear him howling up until about a half hour ago and it was deafening to me. I buried my journal near him. I figured there wouldn't be anyone who would dare approach him and that it was safe until Guatusso could retrieve them both.

I'm not sure what I'm feeling right now. My heart is pounding and I'm sweating. It's the first time I've felt really warm in a long time. I think as you begin to lose your soul - your blood literally begins to run cold as well. I suppose in order to survive in this business this long, you have to become cold-blooded. I also have a sense of relief, which seems strange except that when you finally know the end is near, you don't have to be fearful anymore. The worst has happened - although I hear Honduran prisons are pretty shitty. At least I have money and ways to get things. I'm still hoping I can make a deal or that my lawyer can persuade the judge to give me a lighter sentence.

The only thing that truly saddens me is that I may never see Ghost again. I made peace a long time ago that I would never see Alex again and although, there are times when I miss him, I always knew that he would leave my life. Ghost is a different story. I always imagined that he and I would run away together to our treehouse and live out our days. But he's getting up there in age - we thought he might have been a year or two old when I got him from the dump, so I know he won't outlive my sentence.

I'll never regret having him in my life. Just like Machete, he's touched my heart in a very special way. In fact, my love for a very few, reminds me that I haven't lost my soul entirely and I'll forever be grateful for that. I can only hope that prison won't take the rest of it.

Chapter 33: Pancake

After Delia's disappearance, I stayed in her beach house through the summer and into the fall. If I was honest, I didn't stick around because Veronica or the DEA expected me to - it was partly to piece together Delia's story after reading the rest of her journal and some part of me was hoping I'd receive word from her that she was okay, wherever she'd ended up after her escape.

I did finally make it back to New York city for the tail end of autumn to enjoy wooly sweaters and big mugs of coffee once again. There's a part of me however, that missed the island - and of course, missed Delia and her stories. Some nights, I would leaf through her journal or just allow it to open to a certain page and read something she'd written. It made me feel closer to her. Inside the pages of her last entry, I had tucked the worn photo of her and Ghost. I thought of how hard it must have been for her to tie him to that tree and leave him behind. I wondered, if she'd ever felt the same way about me.

Eventually, fall gave way to winter and in early December, I got an answer to that question. I came home to my condo, to find a postcard from Honduras in my mailbox.

Crystal waters in paradise, where the diving is spectacular. Honduras.

"God calls you to the place where your deep gladness and the world's deep hunger meet."
        Frederick Buechner

Scott Harder

101 West 24th Street

New York, New York

10038

USA

It did not indicate who it was from nor did it have any distinguishable destination other than Honduras. I did however, recognize the handwriting as I'd had many months in which to become familiar with it. I could only take it as a sign that Delia was alive and well and from the quotation she'd chosen, that she had found peace and purpose. These were the two things she'd been looking for when she first embarked on her journey to Honduras and perhaps, for some reason, she had to experience everything she went through - and meet the people she did - in order to finally find them.

I did wonder if the postcard was simply her way of letting me know she was okay or was there something else she wanted me to do? I tried to put her and the whole thing out of my head for months, but well into the new year, I would awaken in the middle of the night thinking about that scene from *Shawshank Redemption* that Delia had mentioned: 'Well, maybe Pancake, someday you'll go looking under a big tree and find a box from me.'"

One night, I got up and went and leafed through her journal to her last entry where she'd written, that beside the tree she'd leashed Ghost to, she had buried her journal. Was it possible that she'd gone back there after her escape and left something else? As hard as I tried, I couldn't shake the feeling that our story wasn't over yet.

It was early March before I'd finally get the nerve to get myself back on a plane and return to Honduras. I didn't go straight to the beach house, however. I went to Mangrove Lane to see Delia's old friends - Guatusso and Ghost. When I walked up the dirt path, I expected to see the large wolf baring his teeth, barking at me again, but I heard nothing. I walked to the gate and pounded on it loud enough that if Guatusso was in his house, he'd hear me.

A few minutes later, I heard the latch click and his skinny face came poking around the gate. "My friend! Wat ya' doin' back in dese parts? Didn't get enuf o'me da last time?"

"Did you need to see my ID again?" I quipped.

"Don't be silly, man! We old frien's, you and I! Come on in!"

I looked around for Ghost, expecting to see him bounding down the path to gobble me up or at least for him to be laying on the veranda, but there was no sign of him.

This made me sad. I assumed that Delia had been right and the old boy hadn't lasted long after her escape. I didn't want to ask or know the truth. I simply followed Guatusso up the steps to his veranda and sat and waited for him to go fetch us a drink. There was no limonada this time - this time, it was Salva Vida.

"Are ya hungry, man? I got some fried fish from da night befo'?"

The truth was, I was so anxious about being back in Honduras that I didn't have much of an appetite. "No, I'm good. Thank you, though."

"No problem, man. So, what brings ya back to dese parts?"

"That's a good question!" I took a sip from my beer and drew in a large breath to get the nerve up to tell him. "I got a postcard in the mail back in December - it was from Honduras."

"Still got some friens' here, do ya, man?"

"Well, one anyway!" I kind of chuckled thinking that Delia could be considered a friend now and not simply someone I was interviewing. "I think it was from her."

"Could be, man. What makes ya tink dat?"

"The quotation that was on it. It reminded me of something she said once about looking for peace and for purpose in her life."

"I see! So, what you want here, man? What can I do for ya?"

"I was going to go back to her beach house - to the place you found her journal. I thought maybe - maybe she'd left something else there."

"Well, I didn't see nuttin' else dere 'cept her journal, but then that was over six years ago. I suppose she coulda gone back dere at some point. It's still her property."

"Are you still renting it out?"

"Nah! It's been sittin' empty since you left. I tought maybe - well, it sounds silly, but if I left it empty, she might come back there someday."

"It doesn't sound silly to me. I've had similar thoughts regarding her."

"So, yeah, were you tinkin' bout renting it again?"

"No, I think my place is in New York now. I'm back working with *The Times* and I have her story to publish at some point."

"You mighten' want to hold off on dat, just a little longer."

"Yes, I thought the same thing."

"Yeah, good idea to keep that stuff to yourself for a bit."

"I wondered if I might be able to see her painting one last time. I mean, I know I have the photo, but it's really worn and well-"

"I ain't got dat paintin' no more."

"What? What do you mean? Where is it?"

"It got sold. Somebody bought it."

"Who? Who would buy it?"

"Somebody who liked it, I guess."

"Was it somebody who knew her?"

"I suspect so. Why else you'd want a paintin' of a woman and her dog?"

"Can you tell me who it was?" All I could think of was that maybe it was someone who knew her - and was as curious about her and her life as I was. Maybe I could talk to this person.

"I can take you to'em, if ya like?"

"Really? That would be great!" I was viscerally tingling all over my body at the thought of meeting someone else who cared about Delia.

"I can, but now, dis person is a real stickler 'bout his privacy. He don't want nobody knowin' where he's livin' so I'd have to blindfold ya if I was gonna take ya dere."

"I guess I'm okay with that. I mean, I don't think you'd kidnap me, would you?" I chuckled nervously, after I asked him the question. Honduras did have one of the highest kidnapping rates, after all.

"You got anybody back home dat would pay a good price fo yo' ass?" He chuckled too, which unnerved me just a little bit.

"Nope! Nobody gives a hullabaloo about me! No money to be had!"

"Just as well! I don't really wanna end back up in da slammer, you know? I already been dere three times!"

"Right!" I nodded and smiled slightly.

"Well, we can't leave 'til tomorrow. The seas too rough dis afternoon. You can stay in Delia's beach house for da night and meet me here at first light - around 5:30 am and we'll set out. Bring some bug spray and some water with ya' - it's a bit of a haul 'cross the waters and den into da jungle. You don't wanna get none of dat Dengue fever dat's goin' 'round da island."

"Okay. I'll be ready."

"Good. I'll see you tomorrow mornin' at first light."

I took my leave and walked down the steps to the dirt path. I looked back around one last time, thinking I might see Ghost, but still, there was no sign of him. I breathed deeply and walked into the sunshine to hail a taxi back to the house on the beach.

***

Being blindfolded is one thing. Being blindfolded on a moving boat, is quite another. I had no idea where - or how far - we were going and so that made it worse. I tried to sit and hold onto the wooden plank that served as my seat, but the waves were knocking the boat so hard, I was being tossed into the air and then slammed back down again. It was a nightmare trying to stay in one place. I also began to feel seasick and hoped I wouldn't have to barf right in front of Guatusso.

He'd shared with me that morning while we sipped very strong coffee on his veranda that when he was a young boy, his father got recruited by some men that came to the island of Guanaja to see about hiring captains for their boats in Dubai. Legend had it that the fishermen and sailors of the Bay islands were the best sea Captains - and navigators of rough and shallow waters in the world and apparently, they needed them to run oil boats back in the 1970's. His dad had passed away, but not before teaching Guatusso how to run boats amidst the islands. I was grateful to hear that!

I estimated that it must have been about two hours that we were at sea and I'd never been so happy to feel land under my feet. I was still blindfolded, so Guatusso helped rig my backpack up on my shoulder and then led me along what felt like a sandy beach. It gave way to some tougher terrain, so once we were off the open beach, Guatusso told me it was okay to take off my blindfold. He walked ahead of me with his own bag strapped to his back and a machete in his right hand.

"Dese come in handy when you in dis kind of jungle. Watch now, you stay on da path cuz dere's some snakes and lizards you don't wanna mess wid!"

I wondered what I had gotten myself into! I was nervous and excited at the same time. I had many thoughts running through my mind. I imagined that this person might be the allusive DEA agent - who had also disappeared at the time of Delia's escape - or maybe it was some famous actor or celebrity that had heard about Chihuahua's escape and wanted a painting of her. Whoever it was, he was going to great pains to not be found as this island appeared to be very small and remote. We walked for about another half hour, before Guatusso came to an abrupt stop on the path. "Dis is where I leave ya. I'll be back later - after I do some fishin' for dinner."

"You're leaving me? How do I know where to find this person?"

Guatusso turned sideways. "Just follow dese steps up and keep goin'. You'll find your way. Just don't sneak up on him - he's likely got a gun and you don't wanna get yo'self shot!"

"Great! Thanks! I feel better now!" He patted my backpack for reassurance and disappeared back down the steep path we'd just come up. I hope he would at least catch some fish as I was ravenous. My sea sickness had subsided, thank goodness and the thought of fresh fried fish sounded very appealing. I breathed in deeply and began the steep climb up the stone stairs.

I looked up a few times to see how far I had to climb, but the jungle canopy was so thick, it made visibility poor. It was very dark amidst the jungle, despite it only being about eleven in the morning. Eventually, the stone steps gave way to yet another steep wooden staircase. I looked up and for the first time, I could make out a wooden structure above me. It was so high, I almost felt dizzy. I continued, despite my hesitation because I knew there was no turning back. I finally came to a landing and took a minute to rest. I looked up and tried to see how many more stairs I had to climb.

It was then that I caught sight of a large shadow moving very quickly above me. When I realized it was making its way down towards me, I froze in fear. I didn't know if it was better to start running back down the steps or just stay frozen and hope it meant me no harm. I actually closed my eyes for a split second to think clearly and when I opened them, there it was - the massive, wolf-dog coming at me. When he reached me, up he went on his hind legs and shockingly, instead of taking a chunk out of my face, he licked me!

"What the hell?" I said out loud before realizing that I had Ghost's front paws in the palm of my hands.

"What the hell, is right!" I heard a familiar voice from behind the attack dog. "Am I ever going to be rid of you, Pancake?"

"Delia?" I looked around Ghost and there, standing no more than ten steps away was none other than the escape artist herself. "What the hell? You mean, Guatusso knew it was you the whole time? You're the one who bought the painting?"

"What'd you think that grand I had you deliver to him was for? Drugs?" She laughed out loud. She still looked aged, but there was a glow and colour to her face that I had never seen before. "Are you going to come up, or are you going to stand there dancing with Ghost?"

"I'm coming up!" I said, and secured my pack on my shoulder and rushed up to her. It was the first time that she and I ever embraced and it was the best feeling in the world to know for a fact that she was alive and well and free. "I've missed you!"

"Now, don't get all mushy on me or I'll kick you off my island!"

"Your island? You mean you own it?"

"Where else is an escaped convict going to go? I couldn't very well rent a hotel room or go back to my beach house! I heard you stayed there for a while after I disappeared. How'd you like it?"

"It's beautiful. Great views and spectacular sunsets."

"Yes, it was beautiful, but this is pretty sweet too. Come on, I'll show you around my treehouse! We get spectacular sunsets here too. I have a landing where you can sit and watch the sunset and on the other side, you can catch the sunrise."

"It's like a jungle paradise in here! All you need is your Tarzan!"

"Yeah!" She said and lowered her head. I wondered if she was thinking of Alex in that moment. I wanted to ask her if he had come with her, but I refrained. I didn't want to overwhelm her with questions right away, although I had quite a few of them.

After showing me around her treehouse, which was a phenomenal three-story creation with windows on each side that captured the ocean views from every angle, we passed the afternoon on her sunset landing drinking beers and she shared with me what had happened in the days leading up to her escape and of course, afterwards.

She told me that the guards got wind that there might be a riot by the inmates and that's why they had toughened up security and been so invasive that last day I was there to visit her. Sure enough, some of the girls who had had enough of the conditions and the higher prices planned an all-out revolution in the prison.

Mava - Osito's sister and Eye had come to her a couple of days before and said that there was a seasoned guard - a female that, for the right price, would help Delia escape while everyone else was distracted by the riot. She was in desperate need of money after her husband had left her with six kids to feed. She was on her own and would risk helping Delia if it meant feeding her children. Delia saw it as a win-win for both her and the guard - and of course, she gave Mava and Eye most of her things and some stashed money before she left.

She told me that Osito had survived the shooting in the mangroves as he'd crawled to get help, but he had pretty much stayed clear of the drug trade since then. They never saw each other again - but he had often made arrangements to get her things in prison - and any protection she needed - after her arrest. She had never incriminated him after she was arrested - and he never spoke to anyone, except his sister Mava, of ever knowing the infamous, Chihuahua.

After her escape, she managed to make it as far as Le Ceiba, where Alex was waiting for her to take her by boat to a place where she could stay hidden until things died down. They docked in a cove off a cliff on the mainland's shore for three days and then had planned on heading to the island that she'd bought years earlier. They were intercepted by a fishing boat with three men on board. Unfortunately, one of them recognized Delia right away. Two of them were locals, but the third one was the yahoo from Ripon, Wisconsin. Funny enough, Delia said, he was still wearing that dirty neon-green hat! When he recognized who she was - he wasn't long in telling his two buddies. They threatened to report them if they didn't hand over all the money they had.

Alex, who had a gun, managed to shoot and kill two of them, but Kenny shot back and then jumped overboard. Alex dove in after him, as he knew if he made it back to shore, he'd report them and Delia would be taken back into custody. Neither one of them resurfaced.

Delia was beside herself - but with one fishing boat with two dead locals, a missing American and no sign of Alex after two hours, she had no choice but to take their boat and get herself far away from the mainland. She landed on

Roatan at dusk and managed to pull the boat to shore. Somehow, she swam and crawled her way through the thick mangroves until she got to Guatusso's house. The next morning, he got her in a boat and far away from Roatan.

I just shook my head at hearing the story. If I wasn't sitting there right in front of her in the very treehouse she had purchased for just such an escape, I wouldn't have believed it. I was sorry to hear that she had lost Alex. It seemed like she might have almost got her happy ending, but with most things in life, they don't turn out the way you hope.

"So how did you get your painting and Ghost here?"

"Well, this isn't Guatusso's first visit to the island, obviously. He came back a couple months later with both of them. He told me that you'd come to see him a few weeks after my disappearance and paid him. Thank you for that, by the way! At the time, when I asked you to do that, I didn't think I'd ever see Guatusso - or Ghost - again. I guess, it all worked out."

"Can I ask you something else?"

"Sure."

"In those last few weeks before your escape, what made you try to take your own life?"

She looked at me, took a sip of beer and put it down. "I got word about my friend-"

"Bernie, right?"

"No. Chacarron -"

"Wait a minute, Chacarron? I thought he quit working for you years before?"

"He had, but before I got arrested, I asked Bernie if he'd make sure Chacarron was taken care of - financially, I mean."

"That's pretty generous of you, considering he cost you sixty grand."

"It was a lot of money to lose - although we managed to get back some of it when their yacht blew up, but I'm not going to say anymore about that. Anyway, I think Chacarron lost a lot more in that deal than I did. When he found out that I'd made arrangements to keep him and his family living well, he started to visit me in prison every couple of months. He used to bring me stuff to help me out and I started to really look forward to his visits. Anyway, word came to me soon after you started coming to interview me, that he'd gone back in the business - got himself tangled up with Lombardi and was shot when a deal went sour.

"I guess, when I heard that and then followed by Bernie's death, it just kind of sent me over the edge. I kept holding on to hope you know, that things would get better - or maybe in the end, my few acts of kindness would help things turn around for my friends - and for me. When I heard Chacarron had been killed and Bernie had died of AIDS, I just lost all hope."

"Why didn't you tell me that Chacarron had been coming to see you?"

"I don't know. Maybe I was trying to protect him - or maybe I was scared you'd stop coming as often if you thought he was bringing me stuff. He was also keeping me apprised of a lot of what was happening on the island and I didn't want you to ask me too many questions. I'm sorry! I just thought it was for the best."

"I guess that brings me to my other burning question. Why did you tell me you'd found a package, instead of the truth? Was the story about opening it and getting it all over your face, all bullshit too?"

"No, that really happened! When I opened my first bag of it down here to test it, I was a little over zealous, I guess. It did blow up all over my face and I did talk Bernie's ear off that night on the yacht. In regards to finding a package, I suppose I'd told myself that lie so many times, I started to believe it. People seemed to buy it and ask me less questions about how I'd really got into the business. Maybe it's because I wanted to believe that the white shark came looking for me - instead of the other way around because that way, I could still tell myself I was just a victim in all of it."

"You know Delia - you were someone's victim. David Fisher – and Peter Manning - preyed on you - and your passion for wanting to help others."

"Maybe! Maybe I just liked the thrill of it - like being a journalist and going after the most exciting stories. This life of mine sure has made for a pretty interesting story!"

"No doubt about that! I think perhaps, it's a story I need to put on the shelf for a while."

"I'd appreciate that!"

"Anyway, I'm sorry about Chacarron and the other losses you've had."

"It goes with the territory I guess - except that when I was a young girl and looked out to the horizon, this kind of landscape, was never what I imagined. I was going to go around the world and help people, remember!"

"I do remember. Well, if it's any consolation, I think you have! I saw Velvet."

"Yes? How is she?"

"She's great. Working away. I can only assume you know what I'm talking about."

"Our school?"

"Yes, your school! What else? Why didn't you mention it to me?"

"To what end? I didn't want anyone to know! I certainly didn't want my name on the blasted sign! Velvet went ahead and did it anyway! I was so angry with her! Don't people know by now that any known association with me, could be dangerous? Including you!"

"Well, don't worry about me! After this, I'm heading back to New York to lay low for a while!"

"That's probably a good idea! You'll have one of those succulent Knackwurst for me, right?"

"Absolutely!"

"With loads of Sauerkraut too?"

"Of course! God, now I'm really hungry! Where's Guatusso with those fish?"

"He'll be back soon!"

"You know, before he gets back, I want you to know that you aren't just helping those kids. You've helped me too!"

"Yeah, how's that?"

"I've always been so hell bent on making a living - making money to live well in New York that I was caught up in a life that would have killed me eventually. I guess spending time with you - and on these islands, has taught me there's more important things in life."

"Well Pancake, here's to friendship!"

"Here's to friendship!" I heard Guatusso's voice behind me. I turned to see his smiling face and in his left hand was our dinner of fresh fish and crab. "Where's *my* beer?"

That night spent on Delia's island was one of the best nights of my life. Guatusso, Delia, Ghost and I watched the sunset while savouring fresh fried fish and sipping Salva Vidas. At one moment, I happened to look over at Guatusso who must have been wearing Delia's rose-coloured aviators. I smiled at how regal he looked.

"Hey JLo! Want me to take your picture?"

"I don't tink so, man! Da only time I e'er get my photo taken is during mugshots!" He laughed and then continued to eat his fish with his fingers.

"Hey JLo!" Delia quipped, "You want a fork?"

"Nope!" He held up his right hand and waved it. "Dis all the fork I need when I'm yammin! And besides, dis utensil got five prongs and a fork only got four!"

"So, Pancake!" Delia turned to me. "I guess you're officially part of this pack as you finally nicknamed someone down here! Congratulations!"

"Thanks!" I said, and began eating my fish with my fingers.

We shared many stories - and laughs - well into the starry night, as if we'd been friends our entire lives. In the end, the fact that Delia had been reunited with Ghost and escaped the belly of that dank, despairing prison was happy ending enough. I was grateful to have been a part of it and to witness my friend, safe and finally free of the drug trade. This is perhaps what happens when kindred spirits are brought together in the strangest of ways and become a part of each other's story. I wouldn't have changed a minute of it.

Chapter 34: The Dress Thief

I wasn't back in New York even a month before I got a visit from Peter Manning. I use the word *visit* very loosely. I had a six sense I was being followed – and since I knew he'd been released from DEA custody – thanks to an unwanted, but appreciated call from none other than Veronica – I decided to nickname her the *She-devil* instead of her alias, *Angelica* - I figured out who was following me pretty quickly. Instead of waiting for him to jump me or stick me with a gun, I decided to turn around in the street and face him.

"What the fuck do you want?"

"I want my money!"

I laughed in his face. This didn't impress him very much and the next thing I knew, I was being held up against a brick wall on a dark street in New York. It was my worst nightmare coming true, except that something deep down had changed within me. Perhaps, my experience with Delia or watching what she'd had to endure and was able to come out the other side, I suppose I felt a little invincible. "Why do you think I have anything of yours?" I asked him as much to provoke him as to really hear his answer.

"I know she's got it stashed away. I know David sent her something to buy her off!"

"Well whatever it is – or where ever it is – I don't have any idea buddy. What I do know is that you're a fucking thief and there's something wrong in your head when you steal a woman's dresses and the meat out of her freezer!"

"What the fuck do you know about it?"

"Enough to make me think you've got some strange fetish for dressing up meat – or maybe yourself - in women's dresses, you fucking freak!"

The provocation worked. He hauled off and drove me right in the stomach and I was down for the count. He knocked the wind out me. I hadn't had that happen since the sixth grade when a boy was picking on a younger girl and I stood up to him. He knocked me down too, but the smile that little girl gave me, was enough to make up for it!

Lying on the pavement, writhing in pain and trying to catch my breath, I imagined Delia in her treehouse high atop those La Ceiba trees, smiling, followed by shaking her head and calling me a *tonto*. That image was enough to get me back on my feet and when I got home, I knew that whatever penance I felt I needed to pay for my sister, Sarah that I had paid it. I slept better that night than I had in years.

It wouldn't be the last I heard of Muttonhead. He continued to harass me and made a few attempts to extort me over the next couple of years. He threatened to go to the DEA and tell them that I was part of Delia's trafficking business in Honduras and that's the real reason I went there. He seemed desperate and that's the part that concerned me. Desperate people do desperate things. He must have had reason to think that David had paid Delia for her silence – or perhaps it was part of her cut. In any case, he was determined that she was holding onto something here in New York, that I knew about it and that somehow, he was entitled to it.

I suppose I could have called Veronica and told her about his harassment, but to be honest I didn't want anything more to do with the DEA. I didn't trust her – or the organization, any more than I trusted Muttonhead. I wanted to be left in peace. After a few years, I didn't hear from Peter Manning again and I figured he'd either left the country or been killed. I would get my answer, eventually.

Epilogue: The Hourglass

15 years later

I had listened to Guatusso's wisdom regarding waiting "a little longer" to publish Delia's story. That little while turned into fifteen years. I knew if I ever went public with it while she was alive, I'd have to divulge her whereabouts and that was never an option I entertained. I managed to visit her and Ghost - a few times over the years, and then later, her alone after Ghost passed away, but very sporadically as to not bring attention to their location. As it was, I was still always looking over my shoulder.

Eventually, after Ghost died, Guatusso moved to the island to keep Chihuahua company. When she passed away, he buried her alongside her best friend under a La Ceiba tree as she requested. She got to enjoy her treehouse for those fifteen years - and the two friendships she'd cherished the most.

When I returned to New York after my first visit to her treehouse, I had two of her possessions with me. The night I spent alone in her beach house before Guatusso took me to see her, allowed me to go to the large tree where she'd leashed Ghost and buried her journal. I began to dig around and sure enough I found a little tin box. Inside was the diamond brooch her mother had sent her - she - or perhaps Guatusso - must have gone to retrieve it from her friend Bam Bam at some point and the second item was a key. She had asked that first night in her treehouse if I ever found the tin box, but Guatusso was there by then and I had simply nodded, but said nothing. The items were wrapped in a piece of cloth and beside them, was a note.

Dear Pancake

I don't know if you'll ever find this, but if you do, know that I'm well and with the love of my life - Ghost. When you return to New York, would you please see that my mother gets my brooch and tell her that I'm okay and that I love her. The key is yours to do with what you will.

"Abacus Federal Bank."

With love, your friend,

Chihuahua

I dropped off the brooch to her mother one afternoon about a month after I returned. I told her I had been a colleague of Delia's and that in one of my visits to her in prison, she had asked me to return it to her mother. I know her mother wanted to ask me the one question that had been eating her up inside, but I also knew that she couldn't bring herself to hear the answer. Before I turned to leave her residence, I did what Delia had asked me. I told her mother that her daughter was okay and that she sent her love. Her mother inhaled a large breath and wrapped her arms around herself. A few moments later, she let out a deep sigh and smiled. I heard a faint whisper reach her lips. "Thank you," and she closed the door.

I didn't visit the Abacus Federal Bank until just recently. Delia's been gone for a few months and I've kept that key hidden for almost sixteen years inside a shell that I picked off the beach near her house and smuggled home in my dirty clothes. Some might think I'm crazy, but I was always too afraid of what that key might open, and like Delia, I'd be faced with a decision that was too difficult to make.

I was also afraid that Muttonhead might turn up one day looking for his cut. Recently, however, there'd been a story at *The Times* that came across my desk. Apparently, the DEA had finally extradited David Fisher on charges of drug trafficking and embezzlement and Peter Manning had been taken into custody as his accomplice. I wish it had happened while Delia was still alive. But, in the end, she had always wanted it to be her game and to play by her rules. Perhaps, this was the real reason she had wanted to convince people she'd found a package, instead of being Fisher's pawn - and so, Fisher and Manning were in many ways, irrelevant to her story.

When I opened her safety deposit box, the only thing it contained was an hourglass. I laughed out loud when I saw it. I thought of David's message to Delia: *Look into the Hourglass!* and wondered what it was he was trying to convey to her all those years before. I tucked it into my pocket, locked back up the security box and exited the bank.

When I got home, I managed to pry open one end of it, in some vain attempt to actually count how many grains of sand it had. When I shook the contents out on my coffee table, I discovered that it wasn't sand at all. It was a small amount of white shark, probably not worth much even on the street and at its very center, was what I thought was a tiny stone. When I picked it up, I realized that it was actually a *rock* – the kind that cuts glass. The kind that makes way for a journalist from New York to retire early and go live in a treehouse in the Caribbean!

I could only assume that David had given it to Delia at some point after she'd returned from Colombia, perhaps to silence her – or repay her for the favour she'd carried out for him. I sat there and stared at the diamond for a long time and then to the white powder sitting on my coffee table. It dawned on me that I had only ever tried Cocaine once at a frat party way back in university. I vaguely remembered how to cut it and then snort it. Who knew if it would be any good, but there was only one way to find out!

***

I sat there in my living room at almost fifty years old, high on cocaine and I could have sworn I saw a huge wolf-like dog and a beautiful woman in an ivory gown pass by me. I smiled, feeling a euphoric gratefulness that the sand in my hourglass had come into contact with Delia's.

My epiphany that evening was that it doesn't matter how many grains of sand there are in each one of our hourglasses, as long as we make the most of the ones we get. I hoped that in the end, Delia had felt she had made the most of hers. I knew for certain that even if there was never another story for me to chase after, that Delia Russell's story had been more than enough in my journalistic career.

Manufactured by Amazon.ca
Acheson, AB

12409182R00182